Shut out the noise and listen to your heart . . .

Worse than a one-hit wonder, Tassia Hogan is a one-line wonder. Infamous for a memorable, extremely provocative verse, her music career is going nowhere. Finding a decent man to date has also proven fruitless. They all think she's as wanton as those lyrics. But now her label is offering Tassia the chance to shine—with a catch. The album is duets. Her partner is a Country Western singer. And he's just as reluctant to agree as she is.

Hyde Love has been in the music business since he was eleven, and he's becoming more and more disenchanted with it. Collaborating on an album seems great in theory, but Tassia is an R&B singer. Melding their sounds and personalities will be difficult—though not as tough as keeping things strictly business. Getting involved with his partner could prove career-wrecking, yet discovering the real Tassia could be earth-shattering.

Visit us at www.kensingtonbooks.com

Books by Crystal B. Bright

The Love & Harmony Series
Crazy in Love
Love Like Crazy
Crazy On You

Mama's Boys Series
The Look of Love
Forget Me Not
Head Over Heels

Published by Kensington Publishing Corporation

Crazy on You

The Love & Harmony Series

Crystal B. Bright

LYRICAL PRESS
Kensington Publishing Corp.
www.kensingtonbooks.com

LYRICAL SHINE BOOKS are published by
Kensington Publishing Corp.
119 West 40th Street
New York, NY 10018

All Kensington titles, imprints, and distributed lines are available at special quantity discounts for bulk purchases for sales promotion, premiums, fund-raising, educational, or institutional use.

Special book excerpts or customized printings can also be created to fit specific needs. For details, write or phone the office of the Kensington Sales Manager: Kensington Publishing Corp., 119 West 40th Street, New York, NY 10018. Attn. Sales Department. Phone: 1-800-221-2647.

Lyrical Shine and Lyrical Shine logo Reg. U.S. Pat. & TM Off.

First Electronic Edition: February 2019
eISBN-13: 978-1-5161-0473-4
eISBN-10: 1-5161-0473-0

First Print Edition: February 2019
ISBN-13: 978-1-5161-0473-4
ISBN-10: 1-5161-0473-0

Printed in the United States of America

Ever posted a picture on a social media site or did something crazy at a party or gathering, and you were forever labeled as THAT person? Were you the "wild and crazy" girl when really you were just living life and being free? Or were you labeled as a "jump in the pool with all of your clothes on" partier when really you just tripped and slipped in the pool by mistake?

Sometimes, you can't live down one mistake or event. For those times, keep your head up and know that you are the ultimate author of your own story. This book and the entire Love & Harmony series is dedicated to people looking for redemption and second chances. Don't like the ending of the story that's been said about you? Change it. The key to life is to make yourself happy.

Acknowledgments

Thank you to all the readers who loved the Mama's Boys series and asked for more work from me. The reaction was gratifying and unexpected. I appreciate each and every one of you.

Thank you to Martin Biro and Renee Rocco for giving me the chance to do another series for Lyrical Press. I sincerely hope I can continue with this relationship.

Thank you to my editor, Mercedes Fernandez, who keeps me on track and in check. I appreciate our working partnership and hope it's producing great work.

The only way I'm able to keep sane while writing is due wholly to the love of my life, Jim Stark. Thank you for letting me be when I needed it, and for being my rock. I love you.

Author's Foreword

Sigh. Another series comes to an end and already I miss it. Just like with the Mama's Boys series, I feel happy to wrap up all the stories, but a little torn, too. I've grown to love these characters, and I hope you all have as well.

Tassia and Hyde are both tough in their own ways, but I hope readers can see that they belong together.

Please enjoy the third and final book in my Love & Harmony series. And if you haven't done so already, pick up my Mama's Boys series and give that a try.

Keep reading,
Crystal***

Chapter 1

Tassia Hogan sat in a makeshift director's chair that reminded her of the chairs on the set of the TV show she had done as a pre-teen called the *Ratty Rat's Fun Crew*. Fifteen years later and she still liked to sit in the taut cloth seat with her leg draped across the arm, leaned back against the stretched black fabric. Anything that relaxed her before a show fit the bill right now.

Since she sat backstage with Aaron's back-up singers and dancers, she felt comfortable with this group. She wore black shorts along with her black leather bra until showtime. Then she would swap the shorts for a matching black leather skirt and heels that would kill her feet as she danced around in them for over an hour on stage. Thankfully, tonight would be the last show on the tour.

The limber dancers all stretched in different corners of the room. Even in a room far away from the main arena area, Tassia heard the crowds all chanting Aaron's name, which sucked for the opening act on stage at the moment. She could relate. Tassia knew full well that the sold-out arena full of people would have their full, undivided attention on the headliner, Aaron. She just happened to sing a hook on his latest hit song. One day she would gain some respect and have fans of her own. Now that enough time had been put between her and that kids' show, she could start making a name for herself.

"Oh, shit."

Tassia rarely gave her attention to the generally foul-mouthed crew that surrounded her.

Most times the backstage area sounded more like a teenager-filled locker room than a room full of professionals working for one of the highest-paid rappers in the game. When she heard the expletive she didn't flinch. Like she did at ten years old when she had worked on the show, she swung her leg back and forth. Then she heard her name.

"I can't believe they still play this show."

The hairs stood on the back of Tassia's neck as she dared to bring her attention to the wide-screen TV that hung on the wall. It didn't take her long to notice the taped opening to *Ratty Rat's Fun Crew* where she and five other children danced around a man dressed in a rat costume.

A rat. Why the hell did it have to be a rat of all things?

"Aww, Tassia, you were so cute." A female dancer put her hand to her chest.

"Yeah, look at those pigtails." A back-up singer pointed to the screen.

Tassia didn't need to look. She knew what she looked like. For a year, the show pressed her natural hair using a blow dryer and a hot comb so that she could achieve her straight-hair look. With all the dancing she did on the show, by the end of the day, the sweat that had poured from her reverted her hair back to its naturally wavy pattern.

Thankfully with wigs now, she didn't worry about her hair, still in its natural state. Pretty soon she would see a stylist to get cornrows in her hair to get ready for her vacation. Fuss-free hair on a drama-free vacation.

Although she fought hard to avoid looking at the screen, her gaze fell on one of her kiddie co-stars. Tassia remembered Hyde Love being shy and quiet.

As though a back-up singer had read her thoughts, the woman said, "I can't believe that chubby kid turned out to be the biggest star out there." She turned to Tassia, who now had to bring her leg down and squeeze them together when that familiar school-girl crush returned. "Did you know he would blow up like he has?"

Tassia shook her head. "We were kids. We didn't know what would happen in the future."

Yes, she wouldn't have known that this man would stab her in the back, not once, but twice. It was too bad because at one time, she completely thought the world of him.

Immediately, Tassia went back to her ten-year-old self on the set of the TV show. She remembered how much she hated the waiting. She knew her lines, could sing her face off according to the producers, and she could dance circles around most of the girls in the show, but at her young age, patience had never been her strong suit.

She sat back in one of the director's chairs that littered the dim area of the sound stage in California while grips and stagehands milled around her, setting up the set for the next scene, one where she would dance around with an eight-foot rodent that wore a sideways-facing blue baseball cap and sunglasses.

She shouldn't have complained about all the waiting. What other ten-year-old girls could say they co-starred on a TV show where she could sing and dance as her job? She could do this for the rest of her life. She knew better though. Eventually, she would get older and her part would be recast with someone younger, at least that's what her father, Burt, had prepped her to expect. No love or loyalty in this business.

"Are you doing okay?" She remembered Burt had stood in front of her and blocked her view of the brightly lit set. As usual, her rock of a father, with his dark skin and glasses resting on his thick nose, carried a harried expression as he tugged on his blue-and-white striped suspenders.

Burt had never come across as mean or as manic as the other stage moms there. Tassia appreciated that aspect of her father. She had watched the parents of the other kids in the show and hadn't liked what she saw. Pushy, demanding and demeaning, and all out rude. Her dad never carried himself that way. He had always told her whenever the show or being in the business stopped being fun for her, she could go. Knowing she had an out plan made the experience all the more fun.

"I'm cool, Daddy." Tassia nodded while she had her leg draped over the arm of the chair.

"Leg down." Burt tapped her against her knee. "Always be a lady."

She groaned and brought her foot down. "I just wanted to be relaxed. No one is paying attention to me." Particularly not the very cute Hyde Love, one of the many co-stars in this children's show.

Too bad Hyde's attention stayed on his career and nothing else, which probably explained how he rose to mega-stardom and she fizzled to the middle. What else could she expect from an eleven-year-old boy? Tassia had kind of hoped that the writing team would be a little progressive and write a new storyline that had her interacting with Hyde a bit more. She already recognized the producers' clever trick of hiring all races for the show. Tassia represented the African-American group. Hyde had to be the poster child for middle-American white boys, complete with blond hair and the most interesting green eyes she had ever seen.

"Have you talked to Mommy today?" Tassia swung her leg back and forth as she awaited the answer.

Burt glanced at his watch. "Uh, yeah. She's fine. She said hi." He looked away.

Tassia's heartbeat slowed down a little. She knew both parents couldn't be with her. She had hoped though that her dad would have given her more information, or, better yet, allowed her to talk to her mother at least. Between work and the tutoring, she barely had time to be a kid. At the end of filming season, Tassia loved going home. She hoped she would have that chance in a few weeks.

"I need to have a word with the producer. You're going to be all right here?" Burt started heading toward a table off to the side filled with men and women who mingled with the writing team.

Tassia nodded. As soon as he walked away, Christina, one of the bubblier cast members, plopped down in the matching director's chair beside her. Tassia always felt more mature for her age, but being around Christina made her seem almost parental.

"I love filming day." Christina pumped her little fists in the air.

Tassia gave her a polite smile and nodded. Her mother would have appreciated that gesture.

"Did you hear the news?" Christina hopped up on the seat of the chair and faced Tassia.

"We're filming two episodes today? Yeah, I heard." Tassia had practiced the dance routine so many times, she could do it without music.

"Yeah, and they're planning on something special." She wagged her backside, resembling a dog shaking its tail.

"Special? How?" Tassia shrugged.

"Well, there are six of us." The young Latina's light-brown curls bounced around her cherubic face. "Rumor has it that we'll be paired up."

Tassia perked up. "Paired up how?"

"You know, like singing partners and stuff. I think it sounds like fun." Christina patted Tassia's arm. "You want to be my singing partner?"

Ordinarily, Tassia would have said yes, ever the agreeable worker. Then she caught Hyde Love across the room. He sat on the floor by himself with a piece of paper and a pencil. He had on a bright red baseball cap that he wore backward on his head and had now become a part of his official look.

"Tassia." Christina patted Tassia's arm again. "What do you think?"

"Sounds great and fun, but you know the producers will decide who gets paired up if that's going to happen."

Christina scrunched up her face. "That's true."

Tassia slid off her chair. "I'll be right back."

Activity around the room seemed to have ramped up a little, meaning filming would start again soon. Tassia had only a moment to get some quiet time with Hyde. Without invitation, she plopped down next to him, but he kept his head down while he continued writing.

"Hey." Tassia stretched her legs out in front of her. She noticed Hyde glanced at her legs very quickly before going back to work. "We don't get to talk a lot between takes."

He gave her a nod before returning to his writing.

She had to do something to break the ice with him. He had been the only cast member she hadn't really connected with since starting the show a year ago. "What's your favorite ice cream?"

He wrinkled his nose when he looked at her as though her words contained a smell. "What?"

"Ice cream. You eat it, right?"

"Are you making fun of my weight?" He glanced to someone behind her. "I told my dad I'm trying to lose it."

Tassia started to look behind herself but decided that she needed to stay connected to him. "I don't think there's anything wrong with how you look now." She smiled to back up her supportive words. "My favorite is something called kitty tracks. It's vanilla ice cream with chunks of chocolate and peanuts and caramel. It's so good." She knocked her shoe against his foot.

Hyde scooted away from her. For being the most energetic of the kids when he performed, he sure did come off stiff and quiet. "Vanilla. Just plain vanilla."

Tassia had to hide her surprise that he had even answered her. "Favorite candy?"

Again, he peered toward the area where his father stood before he answered. "Snickers." He smiled. "I like chocolate."

She beamed. "Me, too. I like them frozen."

Hyde wrinkled his nose. "Frozen?"

She nodded. "You haven't lived until you've eaten a frozen Snickers."

"I like them melty. The caramel strings out when you bite into it." To demonstrate what he meant, Hyde held his hand up to his mouth before drawing it out in front of him as though the caramel could get out to over a foot.

"I'm also a huge fan of sour apple Now and Later." She drew her cheeks in. "So good. Okay, favorite meal ever?" Now that she had him engaged, she didn't want to stop talking to him.

"You like food, huh?" He chuckled.

"It's universal. We all eat. My favorite meal is when my dad cooks anything out on the grill. Steak, hamburgers, hot dogs, even corn on the cob. It makes the food taste so good. What about you? What do you like?"

He shrugged.

"Come on. I can't be the only one revealing stuff. If today was your last day on earth, what would you want?"

Hyde drummed his pen on the pad of paper he held before he answered. "My grandmother's fried chicken, green beans, mashed potatoes and gravy. Oh! And her rolls. I love her yeast rolls right out of the oven with butter. She makes the house smell like a bread store."

"You mean a bakery?"

Hyde snickered. "Sure." Then his smile melted. "I miss my grandparents."

"Oh, did they pass away?" She wanted to reach out to him, but she had already seen him move away from her. She didn't want him to totally recoil from her.

Hyde shook his head. "No. Too much work and school. We never have time to stop and visit like we used to." He sniffed and ran his finger across his nose.

Tassia tapped his pad of paper. "What are you doing?"

Hyde peered up at her. His hypnotizing stare froze her in her spot. She had even stopped breathing for a moment, which made her nervous. She never got nervous around boys.

"Writing." He quickly dropped his stare back to the paper and adjusted his cap.

"Oh. Homework?" She snickered. "I hate having to do that."

He shook his head. "Writing songs." He smiled. "I like writing songs, and I'm learning how to play the guitar."

She sat up taller. "Really? My daddy put me into piano lessons." She scooted over closer to him. "So what kind of songs are you writing?"

"Um, country songs. I like the ones I hear on the radio." He nodded toward the person she assumed had to be Hyde's father. "My dad, who is also my manager, thinks he can get me a recording deal."

"Wow. That's cool. I wouldn't be surprised if you did get the deal. You're the most popular one here in the R.R.F.C." She drew her knees up and wrapped her arms around them. "Can I see what you're writing?" She leaned closer and reached out to him, and he recoiled back, a reaction that felt like a punch in her stomach.

"No. It's not ready." Hyde shook his head hard enough that his hat had almost flown off his head.

Tassia drew her hand back. "Oh, okay." Not willing to give up this conversation, she continued. "Christina just told me about a rumor she had heard."

"What's that?" Hyde put his paperwork down for a moment to give his full attention to her.

"That the writers are going to pair us up. I mean, not you and me necessarily. But that could happen. Wouldn't that be cool?" Tassia remembered how her stomach knotted as she waited for his response.

Hyde shook his head. "Sounds like you won't have an opportunity to shine on your own."

Tassia knew her heart had stopped. Sounded like Hyde didn't want a singing partner or to even be on a show with other children.

He looked at her. "We can't keep doing this show for the rest of our lives. That's what my dad always says." He pointed to his dad, who had his arm draped over the shoulders of the set nurse. He seemed to make friends a lot with various women around there. "What do you plan on doing when our time ends?"

"Um, I don't know." She looked down at the paper he held. "Maybe write songs, too. I sing really well, so maybe start singing, too."

"You write songs? I'd like to see them." Hyde's eyes widened.

Tassia hadn't even finished her homework let alone written a song. Why had she even lied to this boy? Her parents would have been so disappointed had they heard her telling these tall tales.

Before she could explain herself, she heard raised voices, and one sounded strangely familiar. She peered across the room and saw her normally cool and calm father storming toward her.

"Is that your dad?" Hyde pointed to him.

"Yeah, he looks kind of mad."

The story about her little lie couldn't have gotten to him yet.

"Looks like he cares." Hyde returned his attention back to his paper.

"Come on, baby girl. We're leaving." Burt put his hand out to her.

"Leaving? What do you mean, Daddy? We're about to start filming soon." Tassia pointed to the crew, who now had all stopped moving to look at the spectacle in the room.

"You don't have to worry about filming. You no longer are a part of the Ratty Rat family." Burt looked back over his shoulder to the table full of producers. "You and your talents aren't appreciated here." Then he had glared at Hyde, who looked shocked. "It's apparent who they think is the true star of this show. Let's go."

Tassia grabbed her father's hand and he helped her up to her feet. "But—"

"We'll go home to Maryland. You can go back to being a kid."

Sounded nice except Tassia had started to like this grown-up world of filming and being on a TV show, even one on a public TV channel. She also started to like Hyde, even with the little bit of interaction they had between takes. With this abrupt exit and now that she would be going back to the east coast, she knew she wouldn't see Hyde again. At the time, she didn't even know if she would be continuing in the business. Fortunately for her, Tassia had continued on her own.

She jumped out of the chair. "Turn that off."

"Aww, come on. Isn't it nice to reminisce?" One of the dancers asked.

At that moment, a back-up singer started singing the Mary J. Blige song of the same name and getting the entire room, except for Tassia, to sing and dance with her.

When the song ended, a female dancer looked at the screen and shook her head. "Even as a chubby kid, Hyde was cute. Now he's F.I.N.E., fine." She grunted. "I mean, did you see his last video where he was singing in the rain and not wearing a—"

"No." Tassia snatched her skirt from her case because she knew—or at least hoped—that they would be on stage soon and could stop talking about Hyde Love.

Truth be told, Tassia hadn't really stopped thinking about Hyde Love, but only when he became an adult and really blew up in entertainment. Time did right by his body. He no longer carried extra weight around his middle. He had a swimmer's body, long and lean with just enough bulk to have her fantasizing about holding him.

Of course, she had seen the video that the dancer had mentioned. Who hadn't? In the video, Hyde wore jeans, boots, and his trademark backward baseball cap, now in blue. For whatever reason, the director had him singing his song shirtless in the rain. Tassia had never wanted to lick water off a man's body more than in that moment.

They must have kept that set cold. Hyde's pink nipples looked small and hard. His large hands had Tassia wondering what he could do with them on her. Where would he touch her? How would he touch her? Would he stare into her eyes as he did?

Those same mesmerizing eyes that stunned her as a kid still did that when she had seen one of his videos or saw him in a magazine. Whenever the memories of their tainted past came back to focus, she gave up the fantasy.

"I've been too busy with my own career to pay attention to old colleagues."

In unison, the group screamed, "Colleagues?"

A male dancer stopped her from going into the bathroom to finish changing by draping his arm around her shoulders and facing her toward the TV. "I mean look at the two of you. You in pigtails, and him in overalls. You two could be the country and R&B versions of Beyoncé and Jay-Z."

The group laughed. Tassia found no amusement in his teasing.

"I don't think Dorian would like hearing you marry me off to another man." Tassia jabbed her elbow into the dancer's muscled side.

"That stagehand?" He snickered. "Your boyfriend is a stoner and a wannabe rapper. You need to cut your losses and go." He jutted his thumb over his shoulder. "Drop that zero and get with a hero."

Tassia stared at the screen. For a brief moment, she had worked with the talented star for only a year. In the shot, they both sang the kiddie version of a current popular pop hit. Hyde glanced at Tassia. Back then and now, her breath stopped. Hyde had that certain thing about him that she couldn't explain.

"I haven't seen Hyde in years. He probably wouldn't know me if he saw me in public." She shook her head.

"But you know—"

"And there's nothing I need from him." Tassia went into the bathroom and had to lean against the door to collect herself before changing into her skirt.

She didn't need to tell the group in the room how Hyde had dismissed her, not once, but twice. Actually, the first dismissal came by way of Hyde's father. It had happened on her last day of shooting. When Burt had removed his child from the set, he had revealed to her in the car all the changes that the producers had wanted to make, and they all involved Hyde and only Hyde.

Tassia couldn't blame Hyde for that. No way a kid could manipulate adults like that. Her second run-in with him had been different, and placed the nail in the coffin on this former colleague at least being friends with her. Being ignored hurt her, but she refused to wallow in the memory or let it break her. She had a job to do…whether she liked it or not.

* * * *

"Baby, let's get naked and let me ride on you all day." As soon as Tassia sang the infamous hook in the popular song by Aaron, another Charisma artist, her stomach knotted despite the smile on her face.

Singing the song with the chart-topping R&B artist, who the media loved to link her with romantically, didn't help her current relationship situation. She glanced off to the side of the stage and spotted Dorian sitting on a large black-and-silver crate backstage while he busied himself on his phone, his other constant companion when he didn't consume all his time with work.

Hell, even wearing a skirt short enough that the front row could see the color of her underwear and singing a seductive song like the one she sang now that put her name on the musical map couldn't hold her man's attention.

Tassia didn't need any more signs to let her know what she felt in her heart. Even the dancers and back-up singers knew she and the immature roadie didn't belong together.

The sudden brush against her body by Aaron when he danced by her snapped her out of her personal thoughts and back on her performance.

She smiled. She swayed her hips. She sang her hook. Then she employed every muscle in her body to help hold down the digested food in her stomach threatening to make an appearance.

The large crowd in an arena in Charlotte, North Carolina, screamed as soon as she sang that line. Some of the fans even sang with her. Seeing them mouth the words didn't ease her guilt about singing them in the first place.

Tassia danced around on stage while Aaron commanded the crowd. One day, the roles would be reversed. She would be the lead and she would have others backing her. Hopefully, she would sing something better than songs like "Ride Me."

Singing the tasteless ditty paid her handsomely, better than the Ratty Rat residuals, but at least she hadn't written the song. Tassia would have to keep reminding herself that she could write and had written better songs.

When her part of the song came up again, Tassia steeled her nerves, smiled, and sang her heart out. When she noticed small, pre-teen kids in front of the stage singing that same titillating line, she had to look away. These fans matched the age of Tassia when she worked on the TV show.

She shivered as she thought about her time on the show and her subsequent abrupt departure, courtesy of her father.

Suddenly she felt a body behind hers and an arm around her waist. Tassia turned her head enough to see Aaron's face before she brought her attention back to the audience. Touring for over a year and in every show and rehearsal, Aaron had never touched her. Now the last show of the tour, he must have decided to change it up this time. The unexpected bump-and-grind routine would fan the flames of their rumored affair. None of it true, but the lie the media told attracted more readers and viewers than the truth.

Tassia glanced to the backstage area again where Dorian had been. When she didn't see him again, she decided to go with this impromptu change, moving her body along with Aaron's as he rocked back and forth, occasionally grinding against her.

Despite the close proximity, she felt nothing from him. No hardness. At least Aaron kept himself somewhat composed. That didn't stop her from subtly pushing her elbow back against his midsection to get him to back up a little. Tassia would do anything to put on a great show, but she wouldn't compromise her dignity.

Tassia's part of the song approached. Before she could muster the strength to belt the line again, Aaron planted a kiss on her temple before releasing her to jump around on the stage.

Singing this damaging line did, at least, put her out there in front of audiences. She had spent years in the background singing back-up for lots of singers including Chantel Woodley when she used to be known as Shauna Stellar. She knew she wanted more.

"Thank you, everyone!" Aaron raised his hand in the air. When Tassia came down to the front next to him to bow alongside with him, he immediately said, "Good night!" He walked off without allowing her to bow alongside with him. She had spent all this time on the road with him, and he couldn't give her the courtesy or the consideration to bow next to her, give her a proper and graceful exit.

Now Tassia felt like a prop, like a back-up dancer, good enough to grind against, but not on Aaron's level to bow next to, even at their final show on the tour.

Embarrassed heat flamed her cheeks as she walked off the stage behind Aaron. The singer who had a lighter skin tone than Tassia's chestnut colored one paced offstage as though waiting for something.

Tassia listened to the crowd and heard them screaming, "One more song! One more song!"

Aaron clapped his hands and skipped around. "They want more of the kid. Let's go." He ran back out on the stage.

One of the back-up singers in all black held Tassia's arm. "You going?"

Tassia shrugged. "Why? He's not doing 'Ride Me' again, and I'm done doing the back-up thing." She saw Aaron jumping around on the stage. "You had better get out there."

Tassia continued on to her dressing room. She took the opportunity to get in a shower before the other singers came to the room to strip and do the same. She washed off all the glitter and makeup. As she stood under the hot streaming water, she let everything go down the drain. She would forget about the state of her career or the types of songs she sang for the moment. She would even push out the embarrassing reminder of her time working with a rat…and she didn't mean the guy in the costume.

After the shower, she got dressed in leggings and an oversized T-shirt in time for the other background singers to arrive to the room. Along with them came Dorian. In his oversized button-down plaid shirt and baggy jeans, he looked like he wanted to look like a teenager. It didn't help that he kept his Afro cut in a high-top fade.

When she first met the roadie, she thought he looked cute. He made her laugh, and became the life of the party no matter where they went. He made her remember that she should still have fun in her life.

The unfortunate part of her current career had to be that she had become a media darling. She didn't like the media making up stories about her, like the fact that she had left countless lovers in her wake once she hit the music scene, and that she basically slept her way to the middle once she got there. Everything Tassia had she earned through hard work. No one gave her anything, and she didn't have to rely on gimmicks to get to her spot, although after her sudden exit from the children's TV show, her name had been transformed to mud in the industry.

"Right now, I just want to see the insides of my eyelids until I can take a long vacation." She grabbed her suitcases and dragged them out the door.

She would have thought Dorian would have helped her. He followed her out to the tour buses. Gentleman all the way.

She took a breath. For half of the year, her man had been hauling around large crates and cables, making sure the set and sounds stood up to a mega star's standards. He had to be just as worn out as she felt.

Tassia stopped next to the bus. "Look. We've had a lot of fun on this tour."

Dorian reached for her. "Yeah, girl. In the hotel, in the bathroom, on the stage." He licked his lips and leaned down like he wanted to kiss her neck.

"Yes." She smiled despite the public display of affection. Never her thing, but with Dorian, she would roll with it. "And we've both worked really hard. I know you must be just as exhausted as I am. Now we can go off and do that secluded island thing. I know of a great spot in—"

"Whoa, whoa, whoa." Dorian held Tassia's shoulders and pushed her back. "Secluded island? That sounds like we would be alone."

Tassia fought hard not to laugh in his face. "That's the whole point of a vacation."

He shook his head. "That doesn't sound cool to me."

She blinked. "Vacationing on an island with me after the grind of the road after all this time doesn't sound like a good thing to you?"

He snickered and stumbled back from her. "Nope. To be on an island with just you would make me feel like my parents or something, like we should be playing shuffleboard or Bingo." He laughed.

Tassia didn't. "We're both twenty-five. We're young."

"Yep. Young, black, and gifted." He nodded while keeping his hands on her hips.

"So we can walk around on a beach and wear bathing suits all day if we want. And now that the tour is over—"

"Yeah, now that the tour is done, we can go off and do our own thing… with other people." Dorian's face became solemn. "This was all for fun, right? I mean you had fun with Aaron, right?"

Tassia stared at Dorian. *"Singing.* That's it." How could she miss seeing that he hadn't taken her or what they did together seriously? "You don't want to keep seeing me?"

Dorian shrugged. "I just see two different things for us. I'm working on my career."

"As a roadie? That's your career?" She put her hand to her head.

He nodded. "It's what I want to do, babe. You'll be going on other tours. We'll split up. A relationship like that won't work." He pulled a joint from his pocket along with a lighter. "Besides, everyone knows you and Aaron are kicking it."

Tassia shook her head so hard that her neck hurt. "Will you stop saying that? We're not. I don't know why he did that whole dance thing on stage tonight. That wasn't my idea, and we hadn't talked about it." She pointed at him. "How could you, of all people, think that? If I wasn't on stage, I was with you."

Dorian shrugged. "There are rehearsals where you're alone with Aaron. And roadies are on a different bus, so…"

"You've been with me this whole time but thought that I was cheating on you?" She had to put her hand to her chest when it felt like her heart would explode at any moment.

He snickered. "Yeah, but to be linked with Aaron and have folks thinking that I'm tapping the same girl he's hitting, that's tight."

"No, that's pathetic." Now she had to move her hand to her stomach when it lurched.

Dorian started to move back from her. "I'm sorry if you felt like this would go somewhere."

No use feeling sorry for herself. She should have seen the writing on the wall, but she had hoped that Dorian would have been different since he didn't sing for a living. She should have stuck to her rule when she first got into this business: stay away from men in the music industry. Now she would have to include roadies in that group.

"Thanks." She started loading her luggage on the bus by herself. "I can't believe this is happening. You used me."

He snapped the lighter before dousing it. "Don't be all like that. We used each other. You needed a distraction on the tour." He licked his lips. "I wanted the 'Ride Me' chick."

Tassia could have reminded him that the few times she did have sex with him, it had felt more like a chore than pleasure. She wouldn't stoop to that level. She still had to leave this situation with her head held high, and she had a good opportunity for that as long as Dorian kept his attention on his recreational distraction and not on her.

"Fine. Have a nice life, Dorian." Tassia headed to the open door of the bus.

"See you, hotness. Hope you're not simply a hook girl." Dorian sneered at her before he walked away.

Damn. Dorian voiced a concern that she also had. Would her mark in music be reduced to a line she hated singing night after night? Something would have to change.

Chapter 2

"I love you, Hyde!" A female fan screamed through the darkened window of his limousine.

Thankfully the fan couldn't see Hyde's expression. Even his deep love of his fans got beaten down by exhaustion. He rubbed his eyes while hanging his head down. "Can we go, please?"

"What? You don't like this attention?" Hyde's father looked at the chaos happening around the car. Clever Love, who liked the media's moniker of C. Love, enjoyed this attention more than Hyde, especially when the young women pulled their tops up and pressed their naked breasts against the glass.

The first time he saw faint pink nipples and areolas, Hyde couldn't believe his luck. Of course, he saw his first set of naked boobs when he started in this business at eleven. Fifteen years later, the allure of this strange unconditional love from people he didn't know all seemed foreign, unreal, unnatural. After all this time, Hyde longed for something real, something substantial.

The limo eased up a little before finally pulling away from the ravenous crowd. Once on the interstate, Hyde removed his blue cap, now an expected signature trademark since his days on the *Ratty Rat's Fun Crew*, and tossed it on the seat next to him.

"Great show." Clever pulled out his phone and started typing over the screen. "Put the hat back on and smile." He held his phone up to Hyde's face.

"Will you give me a break? No photos right now, all right? I just want to chill. Can't I just…" He leaned back, kicking his legs out in front of him and crossing them at the ankles. He couldn't wait to remove his boots.

"Your fans want to know all about you." Even with his eyes closed in the darkened ride, he saw a bright flash through his eyelids. "They'll have to accept a picture of you sleeping."

"Damn it." Hyde shook his head. "Does every part of me have to be for sale?"

"If you want to sell records and sell out arenas, yeah. You have to give up a bit of yourself. Besides, you have more sales that that Justin kid out right now doing the pop thing. That's unheard of in country. Not since Garth Brooks and Taylor Swift." Clever knocked his foot against Hyde's. "You have broken barriers, but there are still some walls you can break through." He cleared his throat. "That reminds me. Are you awake enough to discuss business?"

"No," Hyde replied flatly.

He really didn't want to talk about anything except for maybe a scheduled break. He hadn't had one of those in several years. Between recording, touring, interviews, and other appearances, Hyde's life no longer belonged to him. Record labels and fans dictated every part of his existence.

"Fine. Let's talk about you and Shelby Lynne."

Hyde groaned and lifted his head. "I damn sure don't want to talk about her."

What started off as a promising relationship turned out to be an orchestrated pairing set up by his own father and Shelby Lynne's manager. Hyde put himself out there more in the relationship, something he never thought he would do. Then the truth came out.

Even their breakup had been carefully scripted. Hyde couldn't have cared less what anyone thought of him severing the fake relationship. From the way the rising country singer bounded onto her next relationship, it looked like Shelby Lynne bounced back without a scratch. Meanwhile, Hyde looked at every woman with a suspicious stare. Could anyone be trusted?

"Shelby Lynne has dropped her newest album." The hopeful lilt in Clever's voice snagged Hyde's attention.

"Is that supposed to mean something to me?" Hyde glared at the man he should have been able to trust with his life but couldn't.

Hyde couldn't forget his father's critical comments about Hyde's weight as a youngster. Too bad the man knew how to conduct business and get Hyde in front of the right people.

"Yeah. Might be a great time to rekindle the relationship." Clever rubbed his hands together. "People love second chances, and they loved you two as a couple." He nodded. "You and a cute little blonde on your arm."

"Who just loved the fame and limelight as much as you." Hyde widened his eyes. "Hey, maybe you two should hook up. You could do wonders for her career."

"I don't think you want a stepmother, particularly not her." Clever snickered. "Might be a little awkward around holiday meals."

No, Hyde knew his father didn't want a wife. Maybe the fact that Hyde's mother simply walked out of the marriage to his father, according to Clever, should have reflected more on Clever than his mother.

Hyde scratched his head. "Besides, you're overlooking two important aspects in your suggestion. One, I don't want to be with her anymore, and two, she's moved on to someone else already. It's apparent she no longer wants to be with me, either."

"I'm going to chalk up your salty attitude to lack of sleep and food." His dad returned his attention to his phone. "I have a spread waiting for you back at the hotel."

Sounded good, but Hyde wanted to conk out on his bed, preferably for days. Unfortunately, he didn't have that luxury. Always another show, another interview, another appearance. When would his life be his?

"That's all that had better be waiting for me in my room." Hyde didn't need any surprises like he had gotten a week ago when Clever filled his room with groupies willing to do anything for Hyde.

As tempting as the prospect seemed, Hyde knew not to use women like that. Plus, none of the women saw him as a normal man with an unusual job. They all saw Hyde Love, the country music star.

"You seem chatty now. Care to talk about—"

Hyde cut him off. "No." He wanted sleep and peace more than anything. He also had to get something off his chest. "I don't want to talk about business. The last day of my tour is in two days." He took a deep breath and cleared his throat so that his words would come out clearly. "I want to take a break." Recognizing that he sounded like his eleven-year-old self, Hyde quickly amended his comment. "I'm taking a much-needed break."

Clever held up his overly tanned hand that went with the rest of his leathery body. "Whoa, whoa, whoa. Hold on, champ."

Hyde shook his head. "No hold on. I've been busting my ass ever since I can remember. Home schooling, acting, recording, touring, performing, interviewing. I'm exhausted. I just need a break before I break." He didn't think he would have had to beg for this time, but considering his current circumstance, he knew he would have to assert himself.

"I understand, kid." Clever adjusted his jacket. "You're tired. I get it. Let me look at your schedule and see where I can fit in a week or two."

Hyde snickered. "A week or two? Great." He leaned his head back. "I guess I had better get a jump on some sleep, then."

"Okay, I'll tell you what I wanted to mention before. If you fall asleep and miss what I'm saying, I'll tell it to you again later." Clever clicked the overhead light in the limo.

"Light off." Hyde didn't ask for much, and he couldn't really be qualified as a diva. Quiet and silence came at a premium. Whenever he could get it, he demanded it.

"Fine." Clever turned the light back off. "So, I had an interesting conversation with Truman Woodley."

Hyde lifted his head and tried looking at his manager in the darkened car. Although Truman started recording professionally only a few years ago, Hyde liked his style. He especially liked the fact that Truman recorded songs with heart and substance, post "Beer and More Beer." Being married to Shauna Stellar must have changed his whole perspective.

Hyde almost wished he could find a true love like that. In this business, he didn't know who wanted what from him. Fans wanted his time. Some women who went after him wanted his money. Other artists, especially the newer ones, wanted his fame. Truman didn't seem to fit in either of those categories. Truman had married the most famous woman in music.

"What did Truman say?" Hyde hated that his father baited him into this conversation. His curiosity got the better of him.

"Truman and Chantel are looking to do an album of duets. They checked out your catalogue of music, and they like your style. They want to know if you want in." Even in the darkness, Clever's teeth shined brightly.

"Are you serious? Truman wants to do an album of duets with me, not his ultra-famous wife? Doesn't make sense." Hyde sat up and drew his feet back.

"The duets wouldn't be with Truman or Shauna or Chantel or whatever she's calling herself nowadays. It would be with you and one of their artists." Clever looked at his screen and started typing something over it.

"Do you know who? They have lots of different artists signed to them."

"You're interested?" Clever nodded.

"I'm curious. There's a distinct difference." Hyde scratched the back of his head.

"We're in North Carolina. It's a hop, skip, and a jump to Virginia. I can set up a meeting with Truman and his wife. That is if you're still *curious*." His dad had a playful inflection in his voice. "I can fit it in after your final show."

Hyde thought about the possibilities. Lately he had lost the love he had with country music. Maybe this would give him the boost he needed.

Then he shook his head. "No. I need a break. I can't go into another project, especially one where I don't know all the details."

Clever chuckled. "That's the easy part. *They* called *me*. They're waiting to hear back from you. The ball is in our court. All they need is the word and they'll meet and give you all the details." He leaned forward and put his hand on Hyde's knee. "What do you say? This could be big. You saw last year the two of them got Album of the Year at the Grammys." He patted his knee. "You could have the same."

Despite the money and fame, industry recognition eluded Hyde. He assumed since he started recording at such a young age and because of that kids' TV show that he had done at age eleven, that no one took him seriously at his craft. As much as he needed the break, he wanted the respect more.

"Set it up." Hyde settled back in the seat.

"Done."

Hyde would see if this new project would give him the love that he lost in music and the respect he thought he should have earned over the years. If it didn't, it would give him the reason to take a break. Or maybe he had to reevaluate his desire to stay in the business.

Maybe the new pairing would expand his musical career to morph into continuing as a duo. He could be the next Brooks and Dunn or Big and Rich. At least with a partner, the other person could shoulder some of the work and burdens.

At the hotel, the limousine pulled around back to allow Hyde to go into the building relatively unbothered. Fans normally didn't crowd around the back doors. No. They made their presence in the front of the hotel and the lobby.

A hotel staffer escorted him in the service elevator up to the top floor that only housed Hyde, his band mates, and Clever, who always demanded a room on the same floor as his son but on the opposite end. Hyde trudged to his room with Clever fast behind him.

"I'll call you around seven so that we can hit the road early."

Hyde heard his dad talking behind him, but his full focus went to getting to his room and going to bed. He swiped his badge over the reader and opened the double doors that went into his suite.

Before taking off a stitch of his clothing, he did what he had always done in hotel rooms since he started touring. He looked under the bed first before opening the walk-in closet and looking behind his clothes to make sure no fans camped out in those locations. He even checked in dresser drawers and the in-room refrigerator for recording devices.

Satisfied with his search, he sat on the bed and removed his boots first before resting his back against the headboard and crossing his legs at his ankles. When he could muster the strength, he would get up to take a shower before sleeping off the day's events.

Hyde turned on the flat-screen TV that hung on the wall in front of the bed before the smell of the food his father had ordered him caught his attention. He peered over at a table in the dining room area of the expansive hotel room.

His nose hadn't betrayed him. He thought he smelled the distinct aroma of red velvet cake with cream-cheese icing. Sitting in the middle of the spread sat a slice of cake along with lobster, fruit, vegetables, breads of all kinds, and steak.

Clever definitely didn't want Hyde to starve. The gesture resembled the most fatherly act Clever had done in years. Hyde brought his attention to the TV screen and absentmindedly flipped the channels. He only stopped when he caught the local news and spotted performers on a large stage.

Hyde assumed the news story would be about him and his band performing that night. Instead the newscasters mentioned a rapper, someone named Aaron. Hyde had heard of him, although he hadn't listened to his music.

He started to turn the channel when he caught a voice that grabbed his attention. The singer on stage with Aaron sounded good until he really listened to what she had said.

"Christ. Did she just sing about wanting to ride a guy?" Hyde snickered and shook his head until he spotted the singer.

The African-American woman wore a short black leather skirt with a matching bikini top. With a body like hers, she didn't need to sing a song about wanting to have sex with a man. Men probably lined up to be with her.

Her cascading brown, wavy hair caused his fingers to tingle like he wanted to dive his hands through it. When she turned to the camera, Hyde bolted up in bed.

She looked so familiar. No way could he have encountered this woman and not remember her. Her green eyes had him spellbound along with her bow-shaped full lips. It hit him when he really looked at her eyes. Tassia Hogan. How could he have forgotten about her from his Ratty Rat days?

He still remembered her final day on set when she had struck up a conversation with him that at the time he had wanted. As a shy kid except when the cameras focused on him, he didn't put himself out to meeting new people, not even the kids performing with him. Tassia had been different. He recognized that early.

His father must have noticed something as well. After her abrupt exit, Clever had shared that Tassia's father had tried minimizing Hyde's role on the show. When the producers didn't want to do that, Tassia's father took her away.

Good riddance.

No matter how adorable she used to be back then, or how hot she looked now, no one used him.

When Aaron got behind Tassia and wrapped his arm around her waist, Hyde settled back on the bed.

The way the two of them looked, he wouldn't be surprised if they dated or hooked up as Hyde's contemporaries would say.

He lifted his hand to change the channel when something caught his attention. Hyde thought he spotted a shadow on the floor moving behind the bathroom door. Hell, he hadn't checked that location when he had gotten to the room.

Hyde placed the remote on the bed and slipped out of it slowly. He padded over to the buffet of food first where he knew a knife would be with the steak. He picked it up before creeping over to the bathroom.

His heart pounded with each step, but the hell if he would allow someone to scare him out of his place or worse, encroach on his space and time. Hyde took a deep breath before he swept his hand up the wall to turn on the light at the same time he rushed into the room.

The cool tile floor under his feet covered in thick socks couldn't calm him down.

"Haa!" Hyde screamed as he pulled the door to look behind it.

He held the steak knife up to a pair of young girls who clutched each other and screamed. They reminded him of young deer when separated from their mothers. Collectively, their ages together probably equaled Hyde's age.

"What the hell?" He lowered the knife and ran his fingers back through his hair. "What are you doing—"

"I'm sorry. I'm sorry." Tears streamed down one girl's face.

"I told you we shouldn't have done this." The other girl peered down. "He was going to kill us."

Hyde dropped his gaze to his hand. "No. I didn't know who was in here." He stopped when he heard banging on his door.

"Hyde! What's going on in there? Are you okay?" Clever's voice sounded both concerned and desperate.

Knowing his father, his concern laid more in losing a client than a son.

"Come on. You two need to get out of here." Hyde stood aside so that the two girls could walk out of the room.

They still clung to each other as they headed to the door.

"I don't know how you got into my room, but you shouldn't have done this." He followed them to the door.

"We just wanted to see you." The girl with dark curly hair spoke first before she sniffed.

"We love you so much." The blonde with big brown eyes kept trying to peer back at him as she continued to the door. "The guy downstairs said that if we were nice to him, he would get us into your room."

Hyde swiftly moved around to the front of the girls, which caused them to gasp. "Nice to him, how?"

The blonde glanced at the brunette and burst into tears before she could say anything.

Hyde shook his head before opening the door to allow in his frantic manager.

Clever stared at the girls before bringing his attention to Hyde. "What the hell? If you wanted some women, I could have—"

"Hiding in my bathroom." Hyde rubbed his eyes. "Call the police."

The girls squealed again and clutched each other tighter.

Hyde held up his hand. "Not for you two. I get that you're fans, and I appreciate that." He stared at his father. "What I don't appreciate is people who use a little bit of their power to take advantage of them." He raised his eyebrows in hopes that he wouldn't have to say more than that. When Clever still looked confused, Hyde decided to elaborate. "Girls, I'll sign some posters and stuff for you." He peered back into his room. "I might have some CDs and T-shirts I can give you. I need you two to wait out in the hallway for Mr. Love, okay? And we'll arrange to get you both a ride home."

The blonde nodded and smiled. "Thank you."

When the two of them walked out of the room, Clever wasted no time in talking first. "This is why I insist you have a security detail with you at all times."

Hyde held up his hand. "Not the issue right now. Some asshole took advantage of them. I don't know if he works for the hotel or if he's a part of our staff. I need you to get the police here to get a statement from the two of them and have someone arrested. What happened to them was not cool."

Hyde's serious tone must have registered with Clever. His normally slick-talking father simply nodded.

He put his hand on Hyde's shoulder. "Are you really okay? I can have you put into another room or we can go to a different hotel."

Hyde brushed his dad's hand off him. "I'm fine. I checked out the rest of the room. I just missed the bathroom. My fault. Just make sure those girls are okay. Give me every bit of merchandise you have on you. They need to have something good come out of this."

"Sure, kid." Clever nodded as he walked out of the room.

Hyde walked back to the dining room area and threw the knife on the table. After a situation like this, he now knew that he needed to take a break, remove himself from the spotlight. Forget the duets project.

Chapter 3

Once Tassia got back to her home in Virginia Beach, she visited Charisma Music to pick up some of her stuff and for a meeting. Her shoulders relaxed when she walked in the doors. This building felt like home.

In the open lobby area hung artwork done by musicians. No pictures of current Charisma artists to show any favoritism. The cozy furniture and plethora of plants gave the place a homey feel.

Never did Tassia regret signing her development deal with Charisma six years ago. She certainly had a lot of great opportunities since then. If she didn't have this meeting, she would take advantage of the end of the summer season and enjoy the local beach before going to a more exotic one out of the country. Greece would be nice.

Tassia peeked her head into Chantel's office. Finding it empty except for two high chairs and toys littering the floor, she went to a nearby conference room where she found Chantel's assistant cleaning up what looked like cereal from the long conference table.

"The twins took over." The mature man scraped the strewn pieces into a trashcan. "Looking for Mrs. Woodley?"

Tassia smiled at Earvin. "Meeting. I thought she would be in her office."

He pointed down. "In the studio. Meet her and the mister there."

She raised her eyebrows. "Truman is here, too?"

Tassia shouldn't have been worried. She had done great work for the company. She also knew how volatile and fickle the business could be. One day she could be up like when she had done a TV show at ten years of age. The next day she could be out the door, pulled from the place by her father. She hoped the latter didn't apply to her, particularly since her daddy wouldn't be there to save her.

Tassia got to the studio and heard some tunes coming from the space. It helped that the door had been left open. Had it been closed, she wouldn't have heard anything.

Tassia stepped inside and saw a familiar face behind the boards.

"Hey, superstar." Super producer Laz Kyson nodded to her as he turned off the music. "I thought you were still on tour with Aaron." He stood and hugged her.

"Ended yesterday." She sat down next to him.

The tall blond-haired, blue-eyed hottie didn't look like he would fit in at a record label run by the R&B Princess of Love Ballads. Then again, Chantel's country-singing husband flipped the perception of the recording studio.

The music that came out of the place could best be defined as eclectic. Pop, rock, R&B, country, indie and rap thanks to acts like Aaron. That kind of variety attracted Tassia to the label.

"You just got off tour and you're already working?" He nodded at her.

"Not by choice." She crossed her legs. "I would much rather be lounging on a beach somewhere."

"I hear you." Laz nodded to the side. "You could go out the back door and dip your toes in the Atlantic Ocean." He smiled.

"Sorry. I need a more exotic location, away from hearing about current events and everything depressing going on right now. I only want to hear the ocean, the wind, and some seagulls and not someone screaming for me to sing that one line." Tassia shook her head.

She didn't know what bothered her more, having people who actually recognized her from her days on the *Ratty Rat's Fun Crew* TV show or people who wanted her to sing that one line.

"Speaking of hearing, what were you playing before? Sounded good." She looked in the studio area and didn't see anyone in there recording.

"You like that?" He hit a button on the panel and played a song from beginning to end. "It's called 'Shame' by singer/songwriter Avery."

"Sounds incredible." Tassia nodded.

"It better. If I didn't make my wife sound good, she would never forgive me." Laz chuckled.

Tassia felt hopeful to see so many successful couples in the business. She didn't see that happening to her anytime soon, especially if her last relationship meant anything.

As she thought about the song, the artist, and her producer, Tassia started to put some things together. "Is this a single for Avery?"

Laz nodded. "One from her upcoming album."

Tassia's gut twisted. "Wow. When did she sign with Charisma?"

Crystal B. Bright

"Only a couple of years ago." A wide smile split his head in two. "Avery was offered a development and recording contract the day she graduated from college. I was so proud of her."

"I'm sure you were." The smile she produced probably looked manufactured to Laz, but she didn't want to show her true disappointment in hearing about this new artist, his wife.

She had learned this childhood trick of appearing happy when things upset her. At some point, she would have to stop smiling when things pissed her off.

Not only did Avery get a recording deal, she managed to find the love of her life within the industry. Tassia should have had her life. She'd been with Charisma long enough to have recorded five albums by now. She wouldn't show her jealousy in front of Laz.

No. Not jealousy. More like anger. Why hadn't Chantel and Truman given her the same push? Maybe Tassia had to reconsider her management team, her affiliation with Charisma, or both.

"By the way, the bosses are in the conference room down the hall." Laz nodded his head forward.

She stood. "Do you know what it's about?"

Laz shrugged. "Not sure. But I'm sure you'll be fine."

"We'll see." Tassia hung her purse on her shoulder as she walked down the hallway.

She arrived at the conference room and found Chantel and Truman Woodley sitting at the conference room table. Chantel had her feet up on her husband's lap while he rubbed her soles. The romantic gesture brought a smile to Tassia's face.

"Hi." Tassia stepped into the room. "Is this a bad time?"

Chantel removed her feet from her husband's lap. "Of course not." She padded over to Tassia. "So great to see you again." She gave her a hug.

"Yep. Welcome back." Truman stood and hugged Tassia also. "Please have a seat."

Like a gentleman, he pulled out Tassia's chair and did the same for his wife. Looked like Chantel found the last of the good ones. Dorian couldn't even be bothered to take Tassia's luggage to the tour bus during their last interaction—not that she needed a man or anyone to do anything for her.

"I know what it's like to just get off tour. I'm sure all you want to do is rest and relax." Chantel smiled as she spoke to Tassia.

Chantel and Truman sat at one end of the table. To not make the meeting seem so official, Tassia sat on one side of the table instead of the end and positioned herself as close to the duo as she could. She wanted them to see the intent in her eyes when she spoke to them about the next steps in her career.

"You're right about that. I feel like I've been running for years since I was ten." Tassia noticed the slightly concerned looks covering her bosses' faces. "But you know me. I never turn down work. Bring it on."

"That's good to hear." Truman nodded.

"But I am concerned about something. Since I have you two here, there's no better time than the present to discuss it." Tassia sat up taller.

"Sure. What's on your mind?" Chantel leaned forward.

"When I signed my development deal, I knew that I wouldn't be banging out albums right away. I've been in the industry. I knew it would take time and I would have to work hard." Tassia had to frame this right. She had to show her appreciation.

"And you have worked very hard. Don't think we haven't noticed." Chantel put her hand on top of Tassia's. "I still remember your character on *Ratty Rat's Fun Crew* show."

It still blew Tassia's mind that this multi-platinum artist could be this kind and personable with people who worked for her. Chantel didn't have to talk directly to Tassia. She had people who could have spoken to her, just like Chantel had her management team that included her agent and publicist. Tassia completely believed Chantel had seen her old TV show. She hoped that Chantel didn't see her as that child, or worse, as a quitter.

"Thank you." Tassia patted Chantel's hand. "I hope with all the work I've done that I would have finally earned my spot. I've written hits for you, Truman, Chantel, for the two of you as a duo, and more. And I've sang back-up for a lot of artists."

"And let's not forget that incredible hit song." Truman wagged his finger at her.

Tassia tried so hard not to roll her eyes, but it happened.

"What's that look about?" Chantel cocked her head.

"I'm not ungrateful about that opportunity. Aaron is a hot artist out right now. I was able to be on a successful track. People know me more."

"But?" Truman adjusted his baseball cap on his head.

Tassia took a deep breath. "I don't want to be known as only a 'hook girl.' I'm more than that."

"You are right about that." Chantel held Truman's hand. "My husband and I recognize your talent and hard work. We also know that you've paid your dues. For that reason, we have an opportunity for you."

Tassia felt the tide turning. Since she no longer had any kind of relationship now, she could concentrate on herself. Biding her time would give her a grand reward. Even though she disliked doing that infamous hook, she could use that wave of popularity to catapult her solo career. She could see it all now, and the best part would be that she did it all on her own.

"Do you remember Hyde Love?" Truman picked up a remote.

Tassia wished the two of them referred to her failed love life rather than the mega superstar country singer with the unfortunate name and the curse of giving Tassia a couple of big firsts: her first crush and her first big rejection in the business.

As much as she wanted to push out of her head her failed audition with him and his team to be a back-up singer on one of his earlier tours, the denial still haunted her. She would never forget his expression when Burt had pulled her away on her final day of filming.

"Of course I know him. Hyde and I did a year on that show." Tassia kept her face straight.

"That's right." Truman nodded. "Have you two kept in touch since the—"

"No." No need to tap dance around the obvious.

Tassia and Hyde's lives took drastically different turns in their careers. The determined kid who started writing songs at age eleven now pretty much owned the music and entertainment industry. Had Burt not pulled her away from the show, perhaps she could have had the music career that bubbly Christina, who had ended up being paired up with Hyde on the show as she had said, now had.

Truman hit a button on a remote. "I'm sure you're aware now that he's a huge country artist who has managed to cross over to mainstream while still remaining true country." He smiled. "Who would have thought that this would happen for this kid star?"

"Yeah. Who would have imagined?" Although she didn't want to, Tassia focused on the monitor that hung on the wall.

Time had been good to Hyde. She still remembered him as being incredibly shy and quiet except when it came time to perform. Then he appeared larger than life. When she auditioned for her old colleague, he still looked reserved.

A tall, incredibly good-looking man—emphasis on man—populated the screen. At that failed audition, Hyde had sat in the back of the room, keeping his full concentration on a notebook like he had done back in their Ratty days. After Tassia had sung her heart out, Hyde cowardly had his management team dismiss her. He said not one word to her, which after time away from the business to go to school and live life, gave her a quick tutorial back into this world. Friends did not exist, and lovers could not be found there.

Back then, Hyde resembled a gangly boy, despite being about nineteen or twenty at the time. Now he looked tall on the screen, but that could have been due to camera angles.

Through his backward baseball cap, she spotted his now light brown hair. He had grown out of his fair hair. The darker hair suited him better.

His scruffy beard kept him from looking like a teenager like Dorian. At one point, Hyde looked directly into the camera. Tassia had been told that her green eyes looked hypnotic. She didn't see it. Back then and now, Hyde still had that mesmerizing gaze. His eyes drew her in more than the melodic, deep tones coming from his full lips, way different from the way he sang as a kid.

White, black, Hispanic, whatever, this man held her attention. He had *star power* written all over him. Even with his good looks, that didn't stop her from seeing him as a dismissive asshole. She hoped this meeting would be about how through her album, she could be bigger than this guy and break all of his sales records. Tassia wanted that. She wanted to show that she could leave this industry and come back bigger and better than ever.

Tassia looked away from the screen before she got sucked in even more. "Looks like he's a good performer. I see he still remembered some of his dance moves."

"And the singing. What did you think about his singing and the song?" Chantel grabbed the remote and turned up the volume.

Tassia brought her attention back to the screen. Despite working with him in her youth and auditioning for him as an adult, she hadn't been a big fan of country music, even the crossover version. She just needed her foot in the door in the industry before she finally got with Charisma.

Hyde sang a song about one person in a relationship trying to fix the flaws of the other person in the relationship and how that never worked, kind of deep for what Tassia imagined for country songs.

"He sounds good." She shrugged. "Song sounds good. I like that he's singing about more than beer and hayrides."

Truman cleared his throat. "Nothing wrong with songs about beer and maybe more beer."

Damn. Tassia had a feeling she would have to do her research about her boss. She knew Chantel's catalogue. As a fan, she devoured her music. Despite Truman marrying her idol and being her boss, she didn't listen to a lot of his music. She knew that any song she had given him, he killed it.

"What's the deal with him?" Tassia crossed her legs. "Is he a Charisma artist?" A shiver went through her body just thinking about possibly bumping into him in the hallways there.

"Not really. We're trying something new. We *want* to try something new. We've talked with his management, and we want to do another album of duets where we cross genres." Truman paused the video, leaving a close-up image of Hyde's face on the screen.

Oh, no. Tassia saw the writing on the wall.

"We want you to do an album with Hyde." Chantel beamed. "With the twins, Tru and I have been subjected to a lot of kids' programming. Of course, we came across the Ratty Rat show, which they love. We saw a scene you did with Hyde and thought it would be a great idea to put you two back together again, but in an adult version. Bring your soul edge along with his country flavor to make something groundbreaking."

Tassia volleyed her attention between Truman and Chantel. "Like what you two did."

Chantel glanced at Truman. "Something like that. We think that now is the time to cross boundaries, show people that being different doesn't mean you can't work together."

Tassia had to wrap her mind around several concepts. Her first album would be a duet with a country singer she had worked with before but who wouldn't even hire her a few years ago. She wouldn't be doing a solo project after all of these years with the company. It sounded like Chantel and Truman saw this as some sort of political statement.

"I don't know." Tassia shook her head. "I envisioned my first album having my own sound."

Chantel sat up straighter. "It still will. Truman and I want you and Hyde to write all of the music on the album." She jutted her thumb over her shoulder to point at the still image on the TV screen.

"Does the album have to have a political slant? I don't think I want my brand to be that." Tassia tried hard to get out of this situation as tactfully as possible.

Christina may have catapulted her music career by riding on Hyde's coattails. Tassia wouldn't do that.

Chantel furrowed her eyebrows. "You hate being called a 'hook girl', but given the opportunity to do something substantial, you don't want to do that?"

Tassia didn't want to seem ungrateful. She had to turn this around and put this in her favor. "I truly appreciate you two thinking about me for this special project. I can tell it means a lot to you. I don't know if I can give this project the right flavor it needs." She grabbed her purse strap to signal she wanted to go. "Besides, I really should have Norma here with me to hash out deals."

Chantel sat up taller. "We've already spoken to your agent. And we looped in your manager. They were both on board and agreed to sit down with all of us officially with contracts if you were okay with this deal."

Great. Now the people Tassia paid to look out for her best interests hadn't even bothered to contact her to give her a heads-up on this development. Did Tassia have anyone on her side? Did anyone have her back?

Tassia shook her head. "It doesn't seem fair." She wanted to hold back her true feelings, but they came spilling out of her. "I've been busting my butt for you all since I signed my contract years ago. I've been writing, singing, and touring for you all since the day I graduated from college, all in the hopes that one day I'll get to branch out on my own." She jutted her thumb over her shoulder. "I get off tour with the hottest rapper in the game right now to find out that someone off the street is recording her first solo album before I could even get a chance at doing mine, and she has been here less time than I have."

"If you're talking about Avery, you're right about her recording her album before you." Chantel nodded. "You two are a lot alike. You've gotten buzz because of your association with Aaron on his hit song, and the TV show, of course. She made her mark already because of some viral open-mic performances."

"Then why not ask her to do the duet? I've done my time playing back-up." Tassia felt her face becoming hot and her hands trembling. She fisted them to keep some semblance of control.

"To be honest, we did think about her doing this project first." Truman glanced at his wife. "But then Chantel reminded me that because she hasn't performed on a major stage, she may come off as a back-up singer rather than being on equal footing with her duet partner. We know you're strong enough to go toe-to-toe with any singer. And honestly, we thought you would enjoy working with Hyde again."

Tassia snickered. "You're asking me to do a duet with a guy who wouldn't even hire me to sing back-up for him before I started working here at Charisma." She watched Truman and Chantel blink hard before they looked at each other. "Then you want us to record in some mash-up genre that probably won't fly with listeners. And although I'm not getting to record my own solo album, you think I'm strong enough to sing on an album, but only with a partner." She backed up toward the door. "People like categories. They like compartments." She held her hands a few inches apart. "Country." She moved her hands over. "Pop." She moved the duo again. "R&B." Then she shook her head. "Anything muddled will get lost and it'll get no radio airplay because stations won't know what to do with the sound."

Truman cleared his throat. "Sounds like someone who has done a lot of homework on the industry. That's what's so great about this project. You two can make it be whatever you want it to be with our blessing and backing." He put his hand over his wife's. "If the sound you two develop feels more country, go that way."

"And," Chantel quickly added, "if it feels more soulful, you can go that route." She tried hiding a smile as she nudged her elbow against Truman's side.

Tassia stared at the two people she thought wanted her to succeed on her own. Now she only viewed them as puppet masters looking to make carbon copies of themselves. They didn't care about her career, but Tassia had to care.

Suddenly, Tassia could hear Burt in her head telling her she needed to run, go. If these people couldn't see her worth like the people at the Ratty TV show hadn't, then she needed to leave.

"I have to think about all of this. I was hoping to have a different conversation with you two that would have involved me going off and doing my own thing. Instead, I'm still hitching my talent on someone else's wagon. I have no desires to revisit my *Ratty Rat* days, and that includes working with a former castmate." She hiked her purse up on her shoulder. "I'm not really down for a duets album, especially with another male singer, and particularly one out of my genre who, apparently, doesn't like the way I sing. And although people seem to love reunions, I don't see myself jumping on that train. Since I'm at the tail end of my contract with Charisma, I have a lot of thinking I need to do."

Chantel looked at Truman before dropping her gaze for a beat. "I understand. I'm sure you're exhausted. We are asking for a lot from you, probably too much considering you just got off the road."

"Thank you for understanding." Tassia kept her arms tightly wrapped around her body.

"We do. We want you to think about this opportunity, talk to your agent, and discuss what this project could afford you." Chantel stood. "I can definitely see more awards in your future from doing this. You would get the right recognition. I've always told you that you could sing the names in a phonebook and I would listen to it."

Hearing that from Chantel Woodley meant everything. Tassia swallowed to keep from breaking down in tears over the compliment. "You don't know what it means to me to hear that from you."

Chantel smiled, but then it melted almost immediately. "I hope you understand that right now work at Charisma has slowed. Lots of tours are ending, so not a lot of work for back-up singers. Christmas albums have wrapped for the upcoming season. And no need for studio work." She stood. "Did you do any writing while on the road?"

Damn. Tassia had meant to write a song a day, that way she would have lots of options to show Chantel and Truman once the tour ended. Getting wrapped up in Dorian and all his activities put her behind on her goal.

"Um, no." She chuckled. "You know how the road is. When I wasn't performing, I was rehearsing. If I wasn't doing those two things, I was sleeping."

"And dating?" Truman raised his eyebrows at her. "I heard about you and—"

"Done." Tassia cut him off before he could continue. "Road romance." She wiped her hands together. "Broke up on the last day. Now I'm really ready to go solo." In more ways than one.

"That's unfortunate for you personally, but probably a good thing for your songwriting." Chantel glanced at her husband. "Tru used to tell me when he taught me how to write songs that he got a lot of inspiration from being single."

Tassia would have to learn to mine some of that experience if anger didn't fuel her right now. She didn't think music lovers wanted to hear songs about a loser, and she didn't mean Dorian. How could Tassia remain in a relationship with him for so long?

"Enjoy your time off." Chantel put her hand out. "If you change your mind about recording, let us know."

Shit.

Tassia smiled as she shook Chantel's hand. In a nutshell, her boss laid out Tassia's financial future at the label. Do the duets album and get paid, or do nothing and have no work.

"I'll think about it while I'm relaxing on a beach." Tassia beamed.

"Oh, wow. Sounds nice. Where are you going?" Truman draped his arm around his wife's shoulders.

Tassia shrugged. "Not sure yet. I want to go where my heart tells me to go."

Chantel wagged her finger at her. "That line would go great in a song."

Tassia blinked. "Yeah, I guess it would."

"I hope you don't plan on staying wherever you're going for very long. We want to start this album in a month. The process will include songwriting and plotting out the album. Then we'll start recording."

Chantel leaned forward toward Tassia. "We still want you for the album. I hope you'll reconsider."

Tassia had a lot to mull over and not a lot of time. "I'll think about it. I hope you two will think about me doing my solo album." She didn't see much enthusiasm on their faces. Tassia beamed to sell herself more. "I think if I were to release my solo project before this joint one, both could be winners."

Chantel nodded. "We'll see. We would have to see songs for both projects to decide." She patted Tassia's shoulder. "You enjoy your time off."

Tassia knew what that line meant. Unless she played ball with them, they had little interest in pursuing anything else. So much for a summer vacation.

She had to talk to someone, and she knew the right person to call. Not her best friend, India. Tassia hit the speed dial on her phone as she stomped out to her car.

"Hey, baby girl." Despite Tassia releasing her father as her manager when she got back into the industry, Burt never displayed any contempt or hard feelings toward his daughter. "What's going on? Off tour?"

"Yes. Back home in Virginia Beach." Tassia got to her car and hopped inside. She cranked up the air conditioner to cool off since this turn of events made her overheated.

"Good. You can take a road trip up to Maryland to see me." He chuckled a little. "I can make the shaved ice you like, and I'll start up the grill just for you."

Tassia could almost smell the flaming charcoal from where she sat in her car. Then she could calm herself down even more with her daddy's famous shaved ice with blueberry syrup.

She couldn't think about anything refreshing. She needed to vent, and she knew Burt would understand.

"I just had a meeting." Tassia drummed her thumb on the steering wheel.

"Really? With who?"

"With Chantel and Truman Woodley." She took a deep breath. "They made a proposal to me."

"Great. Finally getting that album that you should have gotten years ago?" A lightness filled Burt's voice.

Too bad Tassia's news would deflate him as much as her spirit had been. "They did propose an album to me. But they want me to do a duets album."

"Oh, with one of them? Or both of them?"

"Neither. With Hyde Love."

An uncomfortable silence filled the phone.

Tassia started to fill the gap, but Burt interrupted her. "Leave. You don't need to stay there. They're not making you do this."

Tassia needed to hear someone else's support of her decision.

"What have I told you before? If they don't recognize your talent, you move on to a place where they will. You can do much better, and they'll see that once you go."

She imagined her father stomping around and hooking his thumb around his suspenders. She didn't remember a time when the man didn't wear them.

"You're talented. I told those producers that when you were on that show. They didn't see that. You don't need to do this duets album. You can do better."

Tassia nodded. She still had some thinking to do, but the words from her father helped. If she had to go, she would.

Chapter 4

"So?"

Tassia allowed her father's inquiry to hang in the balance while she continued packing.

"Are you going to tell me what you've decided?" Burt had no patience.

Truthfully, she couldn't hold anything back from her dad. "I'm taking that much-needed vacation."

She'd taken a few days to decide. Tassia would call Chantel and Truman once she landed. She needed to be as far away from Virginia and as far removed from the bad offer as she possibly could. Maybe then she could be allowed to take a deep breath.

And then what? What would she do for a career?

As though her daddy had read her thoughts, he said, "Take your time to decide what it is you want to do. If the money gets tight, you can always come home."

A smile hitched at the corner of her mouth. "Thanks for the offer. I'll do okay with residuals from the show and the single. Hell, there's always *Dancing With the Stars*, right?"

"As long as you get a good partner."

Oh, lord. Her father actually took her seriously.

"How long will you be away?" Burt's choppy words sounded like he did his normal pacing while he plotted next moves.

"Probably a couple of weeks. I'm going with India. I don't think she has the time to stay longer." Tassia returned to her dresser to retrieve some more garments to take.

"Oh, you're going with India." Worry laced his voice.

That tone stopped Tassia in her tracks. "Is there a problem?"

"I don't know. She seems a bit, um, forward thinking."

That had to be code for Burt disapproving of India's choice to date around often and openly talk about her bedroom antics to anyone within a ten-foot radius.

"That's why I like her. She tells it like it is, and you never have to wonder what it is that she wants. Kind of reminds me of Mom." Tassia didn't talk about her deceased mother often with her father, which seemed strange. He should have been the person she could be the most open with when talking about her mom, even with her passing so long ago.

Tassia jumped high enough to hit her twelve-foot ceiling in her bedroom as soon as she heard a loud scream. As she gasped for air, she turned to her doorway in time to see her best friend strolling through it.

"What's going on?" Burt made some rustling noise through the phone. "I'm on my way over there now."

"Don't, Daddy. It's just India. I'll talk to you later when we get to where we're going. Love you."

"Love you, too. And tell that gal to straighten up."

Yeah, easier said than done. Tassia disconnected the call.

"You scared the hell out of me." Tassia abandoned her packing duties to smack her friend's bare arm before she hugged her. "Why in the world are you screaming like that?"

India stuffed her keys into her expensive purse before she threw it on Tassia's bed. "I have been waiting forever for you to come off tour so that we can go on this vacation."

India had to practically take a running start to plop herself back on Tassia's high bed. It didn't help that her friend stood a good foot below her. Even with her short stature, her voluptuous shape let anyone viewing her see that she could not be classified as a child.

"I'm glad you were able to go on such short notice." Tassia would leave out the fact that her original plan had her going with Dorian.

Life had thrown her a major curveball.

India reclined on her side and looked at Tassia with a smile. "I know you were going to go with your boo thang." She nudged her sandaled foot against Tassia's leg. "I also know you two broke up."

Tassia turned her head to her. "How did you know? We didn't talk about that when I—" She stopped when India held up her phone.

"Your boy posts everything. He said he dumped you."

Tassia returned to her packing. Maybe she needed longer than one week in Fiji. Or maybe she should do a week there and then go somewhere cold, like her relationship status. Hot one minute. Frigid the next.

"Doesn't really matter how it all turned out. The fact of the matter is that I'm a single woman, and I'm free." Tassia smiled to prove to her friend that she meant every word.

"Yes, you are." India rolled onto her stomach and rested her chin on her hands. "Don't forget to pack condoms."

Tassia snickered. "I won't need any of those. I'm not concerned about hooking up with anyone while on vacation."

"Then why did you get a full Brazilian?" India pointed down.

Tassia looked down as though she could see through her dress. "How did you know that?"

"Easy. You confirmed it just now." India winked. "I'll throw some in your carryon bag just in case." Tassia started to complain to her friend about butting into her private life when India continued. "What about work?"

Tassia shook her head. "Nothing about me right now. Let's talk about you. You just jetted down from New York to Virginia Beach. Your stylist duties aren't needed right now?"

India shook her head. "It's summertime. Celebs are vacationing. Award season will start up soon and I'll be too busy to breathe then. Until then, you got me." She sighed. "What about you? Now that you don't have anyone to ride at the moment…" She punctuated her statement by doing a dirty grind against Tassia's bed.

"Will you stop that? And don't bring up that line." Tassia huffed.

"Why? That song put some major coins in your pocket. If I were you, instead of saying my name when I meet new people, I would just sing that line." At the top of her lungs, India belted out Tassia's infamous lyric.

Tassia cringed when she heard the words sung by someone else, not because India had a bad voice and couldn't sing. "And that's my fear." She shook her head. "I don't want to be like the woman who sang in that song 'Good Vibrations' back in the 90s. No one knows her name, but they know the song. I want people to know I'm Tassia, and I'm a damn good songwriter and singer."

She struggled with the songwriting at first, but practice made perfect… until she stopped briefly to go on tour. When Truman and Chantel mentioned that she and Hyde would write songs on the new album, that scared her more than being in the same room with her former fellow Rat Crew member.

India sat up and adjusted her shirt and shorts when they bunched around her thick middle. "I can dig it. Did you talk to Norma or Graham about any of this? What about your contract with Charisma?"

Tassia wanted to start her vacation relatively drama free. She knew after a few drinks she would eventually spill her guts to her best friend about her career, her time at Charisma, and that deal they wanted to make with her. She didn't want to talk about any of that right now.

"I'll tell you about all of that and more when we get out of here and get to put our toes in some foreign water." Tassia stretched her arms in the air. "After going from city to city, and from hotel to hotel, it will be great to just relax. I don't want to think about anything."

India clapped her hands twice. "If you want to do all this relaxing, you need to get a move on. We need to be at the airport soon."

Tassia glanced at her watch. "We're fine. We have time." In her bare feet, she padded to her en suite bathroom. "So how many bathing suits did you pack?"

India released a salacious laugh. "One, because I plan on being naked most of the time."

Tassia poked her head out of the bathroom to stare at her friend. "You are not going to be walking around naked with me."

India sniffed. "Fine. I'll go on the other side of the beach away from you. I don't need you messing up my cruising game anyway." She scanned around the bed to the nightstand and must have spotted what she wanted. She picked up the TV remote and turned on the wall-mounted set. "Besides, you'll be too busy moping around or worse."

Tassia rested her fist on her hip. "What's worse than moping?"

"Working." India opened her mouth wide and poked her finger in it while simulating a gagging sound. "I know you. You're going to be writing the whole time, probably about that no-good Dudley."

"Dorian."

"Whatever. I know how you are." She flicked from one station to the next. "You're probably going to write the next 'No Scrubs' anthem song that will get women cheering behind you while shaking their booties."

"Stop it. I'm not even packing a notepad or anything." Tassia pointed to her open suitcase.

India shook her head. "Like I don't know that you do most of your writing on your tablet or phone. You're not fooling anyone. And I don't blame you."

Tassia leaned against the doorframe. "You don't?"

India shrugged. "You're going to need some songs for your album."

This time Tassia snickered. "Fat chance." She knew she should have held her tongue on that topic, but with the mention of the future Tassia wouldn't be having, she couldn't stay silent.

"Uh-oh. That doesn't sound good." India sat up in the center of the bed and crossed her legs while resting the remote on her thick thigh.

Tassia felt the hairs on the back of her neck stand on end the more she thought about the offer she had gotten from Truman and Chantel. "It's nothing."

"That means it's something." India scooted to the end of the bed and let her chubby legs dangle. "Spill it."

Tassia started to turn back into the bathroom to continue collecting her travel items she would need for the trip, but she needed to talk to someone since Norma and Graham both suggested to her to accept Charisma's deal.

"It'll launch your career in a more serious direction," Norma had said.

"It'll make you a bankable commodity," Graham had offered.

Tassia could only see herself playing second fiddle to another star, a bigger star, a *country* star, a former colleague as she had once called him. The country part really didn't bother her. She did wonder if he would use her like a stage prop like Aaron had used her during their last show. Maybe after all these years, Hyde saw her as a valuable commodity, not for her talent, but for wrangling in more fans, which would mean more money.

"Fine. After the last show, I went to Charisma to meet with Chantel and Truman." Tassia crossed her arms.

India wagged her finger at her. "No. Call them what the media calls them. Trutel." She couldn't stop laughing.

Tassia hated the hybrid names the media dubbed celebrity couples. It came off as lazy and as though the two people shared one brain.

"Anyway, they proposed a project to me." Tassia curled her toes under her foot and peered down for a moment before sharing the news. "They wanted me to do a duets album."

India blinked. "That's awesome. With Chantel?"

Tassia shook her head.

India cocked her head. "With Truman?"

"Close, but not him either." Tassia moved back into the bathroom to gather her toiletries. The more she thought about the offer, the angrier she started to get.

"Close? Does that mean they wanted to pair you up with another man?" When Tassia didn't answer right away, India filled in the blanks. "A white male singer?" Tassia started to answer, but India continued. "A white male *country* singer?"

With items in hand, Tassia strolled out of the bathroom. "Ding, ding, ding. Give that girl a prize."

"Really?" India crossed her arms. "Interesting."

"I know." Tassia dumped the items in her makeup bag that would go in her suitcase.

"I'm trying to imagine your sound. Would you be singing country songs or would he be singing R&B?"

Tassia spoke as she went back to her closet. "I wondered the same thing." She pulled out a couple of long maxi dresses and a few pairs of strappy sandals. "I told them that radio wouldn't know where to put our music, which means we would be destined to flop."

When Tassia looked at her friend, she noticed how much she blinked.

"Wait. You didn't tell Trutel that, did you?" India held up her hand.

"Will you call them by their real names? And, yes, I did share my feelings with them." Without care on how her clothes landed in the suitcase, Tassia tossed them inside while India groaned. "What? I've been around the industry long enough to know what's up."

"So have I. I know that when an offer is made, you don't turn it down no matter what." India jumped off the bed and approached Tassia. She held her by her shoulders to make Tassia look at her. "I've seen flashes in the pans come and go all the time. I dress them and listen to newbies talking about doing whatever they want and walking away from deals like they're going to stay rich forever." India shook her head. "You of all people should know better."

"What's that supposed to mean?" Tassia cocked her head and waited to hear what her friend had to say.

"You've been up to bat twice already. Once with the TV show and now with your Charisma contract. You know that a lot of opportunities don't come around that often. Charisma is a good label. You've worked steadily for them for years." She looked around Tassia's bedroom. "You're in a sweet-ass condo down at the Oceanfront. I don't know many people your age who have it like that. You should have said yes to any offer given to you."

Tassia shook her head. "Easier said than done. I walked in there for my meeting and heard that some singer they signed a couple of years ago is working on her album. *Solo* album. That should have been me."

"You can't compare your trajectory to anyone else's."

Tassia stomped into her walk-in closet and opened a drawer in her center island to pull out some undergarments. "That would be fine if she was even considered for it, but I guess she got discounted for her lack of experience. But good ol' Tassia will do it. I'm sure they thought that I wouldn't mind playing in the background to someone else." Tassia rubbed her head when she felt a migraine coming on hard.

She knew she shouldn't have started this conversation now before their trip. She wanted to talk about this once she had some liquid courage to give her some strength.

"Will you at least tell me who you would have been singing with had you accepted the offer?" India stood in the closet doorway and watched Tassia pulling out bras and panties from her drawers.

"Oh, that's the best part. Hyde Love." Tassia walked by India, but didn't get very far before India grabbed Tassia's arm, jostling her enough that she dropped some of her undergarments to the tan carpeted floor.

"Whoa. Did you say Hyde Love?"

"Indy. Girl. Take it easy." Tassia bent over and picked up her lacy items. "Yes. You remember my *Ratty Rat's Fun Crew* member, don't you? And let's not forget that one time I auditioned for him. I certainly can't forget it. 'Don't call us. We'll call you.'"

India blinked hard. "For one thing, your dad pulled you out of the show, not you."

"I know. But even though we worked together for a year—"

"As children."

"He still wouldn't consider me as simply a back-up singer."

"You aren't still hung up on that one audition, are you?" She chuckled. "Even Simon Cowell didn't think Kelly Clarkson would be a star. Look at her."

Tassia shrugged before going back to her bed to pack the rest of her items. "Five or six years ago I wasn't good enough to even sing back-up for him. Now all of a sudden he can do a duets album with me. I don't see the lure for me." She shook her head.

"I do. He's the hottest thing out there in *music*, not just country music. Think of him as the male version of Taylor Swift, but he's staying true to his country roots." India started ticking off items on each finger. "He's sold out arenas. All of his videos go viral. Every time he drops a single or album it instantly goes to number one on Billboard's Hot 100 chart. He's the real deal. Look at what associating with him has done for Christina. They paired up on the TV show, and then she opened for him on one of his tours."

Tassia turned to India. "So just like back then, he doesn't need me. He's got other people willing to ride in his wagon."

"But you might need him. If you do the duet album with him, you'll get—"

"Nothing." Tassia shook her head. "I'll be seen as an accessory like I was when I sang that damn line in that song. I will be the 'hook girl.' I don't want to be that." She slammed her suitcase closed and zipped it up to show India that she wanted to go. "All I wanted was what they promised me when I signed with them five years ago. I wanted to record my own album. Now I'm simply some studio singer good enough to be passed around from one guy to the next."

"Whoa. I don't think Chantel and Truman thought that about you when they made the offer. Maybe they were thinking of our current state of affairs right now. Maybe people need to hear two different voices and backgrounds making good music. Look at Snoop Dogg and Martha Stewart." India laughed. "I love their cooking show. I'm sure people thought those two wouldn't be good together. But they've hit pay dirt."

Tassia slid her feet into a pair of bedazzled flip flops. "Now you sound like Truman and Chantel."

India's eyes widened. "See. They do have a plan for you. Can't you imagine it? You do this album with the biggest star in music right now and it shoots your career out of the water. I'm not simply talking about sales. I'm talking interviews, endorsement deals, award nominations."

"Wait. I got you there." Tassia wagged her finger at India. "I did some research. Hyde Love has been nominated a bunch of times, but he's never won anything. Not one Grammy. Not an American Music Award. Nothing." She snapped her fingers. "Wait. I take that back. He has won an MTV Music Award for Best Video I think. Or maybe it was for Best Kiss in a Video. I can't remember."

"You are so salty." India shook her head.

"I can afford to be. I may not be a top-selling artist now, but I write great songs. If Charisma doesn't recognize my talent, another artist or label will." Tassia picked up her purse.

She didn't need Charisma to keep her career going. She had come to terms with the whole situation from this one conversation. If Chantel and Truman didn't recognize her star power and everything she had to offer, she would go elsewhere. Then she heard India's cackling.

"Where are you going to go?" India grabbed her purse from Tassia's bed.

"I could go anywhere. I hear Section Eight is still looking for a flagship artist to launch their R&B line since they lost out on Avery." That story had been true, but Tassia had no designs on going to that label. She didn't want to be associated with artists who glorified killing and breaking the law.

India's even louder laugh sent a chill up Tassia's spine.

"You want to go to Section Eight? You don't even listen to any of their current artists." India picked up the remote to turn off the TV. Then she made good on her promise and dumped several packages of condoms in Tassia's carryon bag.

Tassia sighed. She would leave them. She knew once they arrived in Fiji, India would need them for herself.

"Fine. Then I'll freelance. I don't just write songs for Charisma. I can write for anyone. Doing the tour gave me a great bump in my bottom line.

The writing sustains me." She glanced at the TV screen and caught the image of a host posing as a daytime talk show journalist, but who really could be categorized as a gossip. "Ugh. Turn that off and let's go. Like you said, we need to get to the airport."

The faster Tassia could get her feet into some warm sand, the happier she would be.

"I'm coming." India paused before she uttered, "Uh-oh."

"What? Some respected person in entertainment or politics get their hands caught in the cookie jar again?" Tassia stood at her bedroom door as she looked at India, who kept her stare directly on the TV screen with her mouth agape.

India only broke her attention once to peer over at Tassia, before she turned up the volume.

Too curious to remain in her spot, Tassia dropped her suitcase and sauntered next to India. She spotted a picture of herself on a monitor over the male host's shoulder. Tassia should have been given points for being able to notice anything beyond the bright, sparkly purple jacket the older man wore.

"What's going on? Why does he have my picture on the screen?" Tassia kept her stare on the man.

"We all know who this woman is. If you don't, then you haven't heard the song of the summer, 'Ride Me.'" The host covered his mouth before adjusting his large square glasses. "This is Tassia Hogan. Besides singing with Aaron, rumor has it that they carried on a hot, steamy affair while on the road."

Tassia turned to India. "That's a lie."

The host continued. "She's also known as a songwriter. At least, that's what she wanted people to believe."

"What?" Tassia put her hand to her chest.

"Turns out all the songs she claims she has written aren't hers. She uses a ghostwriter and is taking the money and credit for each song, including ones written for that dynamic duo, Chantel and Truman Woodley." The host let out a long, low whistle while shaking his head. "Tassia had better make friends with as many people that she can. Her world is about to be turned upside down with pending lawsuits. You can't take credit for something you didn't do."

Tassia balled her hand into a fist and wanted to punch a hole through the lying host's face through the TV. "That's a lie. Every word I wrote in a song came from me and only me." She shook her head. "I can't believe someone is trying to discredit me and my work. This is so wrong."

"Probably so. But with big mouths like this guy and the gossip sites out there, it won't take long for this to spread like wildfire and your name to be mud in the industry. You know that."

"I'm not going to take this." Tassia rummaged through her purse to retrieve her phone. As soon as she touched it, it rang. Seeing her manager's name across the screen accelerated her pulse even more. "Graham, are you watching this crap?" She kept her stare on the TV.

"No, but I've been getting calls back to back, though, about you. What's on the TV?" Graham normally talked slow with a southern drawl that came out as fast as thick molasses being poured from a jar.

Tassia knew even he had to be worried. "That no-good gossip TV host, Chatty Charlie, just announced during his rumor patrol segment that I didn't write any of the songs that other singers have sung. That's bullshit." She paced back and forth in front of the TV.

"Calm down, Tee. We can fix this."

Tassia nodded. "I know, because the first thing I want to do is sue that son-of-a-bitch on TV for reporting that lie. Does he realize that he's ruining my livelihood?"

"I'm sure that's the furthest thing from his mind." Graham's cadence slowed down a little. "We have truth on our side."

Tassia stopped marching. "Right."

"You came on board with Charisma because of your writing, right?"

She chewed her lower lip before answering. "I sang studio work before I let anyone see any of my songs."

She remembered being nervous to show off her work to anyone.

"Oh. That's okay. You did write songs in front of the people you sold them to, right?"

The pause must have made Graham nervous, which, in turn, accelerated Tassia's heartbeat again.

"I like writing alone. It helps my process." She smoothed her hand back through her hair.

"You never collaborated with anyone?" Graham's voice rose.

Like he could see her, Tassia shook her head. "Maybe change a word or phrasing here or there during recording, but that's it." She leaned against the wall next to the TV. "How bad do you think this is? I've got to post something on social media to let people know that this guy is full of shit."

"No." Graham's voice now sounded like her father. "Say nothing right now."

Tassia didn't understand this tactic. Her reputation had been sullied and she felt like she needed to defend herself and her work.

"Right now we need to take the high road and not say anything publicly yet. You'll have your chance to quiet the naysayers."

She snickered. "Yeah? How am I going to do that?"

How would she work in this industry again if people believed this lie? Who would trust her?

Graham took a deep breath before he spoke. "There's a meeting set up tomorrow at Charisma with Hyde Love. I trust you will be in town."

Tassia glanced at her suitcase before staring at India, who looked like she wanted to fly to Fiji naked to get ready for their vacation.

"If going to this meeting will save my career, I'll come tomorrow." Tassia's shoulders slumped down.

"Does that mean you're not going to Fiji with me?" India crossed her arms over her ample chest.

Tassia disconnected the call. "I have to get my career straight. I know you can understand that."

India didn't. This time when India screamed, she did it out of frustration and not excitement. Tassia wanted to join her.

Chapter 5

Hyde sat in Charisma's large conference room, waiting for Truman Woodley and his entourage. He knew the man would be in there with lawyers and business people ready for him to sign all kinds of deals. He wanted to meet Truman first before gracefully bowing out of the project, man to man, face to face. He could have done that easier without being flanked by Clever and three attorneys on Hyde's payroll.

Clever glanced at his oversized, bejeweled watch and let out an audible sigh.

"Truman and Chantel do have twins to take care of." Hyde didn't know where this need to defend the Woodleys came from, but he wanted to go into this meeting with some level of positivity, or at least respect.

Clever leaned in close to Hyde. "Let's face it. In this situation, you are the bigger star, and yet you're here first." He sniffed.

"None of that today." Hyde waved his hand in front of himself. "It's all about the music."

At least, it should have been.

His father laughed. No, more like cackled. The sound bristled the small hairs on the back of Hyde's neck.

"You're not new to this. Everything is about business." Clever knocked his elbow against Hyde's side. "This is a power move. I feel it. The last ones in the room are the ones with the power."

Hyde didn't want to believe that of this duo. He had seen Truman and Chantel at a couple of award shows and shared a cursory "hi" and "good-bye" kind of interaction and nothing more. Hyde figured that despite the fame and fortune, the two of them had to be nice people.

The door opened. On instinct, Hyde stood even though his manager and the rest of his team didn't. Hyde had been taught manners from the champion of excellent southern charm herself, Mrs. Mabel Love, his grandmother.

A mature man strolled in before a harried woman waltzed in behind him. The sight of that twisted Hyde's gut. The guy should have opened the door for the woman even if he didn't know her, which from the way they whispered to each other when they sat at the table, he could tell they must work together. Neither of them introduced themselves to anyone, which he also found odd and a little rude.

Hyde reached over the table. "Hi, I'm Hyde Love." He held his hand up to the woman first, who blinked, glanced at the man next to her, and then finally accepted his hand.

"Uh, hi. I'm Norma Stern." She shook his hand so briefly, she barely left the warmth of it when she drew it back.

"Graham Pontefort." He, on the other hand, gave Hyde a strong handshake but limited eye contact.

Neither stood during their introductions. Mabel would have popped them both had she been in the room.

Hyde nearly took a seat, thinking no one else would be arriving besides Truman and Chantel, when a woman walked in who took every bit of his sense out of his head.

The gorgeous African-American woman floated into the room like she commanded every part of it. Time had been very generous to Tassia Hogan. He noticed she had something that looked like French braids in several rows in her hair that went down to a grouped ponytail that she let rest over her shoulder, different from the pigtails she used to sport as a child. Thin straps held up the very summery dress she wore that whispered over her breasts and brushed the tops of her sandaled feet. Her honey-oak skin tone looked smooth from where Hyde stood.

Without a word, she dominated the room, forcing grown men who didn't bother to acknowledge the first woman who had walked into the room to actually stand when she entered. Hyde had nearly pulled off his trademark baseball cap when he felt a sharp elbow to his side. That motion alone prompted him to follow his original instincts and remove his hat in front of this beautiful woman.

Her reaction to not look at him didn't surprise him. In the last few years, every time he had entered a room, every woman watched him and made a point of getting his attention. Not this cool customer. Their last interaction hadn't been a positive one, so it surprised him that she would want to be a part of this project. Or maybe, like him, she only came to this meeting to turn the project down to his face.

She kept her gaze on the table and the empty chair across from him. When she finally connected her green-eyed stare to his, Hyde stopped breathing. He remembered her having that same effect on him when they filmed the show.

"Long time no see." When he noticed that she stared at him blankly, Hyde decided to break the ice. He held his hand up to her. "I'm Hyde. I don't know if you remember me. We used to work together."

She gave Mona Lisa a run for her money with the slight smile she presented before taking his hand. Electricity shot up Hyde's arm to the top of his head before zipping down to his booted feet that remained cemented to the floor.

"I remember you."

Hyde had kept his total concentration on the way her full lips formed words and sounds that came out of her luscious mouth.

"I can't believe you're here. I didn't know you would be a part of this project." Had Hyde known, he wouldn't have shown up to the meeting. No use dredging up the past, especially after doing so much work to squash his previous entertainment work.

Tassia had him. Between her hypnotic gaze, the softness of her hand that made him imagine that he held velvet covered in mink fur, and her magnetic aura, Hyde couldn't escape. Luckily, he wanted to be trapped in her vortex.

Hyde continued holding her hand as he spoke. "Tassia. You've changed a lot." He didn't know how to react to her. He had already shaken her hand, but because of their humble entertainment beginnings, he really wanted to hug her. "No more pigtails."

"But you still have that baseball cap." She pointed to the cap he held in his hand.

Hyde shoved the rolled-up bill in his back pocket. From the way Tassia crossed her arms over her chest, he figured she didn't want the embrace.

In his mind he did a mental inventory of all the changes. Tassia had sprung up in height. Even at ten, she had towered over most of the boys on set, including him. Not now. From what he could tell from her flowy dress, it looked like she had a nice figure. Her eyes had remained the same. He remembered being eleven and too nervous to stare her in her eyes. Not today.

"We met one time after the show, but I guess you don't remember me." She pulled a chair back on the opposite side of the table from him.

"Maybe what you did wasn't memorable." If Truman and Chantel planned to pair him up with her, Hyde knew he couldn't do this project.

He didn't need the media bringing up their *Ratty Rat's Fun Crew* association again, not when he had successfully managed to get the media to finally stop talking about his early acting work. If he got paired up with Tassia, he would be the laughingstock of the music industry.

"Maybe your taste in quality has changed."

"It has. I no longer deal in childish things." Hyde had to be clear with her. He had no desire to revisit the past. Tassia had to know that. "Besides, you're doing a lot on your own these days, right? You do back-up singing for Aaron?"

The scowl that covered her face could have erupted every dormant volcano in the world. She promptly sat in the chair.

"I'm not a back-up singer. You made it painfully obvious that I wasn't suitable, at least not for you." She sounded like she growled the statement. "If you knew I was coming and you have no interest in working with me, why did you come?"

"I didn't know who my duet partner would be."

Tassia laughed. "Sounds like you still are being treated like a child. I knew you would be asked when I was asked about the project." She cocked her head. "You may want to question your management team about keeping you in the dark."

"Hi, I'm Clever Love, Hyde Love's manager and his father." He shook Tassia's hand.

"I know who you are. I remember seeing you around the set from the Ratty Rat days." Tassia nodded.

"I'm afraid I don't remember you that much from that time period, but it was so long ago, and my son has gone on and done lots of things." He shrugged, and then held his hand up to the two people who had come in the room before the surly beauty to introduce himself to them.

The woman shook Clever's hand first. "I'm Tassia Hogan's agent." She nodded over to the man next to her. "This is Tassia's manager." Then she glanced around the room. "Anyone here on Truman or Chantel's side?"

The rest of the people shook their heads. As though mentioning their names conjured the duo, the door opened and the Woodleys walked inside.

As Hyde expected, Truman held the door open for his wife. When she got to the table, he pulled her chair out for her. Gentleman through and through.

"Please excuse our tardiness. I had forgotten what having toddlers means to your life." Truman sat down after his wife, while a smattering of laughter rippled through the large group.

"I hope you all introduced yourselves and weren't waiting for us." Chantel's naturally husky and rich voice sounded strong, a far cry from the image of her being weak and fragile after her infamous nervous breakdown a few years ago.

"We did, but we haven't formally met." Hyde reached over to Chantel first. "Hyde Love. Nice to meet you."

Chantel beamed as she shook his hand. "Very nice to meet you. I enjoy your work." She pulled her hand back after shaking Hyde's to put it on top of her husband's arm. "Thanks to this wonderful man here, I've gained a new appreciation for all types of music, particularly country. I love it."

Hyde's face hurt from smiling so hard. "Thank you, ma'am."

"Oh, please. Call me Chantel."

"Hi, I'm Truman Woo—"

"Woodley." Hyde nodded. He suspected he must have looked like a wide-eyed fan, but he couldn't hide the fact that he did enjoy this man's music. "I know. Very nice to meet you. I'm a fan of your music." He glanced at Chantel. "Both of you. My grandmother used to make me play 'Love Me, Love Me, Love Me' on the piano when we had company over."

Again, the attendees laughed.

Chantel blinked. "I don't think I've ever heard a man sing that song. I think that would be interesting to hear."

Feeling a bit in control and gentlemanly, Hyde turned to the trio that had come into the room before the Woodleys. "Have you met Tassia Hogan and her team?"

Chantel chuckled a little. "Yes. Tassia actually is a contracted artist here at Charisma. We're very well acquainted."

The picture started to come into focus for Hyde as he assumed his seat. "Okay."

He turned to Clever to get his mind back on business and out of the euphoric fantasy that he had created in his head where he and the Woodleys would have fun jam sessions, and he and Tassia could discuss the tension between them before finally parting ways for good.

"Hopefully, you all know why we're here." Chantel clasped her hands together and rested them on the large, long table that looked like it had been a rooted tree only moments before. A thin varnish covered the sanded down level finish.

"Something about a duet, right?" Hyde glanced over at Tassia, who kept her stare on the Woodleys.

"That's right." Truman nodded. "My wife and I were thinking about our next project. We liked the idea of mixing genres." He glanced at Chantel and smiled. "It worked so well for us."

Chantel gripped his hand.

Hyde had written songs about that level of love and devotion that he saw in Truman and Chantel. He thought relationships like that only existed in books and songs. He wanted that kind of love with someone outside of the industry. Thanks to Shelby Lynne, he couldn't imagine falling for someone in the music business.

"Sounds nice." Graham's voice cut through the still air in the room. "When would you want this released?"

Chantel directed her full attention on Graham. "We're hoping by March of next year."

"March?" Clever put his hand to his stiff peak of freshly dyed hair. "Promotionally speaking, that doesn't give us a lot of time. I mean, we were promoting Hyde's current release a year before it came out. We're already into August, almost September. You want to record an album in that time and have it released by—"

"Spring. Yes." Truman nodded. "It can be done. With the right social media buzz, it could still work."

"We want to release the album that quick to capture the awards season." Chantel sat up taller like she needed to prove something to someone. "We've already been given a time spot to perform at the Grammys and Breakout Music Awards."

"When you mentioned this to me, you said you wanted us to write all of the songs." Tassia pointed to Hyde and finally looked at him.

"What?" As much as he didn't want to, Hyde broke away from her mesmerizing stare to bring his full attention to Truman and Chantel, poised at the end of the table. "The songs aren't written already?"

"We thought you liked writing your own songs." Truman stared back at Hyde.

"Maybe I assumed that because this was some sort of passion project for you that you would have already had some songs in mind for the album." For as much as Hyde had been doing for the last few years of his life, he wanted to be taken care of finally. Pampered a bit, well, if he decided to do the project.

Writing took a lot out of him because he put so much of himself into the work. If the Woodleys expected him to write, record, and promote this album, he definitely wanted to bow out of this effort.

"We wanted you two to have a meeting of the minds and write from your hearts." Chantel volleyed her attention between Hyde and Tassia. "We would open Charisma's studio up to you two for a month to have you write out the songs you want on the album. You'll have access to all instruments."

"Producers?" Tassia asked and leaned her head back as she awaited the answer.

"In-house again." Truman pointed to himself and then his wife. "Me, Chantel, and Laz Kyson."

Hyde hadn't worked with any of them before, but a small spark ignited inside of him. Maybe this creative new direction would be the key to getting his love back into music. The more Truman and Chantel talked, the more he became enamored with the idea. The downside had to be working with Tassia. That couldn't happen.

"What do you say?" Chantel intertwined her fingers with Truman's.

Just as Hyde started to say he wanted to be a part of the project if they didn't involve Tassia, Clever took away his voice with one statement. "No." He shook his head emphatically. "You want my guy to do all the work to bring your singer up."

Truman's eyebrows furrowed. "No. Tassia is a gifted songwriter and singer."

"Not according to every gossip site out there." Clever glared at Tassia. "No wonder your name sounds familiar. You were just blasted for not writing any of the songs that you claimed you wrote." He snickered. "I bet you pocketed all that money, too. And you'll have to give back any awards you've won." He turned to the Woodleys. "And now you want to link her tarnished image to my shining star and think it's going to fly? Not a chance." Then he wagged his finger at her. "I do remember you from the show now. You quit right before a taping. Your father dragged you out. Is that what's going to happen here? You get upset about something and you're going to give up and leave my guy in the lurch?" He glared at Truman and Chantel. "Did you know she did that before you two thought that they would be great back together again?"

Tassia stood from the table, but braced her hands on it to get into Clever's face. "I am not a quitter. You have no idea what you're talking about."

"Oh, so you didn't leave the show? Am I mistaken?" Hyde's father put his hand to his chest.

"No, but I didn't leave on a whim." She gritted her teeth before she continued. "And I wrote every word of every song that I did for other artists. If you were to believe everything you read on gossip sites, then I guess I should believe that Hyde is into underaged girls. There was a report that he had a couple of them in his hotel room recently."

"Lies!" Clever pointed to Tassia.

"Whoa. Hold on, everyone." Truman stood and held his hands up. "Let's all take a breath and settle down."

"No, I'll tell you what's going to happen." Clever stood. "You're going to tell us that these two will split the money for this project evenly, and that's not going to happen either."

"It should if they both write the songs." This time Norma stood.

"And that's a big *if.*" Clever laughed. "I can see the writing on the wall here. Charisma wants the fame of Hyde without signing him because they can't afford him."

"Back up there." Chantel stood. "You can speak for your client, but do not dare to speak for me, my husband, or our business. We came at you two with only one motive: to make great music. There's nothing else on our agenda." She looked at Tassia. "We asked Tassia to do it because she's worked hard and she's talented."

"I can see. She has you two fooled. I don't even know if she can sing anything else but one line." Clever laughed.

Hyde wanted out of this project but not at the sake of this woman's dignity. The sound and cruelty behind his father's words twisted Hyde's guts. Before Hyde decided to pull the choke chain on his manager and bring Tassia down easy, a voice stopped him.

Tassia sang the opening of The Judds' "Love Can Build A Bridge" pitch perfect and without any accompaniment.

Hyde felt his bottom jaw go slack, not only because Tassia knew a country song, but because her voice sounded heaven sent.

At the end of the chorus, she glared at the group. "Sorry this was a grand waste of time for everyone." She grabbed her purse and gave Hyde one last look before leaving the room.

"I'm sorry, too." Clever put his hand on Hyde's shoulder. "Now we can get started on your next album since the tour is over."

Hyde's mind flooded with ideas. Despite seeing Tassia up close and hearing her incredible voice that kept getting better with age, he couldn't see himself doing this project. Actually, he could see himself. He envisioned his younger, fatter version standing alongside the always poised Tassia and feeling inferior...again. That didn't mean he couldn't use this situation to his advantage just like Christina had used their pairing to propel her career. This time, Hyde would be the one to use someone else. So if he wanted to make a move, he had to do it now.

Chapter 6

Tassia knew it. She knew it. Crawling back to Charisma and practically begging for the opportunity to do this project right after the lies had broken that she couldn't write a song if someone had a gun to her head felt all wrong. Both Norma and Graham had convinced her that this would be a positive move in the right direction for her. She didn't believe either of them, but wanted to give this pitch session a chance. Then she saw Hyde. She heard Hyde. He didn't want to do this project, and seemed almost disgusted by the idea of working with her again. Fine. She would walk away. Too bad he looked way different than his show days.

Whoa. The man exuded power and raw sexuality. As a kid, he had captured her attention then. Now, he practically owned her. She couldn't stop looking at him once she finally did.

He looked attractive in pictures. In the era of phone apps with filters, anyone could look amazing nowadays. To see him up close almost broke her down to being just like his fans, who all clamored for his attention. He hadn't lost his appeal, but thank goodness he changed from a red baseball cap to a blue one.

Now *his* green eyes looked otherworldly, like he could see down to her soul and accepted every imperfect part of her like a dream man should. Then he spoke and she knew that would never happen from him. Hyde had judged her from their time together on the same TV show, and her work with Aaron. He made it obvious that unlike Christina, he did not want to work with her again.

She had to force herself to not look at his full lips, surrounded by a subtle light brown scruff. When he smiled, he showed off a great set of straight, white teeth that didn't look like a dentist had manufactured them for show.

All of those amazing aspects hadn't crumbled Tassia. In the back of her mind, she remembered his dismissive demeanor at her audition. She recalled how cold he had reacted toward her by not interacting with her at all. Then she touched him.

Tassia shook his hand at the meeting and the world stopped. The only thing that existed had to be her connection to his tough but smooth flesh. He held her hand like he never wanted to let her go. If only that kind of conviction existed in the men she had dated.

Tassia had prepared to fall on the sword to prove herself in the industry again. She could not only sing, but she could write a hell of a song. Then that jerk C. Love had the nerve to bring up that story, that outright lie, that she hadn't written any of her songs.

"Tassia, wait."

Tassia heard her manager's voice, but that didn't stop her. She continued heading to the front door to go home and sulk. She had already missed her trip to Fiji with India, who delighted in texting Tassia pictures of herself on the beach.

"Don't go." Graham coughed after he made his appeal, and then he wheezed.

So that she didn't tax her team too much, she stopped at the front door and turned to the duo. Norma reached her first before Graham caught up to her.

"You shouldn't have run away like that." Norma shook her head.

Although the dark-skinned woman kind of reminded Tassia of her mother, she couldn't classify as a substitute. Today Norma wore a red pantsuit with a colorful scarf hanging from her neck.

"Why not?" Tassia rested her fists on her hips. "It's obvious that they didn't want to work with me. Did you hear his manager? They believed those stories."

"Yeah, but you shut them down with your voice." Graham tried smiling while still gasping for air.

As much as Tassia didn't want to, she sang the same song she had used during her audition, hoping it would spark some recollection in Hyde or his pigheaded manager. She couldn't believe she remembered the words to the song she had sung to the group.

From Hyde's expression, it looked like he hadn't expected her to belt out that song. Or maybe she had managed to impress him with her voice. Or maybe he did finally remember her audition. At this point in her career, Tassia hadn't expected to keep having to prove herself.

"I knew people would believe those stories." Tassia shook her head.

"Chantel and Truman didn't." Norma put her hand on Tassia's shoulder. "They were the first ones to post on social media that they're standing by you." The stately woman moved in closer to Tassia. "You think they would have put their necks out for you if they didn't believe you?"

Tassia regarded her manager for a moment before crossing her arms over her chest and turning her back on her. "Hyde doesn't want to do it, and even if he did, his dad won't let him. Did you see the way he looked at me when C. Love called me a fraud?"

Graham moved in next to Tassia. "Did you see the way *he* looked at *you* when you called him a pedophile? It goes both ways."

Tassia didn't mean to get down in the mud with Clever Love. When she saw that news story on a gossip site about Hyde and some teenage girls, she didn't believe it, just like she wanted people to not believe she couldn't be creative. When Clever's accusation came out, she had to fight back. She didn't like fighting dirty, though.

"I'm already not feeling positive about all this." Tassia shook her head.

"I don't blame you."

Tassia blinked when she heard a new voice, a deeper voice, a seductive one. She looked in the glass doors in front of her face to see if she could spy who spoke in the reflection. She caught the sight of a shadowy figure behind her. From the height and build, she knew it couldn't be Clever. To eliminate the suspense, she turned.

Hyde kept his light brown hair short, almost military style. He looked different without his trademark backward baseball cap.

"I would feel pretty lousy, too, if I got accused of something I didn't do." Hyde took a deep breath before he continued. "I don't prey on young girls." He glared at her.

"And I know how to write songs and sing." She met his stare with a harder one, at least she hoped she did. "I'm sorry for saying that about you."

"Thank you. I appreciate you saying that. You sure can sing." Hyde took a step forward. "Look. I know we all got off on the wrong foot back there. Can we start over?" He smiled.

The look immediately undid her, so much so that she dropped her gaze to the floor to regain some control. Through his thin white T-shirt, she saw his small nipples poking against the fabric, the same ones she had fantasized about licking whenever she watched his video. When she got down to his jeans, she had to make herself not look for any noticeable impressions around the crotch area. She breathed a sigh of relief down at his feet, thankful he didn't have on cowboy boots. Instead he wore work boots that looked old, worn-in and dirty. This top money-earning artist wore old boots to a meeting. She fought not to smile at that. It still didn't take away from the fact that this man didn't want to work with her again.

"What I heard you sing back there sounded incredible." Hyde's deep voice rumbled the floor.

Tassia felt the vibration through her thin sandals and the tide turning. Did Hyde Love now want to work with her?

"We should talk more about this collaboration. I already have ideas." He rubbed his hands together.

So did Tassia. Too bad her thoughts had nothing to do with writing, singing, or recording.

Come on. Get out of your head. You just broke up with a guy. Not the time.

She peered up at him. "So, you're interested in doing this duets album?"

Hyde glanced at her team before answering. "I am."

Something in his answer sounded like he wanted to admit something else.

"I thought you didn't want to go back to childish things." She wouldn't be letting him off the hook that easily.

"I see this as a great opportunity." His wide smile looked convincing.

Too bad Tassia saw through his cheerful demeanor. She knew he hid something. "What does your father think?" She had seen these types of entertainers before. She'd written for them. Hell, she just left a tour with the poster child of a pampered star. Hyde Love wouldn't be any different.

"My *manager* has a lot of thoughts just like I'm sure your team does." Hyde nodded toward Norma and Graham. "Final decision is always mine. Hopefully, you treat your career the same way." He cleared his throat. "May I talk to you privately?"

Tassia didn't know why, but her heartbeat accelerated at his request. "Anything you say to me can be said in front of my manager and agent."

Hyde glanced at Norma and Graham. "I'm sure business conversations can be."

He let the implication hang in between them until Tassia made the first move away from her team to a more secluded area of the Charisma lobby. With her back to Norma and Graham, Tassia kept her arms crossed as she waited for Hyde to address her.

He sauntered in front of her and looked serious doing so. Tassia wouldn't let that sway her.

"I don't know what you're going to say, but I will tell you this." Tassia pointed to the two of them. "Neither one of us has signed anything. Nothing has gone out on social media about this. No one has to know about this meeting. Let's just chalk it up as a good experiment and move on."

Hyde stared at her for a moment with his head cocked to the side before he scratched the top of it.

"What?" Tassia shrugged.

"I don't know you, but I sort of had you pegged as having a bigger backbone than what you're showing me right now." He brought his hand down to the side of his face and rubbed his barely-there beard.

She blinked hard. "Are you calling me a coward?"

"I wouldn't use that word. Maybe unadventurous or complacent." He snapped his fingers and wagged his index finger at her. "Scared. That's the emotion I'm looking for, like when you wouldn't do that scene with the zookeeper and the live snake on the show."

Tassia felt her eyes go wide before she laughed. "Scared. Really? I see what you're doing."

This time he shrugged. "What am I doing?"

"You're trying to trick me into doing this project. I'm not falling for it."

"Good. Don't do it because anyone coerced you into doing it or on a dare." He moved in close to her.

At his proximity, Tassia caught his heady woodsy scent. Between his aroma and the heat she felt emanating from his body, she could barely keep standing.

"If you're going to do this project, do it because it speaks to you, because you feel like with your words and actions, you can make a difference." He lowered his voice. "I have a feeling that you might have something to prove." He nodded. "I understand."

Hyde started to back up, but Tassia had more questions. "What do you have to prove?"

He continued backing toward the conference room. "That's something I would reveal to a recording partner. Have a good one." He turned and ducked into the room.

Tassia didn't move from her spot. Or maybe she couldn't move. Hyde left a trail of bread crumbs for her to follow. Damn it if she didn't want to join him.

"What did he say to you?" Norma approached Tassia first.

Tassia regarded her agent. "What's the downside of me doing this project?"

Norma chuckled. "There is none. Advanced money they're offering is good. Time schedule is tight, but I know you can handle it. And you'll be recording with the hottest singer out there right now. What do you have to lose?"

Her identity, Tassia thought. Would she just be another back-up singer for a more popular star? Why did this country boy intrigue her so much?

"Are you thinking about doing it?" Graham put his hand on Tassia's shoulder. "Are you ready to go back in the meeting room?"

Instead of verbally answering him, Tassia headed to the war room. She would let her team hash out the details while she figured out Hyde's angle. For a singer who had the world at his fingertips, what did he have to prove to anyone?

As soon as she walked into the room, she noticed a wave of relief washing over Chantel's face.

Truman smiled. "Tassia, you came back."

Tassia took a seat. "The dig about my skills irked me." She glared at Clever, who didn't even acknowledge her until Hyde nudged his manager to do so. "But after some conversation, I think I'm ready to do this."

"No, no, no." Hyde shook his head.

What? Now did Hyde want to back out from this deal? Tassia braced her hands on the table, getting prepared to make her second and final exit.

"I want you to be sure about this. No guessing. Are you positive you want to do this duets album with me?" Hyde stared at her.

Tassia couldn't break the connection. She nodded. "Yes. I think this could be good for my career."

Hyde nodded. "Good. Before we go any further." He turned to his manager. "Isn't there something you need to say?"

Clever worried his brows. "Me? What? Are we ready to talk about money?" He turned his attention to Truman and Chantel.

"We're not talking money or contracts or anything else until you apologize to Tassia for questioning her abilities."

Tassia blinked. In an industry where she, at times, felt powerless and sometimes even voiceless, to hear Hyde not only believe her but make people accountable for their bad actions made her stomach tingle. She had to bite the insides of her cheek to keep from smiling like a goofball. Someone at his level didn't have to go to bat for her. Then again, Tassia had been around long enough to recognize posturing when she saw it.

"You're kidding." Clever kept a confused stare on his star.

Hyde shook his head. "She walked out of here because of something you said."

"She's used to walking. I told you so. And she insulted you, too, with her quip about—"

Hyde held up his hand. "Tassia has already apologized to me. That's why I'm sitting in here with her right now." He remained quiet but his glare to his manager said everything.

With a slow turn of his head, Clever finally looked at Tassia. "I'm sorry for what I said earlier about you not writing your own songs. You understand how the business is. You see stuff on the Internet. Some things are true, and some aren't." He shrugged. "I needed to know for sure that you're the real deal."

"We brought her here. Of course she's the real deal." Chantel's voice cut through the tension of the room.

"Apology accepted." Tassia kept her arms crossed though. She would have to watch herself around this group.

"Good. Now that that's settled, tell us the time schedule for this project and your expectations." Hyde's smile could bring about world peace.

Truman took a deep breath after the tension left the room. "Like we mentioned before, the schedule will be pretty aggressive. We would like for you and Tassia to write and record here in the studio."

"How soon?" Tassia felt the need to insert her voice into this process so that she wouldn't be seen as a prop, an afterthought, a back-up singer.

"How's tomorrow sound?" Chantel chewed her lower lip as she split her attention between Hyde and Tassia.

Tassia opened her mouth to balk at the plan, citing that she would need more time to prepare, when Hyde interrupted her flow.

"Sounds doable. The earlier we can get this going, the better." He rubbed his hand over his short hair. "The more time I have between working, the more I'll want to relax. Now that I have something to do, I don't want to stop." He stared at Tassia.

Although his gaze could melt ice caps, Tassia would be damned if she looked away from him first. "How many songs?"

"Standard album length." Truman drummed his thumbs on the table. "Twelve to fourteen."

"Maybe fifteen." Hyde nodded. "You do half and I do half, and then we'll do one together."

Tassia opened her mouth to agree, but got cut off by one of her bosses.

"We were hoping all songs on the album would be a collaboration." Chantel lowered her voice to something gentle and soothing. "We don't want half of a country sound and the other half sounding like an R&B album. We want you two to blend your ideas."

Tassia swallowed hard at the idea of blending anything with Hyde with his large hands and absolutely kissable lips. She brought her full attention to Chantel to clear her mind. "That brings me to my concern again. How will we be categorized? Pop? R&B? Country?"

Truman shook his head. "Don't worry about that. Just worry about making great music."

Hyde chuckled, which snagged Tassia's attention. "Sounds like folk to me."

Although she didn't want to, Tassia had to smile at his astute assessment.

"No time like the present." Hyde stood. "Tassia, since you're familiar with the studio, will you show me around?"

Tassia looked at her management team for a moment before she could register an answer.

Hyde barreled through his thoughts. "You all work out the details of the contract." He put his hand on his father's shoulder. "Fifty-fifty."

Clever's audible gasp could be heard in California. "You're the big star here." He glanced at Tassia. "No offense. I know you have a hit right now that beat Hyde's latest release, but that's just one hit. Hyde has been at it for—"

"Fifty. Fifty." Hyde spaced the words out so much like he wanted to make sure his manager understood him. "This album is a collaboration. Treat every detail of it like it is, understand?"

Clever cursed under his breath, but Tassia heard him. If she heard him, she knew everyone else had.

"That is mighty generous of you." Norma smiled and it deepened the dimples on the sides of her face.

Hyde walked around to the other side of the table where Tassia sat. She should have stood up. She should have moved. She could have at least said that she wouldn't be going anywhere while negotiations occurred. When she saw Hyde take command of the situation and the room, she couldn't do anything but follow his lead.

Hyde stood next to Tassia and held his hand out to her. "Are you ready?"

Nothing in her life had prepared her for this moment. She slipped her hand into his strong one and mustered a smile.

"Let's go."

Chapter 7

Hyde forgot about the project as soon as he encountered Tassia Hogan and realized he had a way to get his downtime. Although he didn't want to use her, he recognized the opportunity to use this duet as a way to sneak in some time away from the business. Lying had never been a part of his character. For once, he would be selfish and hope that Tassia would understand.

Then again, maybe he didn't have to tell her. He would keep the motivation for doing this deal under wraps. If she balked, he could easily pay her off. It would be money well spent for a tiny piece of relaxation.

After holding her hand long enough to get her to her feet, Tassia broke from the grasp to lead him around the studio located at the beach side.

At various spots in the studio, Hyde caught different aromas. Sometimes he smelled the scent of wildflowers. The fragrance immediately brought him back home to Tennessee and being in the woods behind his grandparents' property. In other sections, the scent of wax and leather mixed in the air, a strange combination. The mixture conjured images of candles burning and musicians with their leather guitar straps circling their bodies. That vision alone had Hyde now imagining himself with his arms around Tassia's body.

Tassia with her luscious curves under her long dress. He even started to like her braids. As he followed her around the expansive studio, his gaze dropped down to her ass.

His grandmother would have yoked him back for objectifying this woman. Hell, he had even yelled at a fan at one of his shows when he caught a guy pulling a woman's tube top down and exposing her bare breasts while she danced around to his music. Here he had those same scandalous thoughts about this woman, wanting to slowly remove every stitch of her clothing and explore her body when only moments before, he had rejected the notion of working with her.

Damn. Had it been too long since his breakup with Shelby Lynne? Hyde really needed to get himself together. He would be working with this woman, closely, for the next few months, and then they would be business partners essentially as they promoted and performed. He couldn't ruin that relationship by mixing pleasure with business. Besides, he figured with her bump-and-grind dance with Aaron that she already had her dance card filled, and wouldn't find the likes of him the least bit attractive or desirable. That wouldn't stop his rampant imagination.

Of course his father would love Hyde's piggish thoughts. Since getting into the music business, his dad reaped the benefits, including scooping up young, willing women. Hyde thanked God Clever and his mother had split before his father lost his mind and his morals.

Hyde would push all illicit thoughts from his head right now to keep his mind on business. He had to give his full attention to Tassia.

"The business offices are on the top floor along with a couple of their recording studios." Tassia glanced back at him as she continued down the hallway. She approached a bank of elevators, looked like she wanted to hit the up button, but then continued to a sign marked *stairs*.

"You're not going to take the elevator to the top floor?" Hyde had to hustle to keep up with her.

"Stairs might be faster." She flashed a nervous smile complete with a twitch as she opened the door and hiked up the front of her dress to ascend the stairs. "I don't trust the elevator."

Maybe she didn't trust herself with Hyde in a confined space. A man could dream.

The door to the stairwell slammed closed behind Hyde as he followed her up six flights of stairs to get to the third floor. By the time they both reached the top, neither of them looked or sounded winded.

She glanced at him. "Need to rest?" Tassia smiled.

Hyde shook his head and took her beautiful smile as payment for the impromptu exercise. "Just fine. I work out a lot when I'm on the road so I can keep up in doing two- and three-hour shows each night." He followed her into a room. "I suspect you must do the same thing."

"Why would you say that?" She turned her back on a closed door and held the doorknob behind her while she looked up at him.

"Because you don't look out of breath. A few nights ago, the news covered the story of your tour with Aaron. That's where I first saw you, well, again." And when she first infected his every thought—again—but he would leave that part out of his story.

"I was playing in another arena close by that same night." In a need to get closer to her, Hyde placed his hand on the doorframe above her head, a feat considering she had to be five-foot-nine or a bit taller.

If she had worn heels, she would be able to look him in the eyes. Hyde kind of liked that idea.

"Was your show sold out?" Tassia leaned her head to the side, exposing her long, graceful neck.

Hyde had to clear his throat when a moan threatened to erupt. "Yes. And your show?"

"*Aaron's* show." She smirked. "Sold out as well. I was right."

Hyde felt his eyebrows knit together from her statement. "Right about what?"

"We cater to two distinct fan bases. People who like your work will probably shy away from the type of songs I normally sing, and vice versa. We might be embarking on a losing battle." Tassia kept her stare on Hyde as though daring him to disagree with her.

"Or we could be doing something great. Wouldn't that be cool?" Hyde watched her staring at him for a moment.

He couldn't be actually considering this. Hyde had had his mind made up as soon as he saw Tassia. Use the situation—not her—as a means to escape. She would sadly be a casualty.

His gaze dropped to her neck where he saw a thick vein pulsating. He had to stop imagining the impossible. Then again, if he had done that, he wouldn't be Hyde Love, mega star.

"That song that you sang just now..." Hyde prided himself on remembering faces, especially one as beautiful as Tassia's.

"The song I just sang didn't stir any memories?" She crossed her arms over her chest. When he slowed to answer, she finally filled in the blanks. "That was the song I used during my audition to be a back-up singer for you." She continued. "I had just graduated college. Charisma had offered me a job, but I wanted to spread my wings, test the waters." She shook her head. "Should have known better. I caught wind about the auditions in Tennessee. I was twenty. I knew you from the show, not that I thought you would have hired me solely on that." She took a deep breath before finishing her story. "I walked in this big conference room. You sat in the back and kept your head down on some notebook or something. It kind of reminded me of the last time we were on set together. You had your head down in the same way."

Sounded like Hyde back when he started his career. He constantly wrote to make sure he could maintain his career. Then after a while, people offered to write for him, and he liked that even more.

"I sang my heart out. At the end of the song, your dad thanked me for my time and had me escorted out. I never heard back about the audition." She crossed her arms and glared at him.

Hyde didn't know what to say, but knew he had to say something. "I can't believe you auditioned for me."

Tassia exhaled. "Yep. And you let me slip through your fingers."

She started to turn away from him, but Hyde put his hand to her shoulder to stop her. "And now we're back together again." He hoped Tassia took him seriously. "Before we go further, there's something we should do." He reached into his pocket and pulled out his phone. "Exchange numbers."

Tassia blinked. "You trust me with your number?"

"Any reason I shouldn't trust that you won't share it with TMZ or some groupie?" He looked up from his phone at her before he continued.

She shrugged. "No reason. I guess it's cool. We will be working together. If we get ideas while we're not recording, we can shoot them to each other." She nodded. "Good plan."

Hyde held up his phone to her. "What's your number?"

Tassia laughed. "Is that how you would ask a woman for her phone number?"

He felt his face go hot with embarrassment, which seemed foreign to him. He didn't want to date her. Or did he? "I would like to say that I'm a lot smoother when I'm pursuing a woman to date. Since we're only working together…"

"Yeah. Just working."

Hyde couldn't tell if Tassia expressed some disappointment with that news. He had to face facts. They would be working together like they did when they were kids. Nothing more.

"Your number." He kept his thumb poised over his screen.

Tassia blurted her number. As soon as she said the last number, her phone rang.

"You might want to answer it." Hyde smiled as he put his phone to his ear.

Tassia pulled her phone from her purse and looked at the screen. She smiled and turned it around so he could see it. "It says 'Might be Hyde Love'. Cute." She answered it. "Hello?"

"Now you know for sure that it is Hyde Love. Save me."

Tassia kept her phone to her ear as she stared at him. If she only knew that he meant his statement in a different way. Something would have to rescue him from feeling lost in the business. Perhaps this new venture would renew his love of music again.

Hyde disconnected the call before she looked at her phone. "So is your name spelled T-A-S-H-A?"

She shook her head. "No. It's T-A-S-S-I-A. My mother got creative. She thought it sounded regal. I think she gave me a name that guarantees I will never find a monogrammed set of ears at Disney World."

"It's pretty and unique." Hyde stopped short of comparing her name to the woman herself. "So where did you take me?"

"In here is one of the recording studios." Tassia strolled inside.

The place looked like every other recording studio he had been in and used in his career. A soundboard sat in front of a large window that looked into the actual recording booth. Two large leather couches sat in the back, one black and the other red.

"I guess the plan is to lock us in this room and have us write our hearts out and then go record in there?" Hyde pointed to the recording studio.

"I'm assuming, although saying that we'll be locked up sounds like a prison sentence." Tassia laughed a little. "I don't think it'll be that extreme." She strolled into the recording studio and looked around the room.

Hyde's full attention went straight to her. He had been in enough studios not to be impressed. He had never been so intrigued by anyone as much as Tassia had grabbed his attention.

Get your mind off her and think about the work.

He snickered and didn't think Tassia had heard him.

"What's so funny?" Her face became somber like his bit of glee had been at her expense.

"I just finished my tour. The plan was to take some time off." Hyde raised his hands in the air. "Here I am still working."

After a slight pause, a small smile curled at the corners of her luscious mouth before she exhaled loudly. "Oddly enough, I was supposed to do the same thing." She glanced at her watch. "By now I should be drunk on a beach in Fiji and diving in deep to crystal-blue water and a trashy novel, not at the same time, of course."

Yes! Hyde had his "in" with Tassia. He wouldn't have to keep her in the dark about his plan to relax since it sounded like she wanted to do the same.

Hyde chuckled. "Our hard work should be rewarded."

"Eventually. Right now we have to get to work." She rubbed her hands together.

Damn. She still took this assignment seriously. Hyde had to revert to the original plan. He had to look out for himself.

He glanced around the room. "You ready to do some writing?"

"What are you looking for?" Tassia also scanned the studio space.

"Pad and pen." He had expected to walk away today without agreeing to do this project. Then he realized the prime opportunity to use this situation to his advantage. Now he came to the studio unprepared to do any work.

Tassia reached in her purse and pulled out her phone. "I keep everything here."

He shook his head.

"What? Are you saying that you're so country that you don't trust modern technology?" She snickered.

Her comment sent an uncomfortable tickle up his spine. "It has nothing to do with my southern roots. Electronics can be tapped and whatever you're working on or trying to hide can be made public. Trust me."

Tassia didn't verbally respond. She lowered her head and typed on her phone. Maybe she felt embarrassed of her words.

Hyde spotted a napkin and a pencil in the room. Those would have to do.

"Oh, wow." Tassia covered her mouth for a second. "I see what you mean. Who took this picture?" She turned her phone around to show Hyde a picture that had haunted his past.

As an impulsive eighteen-year-old young man, Hyde allowed his then-girlfriend to snap a picture of his naked backside right before he took a midnight dip into a lake. The same all-over body heat that washed over him when the pictures first surfaced took over his body now.

"You don't have to look at that." Hyde reached for her phone.

Tassia pulled her hand back. "You shouldn't be embarrassed. You have a really nice—"

"Okay. That's enough." He reached for it again, brushing his body against hers.

"I was going to say..." Tassia stopped when Hyde had to wrap his arm around her waist to keep from falling over on her and toppling her with him. "Um, smile." Tassia swallowed hard as she stared into his eyes.

Hyde hung onto her a little longer than he should have. The warmth of her body became a needed sensation for him. He smoothed his hand up her back before he released her. "I wonder what I would find if I did a search on you." To shake her up, Hyde reached down to his pocket to retrieve his phone. Then she touched the back of his hand.

The connection shook him and he froze in his spot as he regarded her.

"Don't." Tassia shook her head. "Please."

Her whispered plea struck his heart in a way he didn't think would be possible. He resumed his initial position before he spoke to her. "That was done at a different time in my life. I'm not like that guy anymore."

She tucked her phone back into her purse. "That's a shame. That guy could probably write some club bangers for us."

Hyde blinked. "Club bangers?"

Tassia nodded. "Yeah. You know. Hits. Something to get people moving."

"You mean something without substance."

She stared at him for a moment before retreating to the other side of the room. "Tell me something about you." Tassia sat on a stool in front of a microphone. "Let's get deep."

"I thought you Googled me already." Hyde strolled up to her but left a buffer around her.

"I did one search. That doesn't tell me a lot about you." She crossed her legs. "Was the TV show your first big break? When did you leave it? What was the first song you wrote?"

Hyde didn't mean to but he laughed out loud.

"What are you laughing about now?" She crossed her arms as she regarded him.

"Everything you're asking you can get from a ton of interviews I've done in the past."

"Okay. Fine. What do you know about me?" She cocked her head.

He shook his head. "Nothing beyond the show, and even then it felt like we had kept our distance from each other. What I know about you is that you're a great singer who relies a lot on technology." He nodded toward her purse. "I also know that you're no back-up singer, and in a pinch, you studied one country song."

Tassia opened her mouth like she wanted to refute his claim, but quickly settled down. "I learned that song when I thought I wanted to work for you. Too bad you couldn't hold onto me."

That image alone had Hyde needing to take cover when he felt himself throbbing below his belt. "That won't happen again, um, thanks to this project."

"Chantel and Truman told me that they wanted me to do a duets album with you. To be honest, I was going to turn it down."

Hyde had to blink at that admission. "Seriously?"

"Why would I want to work with someone who wouldn't hire me years ago and barely remembered me after we worked together?" She shrugged.

"Interesting." He wouldn't have to lie to her with his response. "I came here to tell Truman and Chantel to their faces that I wouldn't be doing the project."

"At least for them you were willing to look them in their eyes when you rejected them. I didn't get that courtesy at your audition." She shook her head. "Why did you change your mind? You seemed really determined back there that when you found out you would be working with a former *Ratty Rat's Fun Crew* member you wanted no part of this album."

Hyde sighed. Now he had to do something to ensure his care above relaying the complete truth. "After hearing you sing, I realized that we could make magic." She didn't need to know that he had other motives.

Tassia seemed to believe him after regarding him for a tense moment before she backed away from him. "That's going to require a lot of writing and a lot of work. Story of my life."

"Working long hours?"

She nodded.

"Makes it hard to have a relationship, huh?" He heard his heart beating in his head as he awaited her answer.

"I guess you would know that for sure. How many relationships have you been through in your career?" She smiled at him smugly.

He knew her game but wouldn't be falling for hers either. "Enough to know when to throw in the towel." He strolled around the studio, essentially around her. "So how did you get started? What's your story?" When he didn't hear her respond, he walked back in front of her to look her in her eyes.

Tassia smiled. "Instead of me telling you, why don't I show you?"

The idea intrigued him, but he needed to know what she had in mind. "I'm listening."

"Come with me tonight." She hopped off the stool and almost did a twirl in the small space with walls lined in black foam material.

"Go with you where?" Hyde braced his hands on the stool and felt the warmth she left behind. He exhaled and enjoyed this small bit of intimacy from this woman.

"A club. It's a small place, but it's where I cut my chops with singing in front of a live audience once I got ready to come back to work. Sometimes if I go by there, they'll let me sing a song or two." Her smile lit up the space.

Too bad Hyde couldn't join her in her revelry. He winced. "I can't."

Tassia's smile melted. "Oh." Then she snickered. "Should have figured. Busy schedule and all. Probably have interviews to do and stuff."

"No, that's not it." Hyde took a seat on the stool so he could get eye level with her. "My life has changed dramatically the more popular I get. I pretty much have a security detail around me at all times. I would have to get your club cleared by security first, and then an escort to the back door, and—"

"Never mind. Didn't realize I was with royalty." She finished her statement by giving Hyde a sloppy bow.

"I don't think you understand." He followed her out of the room.

"I get it. You want to work with me. You just don't want to hang with me. Too messy."

He shook his head. "Not fair. The reaction I get when I go out is insane."

Tassia stopped and turned to Hyde. "Aww. Poor, rich, successful singer."

Hyde held Tassia's hand.

"What are you doing?" Tassia sounded more curious than indignant. She followed him with trepidation toward the window.

"I want to show you something." Hyde stood in front of a floor-to-ceiling window overlooking the front of the building. "Look down."

Tassia did, and then turned her head to Hyde.

Hyde didn't have to look although he had to give it to Charisma's architect. He couldn't hear the massive crowd gathering around the studio up in the room. "This is my normal life."

"You assume the crowds down there are for you and not the super couple in the other room?" Tassia cocked her eyebrow at him.

Hyde looked down and spotted one poster board sign with, "Marry Me, Hyde!" scrawled across it. "I do when I see things like that." He pointed to the fan. "I'm just concerned about taking the attention from you."

Tassia's mouth hung open. Hyde couldn't tell from her reaction if she believed him or if she liked what he had said. He meant every word, but she didn't know him yet to know the difference.

Before another word could be said, Clever appeared at the door. "There you two are. I thought maybe you ran off with my guy this time." He laughed.

Hyde didn't. Did everyone see him as some spoiled, sheltered man-child? What had his life become?

His father pointed to the elevator. "I think we have the contracts all figured out. Our lawyers are agreeable to the terms, and I think your side is happy with what you have." He nodded toward Tassia. "Equal split."

Hyde could tell Clever strained to smile. "It's the right thing to do." He headed to the doorway for the stairs. As soon as he opened the door, he looked back and saw Tassia getting into an elevator car.

"See you downstairs." She smirked at him just as the doors closed.

Hyde laughed.

"What's that about? And why are you taking the stairs instead of the elevator?" Clever pointed back to the elevator.

"Getting some exercise in." Exercise in patience. "I'll see you downstairs."

Hyde could use this opportunity as a front to finally relax after years of running around.

After all contracts had been signed, the group started to disperse.

"The studio is open twenty-four hours a day." Truman walked beside Hyde. "Let us know when you want to come in to do some writing and if you two need anything."

Hyde tried to get a look at Tassia, who managed to walk out with her management team without a word to him.

"I'm flexible. I'll let you know tomorrow if that's cool." Hyde shook Truman's hand.

"Of course." Truman smiled back at him. "We can't wait to hear what you two come up with."

"Yes. I'm very excited. Reminds me of when we recorded 'Meet Me Halfway.' Remember that?" Chantel wrapped her arm around her husband's waist and leaned her head on his shoulder.

"How could I forget that?" Truman kissed Chantel's forehead.

A strange pang of jealousy tore through Hyde's body. He didn't understand why. He barely knew Tassia. From the way she acted with him, she probably had no desire to know him beyond writing and recording this album.

Clever slapped Hyde on his back. "And, see, you wanted to take some time off." He shook his head. "It's not in you, kid. You need to work and work consistently." He put his hand to his chest. "I recognize that. The fact that you jumped on this opportunity shows me that deep inside, you know I'm right."

To hear that sent a painful wrench in Hyde's belly. Even his own father didn't know what Hyde really wanted in his life. Clever would know soon.

When Hyde walked out through the back door to his waiting limousine, he turned to Clever before stepping inside. "You got copies of everything, right? All contracts and terms?"

Clever blinked. "The attorneys do. You know that."

"Check with them. Since this isn't my main company, I don't want any problems."

Clever looked worried until Hyde glanced over at the security team that stood on either side of the vehicle.

"Okay. Be right back." Clever ran inside.

As soon as the door closed behind him, Hyde made a call. When he heard a click on the other end, he ducked into the car and slammed the door closed.

"Yes?" Tassia's response sounded sharp and uninterested.

"Tell me where you live." He didn't have that much time for finessing.

"Excuse me?"

"I'll pick you up tonight." A pause lingered before he finished.

"You're coming to the club with me?" A hopeful lilt lit up Tassia's voice.

Hyde shook his head like she could see him. "And you're not going there either."

"What are you talking about?"

He could almost see her cocking her head to the side. "I have a plan."

"A plan to take over, because that's what feels like is happening here."

Hyde heard her voice shaking, both from anger and her movement, probably headed his way. Good. He wanted to see her. He looked out the side window to see if he could spot her through the glass at the door.

"I don't want to take over. I want us to get into a creative space to write. All the great collaborations have gone to places outside of the studio to work. We shouldn't be any different, and I have a great place in mind." He smiled. "Come with me."

A pause lingered on the phone.

"Hello?" Hyde held the phone from his ear. "You still there?"

"Uh, yeah. Go with you where?" Tassia's voice lowered.

He smiled. "You just got off tour and wanted a break. I just got off tour and need a break. We both agreed to this project." Hyde saw her silhouette through the darkened door glass. "We need to write. I don't know about you, but I write best in a relaxed setting. I'm proposing we go somewhere."

"Really?" Instead of excitement, Tassia sounded skeptical. "Are you coming with a whole team of people?"

"Nope. Just me and you. What do you say?" He peered out the window and saw Clever approaching the back door again.

"No."

Now he could imagine her head shaking.

Tassia continued. "I'm not going to some unknown place with you alone."

Hyde thought fast. "You and I will ride alone in a vehicle together. No one in my team will be with us."

"Oh, so they'll follow us?" Tassia's voice lightened.

"They will be following." Hyde wouldn't tell her that his team and hers would be searching for them on social media.

"I don't know. We might be working together, but I'm not too keen on going away with you by myself, even with your team there."

"Don't trust yourself with me?" Hyde laughed.

Tassia laughed. "With you? I think I'm safe."

The hairs on the back of his neck stood when she laughed at him. He had to remember that besides relaxation, this trip would be about work and nothing else. Whether Tassia thought of him as some sort of sexual threat shouldn't even enter his brain. Now he only thought about how to carve out time for himself and away from Clever and everyone else.

"If that's how you feel about me, then your answer should be easy, right?" Hyde shifted in his seat when he saw his father. "What do you say? Your bags are still packed from your original trip."

Tassia sighed. "They are."

Clever touched the door handle.

"Good. Text me your address." He heard her sigh loudly again. "Or meet me at my hotel. I'll send you the information. We'll hit the road tonight."

"Where?" Tassia's light voice floated through the phone.

"You'll see. But I think you'll like it." He drummed his thumb on his knee. He had her. Better than that, he would be able to relax.

"God help me."

As soon as he disconnected the call, Clever opened the door to the backseat.

"Everything is all set." His father patted Hyde's knee.

"Good. Before we make any formal announcements, I'll give it a couple of weeks before formally backing out of the project." Hyde took his cap off and tossed it to the side. He didn't care if one of his waiting fans snapped a picture of him without his hat.

"What? I thought you—"

Hyde cut Clever off. "I did. But you were right." Saying that out loud caused his gut to wrench. "I don't need to pair myself up with someone from my past. The initial signing will make me come off as accommodating, but then you can make something up as to why I couldn't do the project. Scheduling conflicts, whatever."

Clever nodded. "I get it. You come off as a big star willing to humble himself, but in the end, you have better things to do. Great move." He leaned back and crossed his legs. "Just promise me one thing, son." He wagged his finger at him. "You let her down easy. She's probably got stars in her eyes now about doing this project. You need to bring her back down to earth gently."

"Isn't that what I'm paying you to do?" Hyde had a need to define all boundaries.

His father laughed. "Yes, you do. Well played. Okay, you give me the word on when you want to pull the trigger. I know Charisma is not going to post anything on social about this project until they see some written songs first. Tassia's team was told the same thing. This can all be done very quietly."

Good. Just what Hyde wanted. He could get his time off like he wanted without the obligations. His plan would work.

"Are you ready now?" Clever sat across from Hyde.

"You have no idea."

Chapter 8

Since her last phone call with Hyde, Tassia had been pacing until she got into this Uber car ride. So what if Hyde Love had called her? So what if he texted her his hotel information? So what if this popular artist now had her number and she had his? Artistry and money aside, the man epitomized fine with a capital F.

Not only did he look good in only a T-shirt, jeans, and work boots, but he treated her like a gentleman. When he demanded that his manager apologize to her before negotiations started, Tassia had to squirm in her chair. Because he seemed so perfect, of course something had to be wrong with him.

Maybe that swayed her to accept his unorthodox offer. Artists working together often secluded themselves in cottages and residential recording studios. What made this situation different had to be that she didn't normally continually think about her singing partner's body.

Except for Hyde's one nude moment caught and preserved for all the world to see, he also seemed a bit uptight, the only reason Tassia even considered this mysterious trip with him. She Googled him and saw he had a relationship with another country star not too long ago. She had moved on, but Hyde didn't. That usually meant she dumped him.

Just so she didn't seem too reckless, Tassia did tell India, although with her friend still frolicking in Fiji, there would be little India could do for her if Hyde turned out to be some homicidal maniac. No use telling her father, although he would have wanted her to share. He still saw her as a little girl needing protection.

The compact ride rolled up in front of a luxury Oceanfront hotel where a group of young women milled around the entrance. Of course they knew

Hyde Love stayed here. Now she would be a part of this ravenous group. How would these women react if they knew she would be getting in a vehicle with Hyde and going away with him?

"Ma'am, are you getting out?" The Uber driver peered over his shoulder in between glancing down at his phone.

"Yeah." Tassia dropped her attention to her phone. "Let me just text my, um—"

"Look. You don't need to tell me about your business." He shook his head.

Her business? Damn, worse than being known as a "hook girl," now this stranger thought that she needed to contact a john. Apparently, he didn't recognize her. With her hair still in vacation mode and no stitch of makeup except for some lipstick, she didn't think she looked like a working girl.

Tassia sent the message but knew she couldn't hold up this entrepreneur. "If you'll help me with my luggage, I'll wait out here." She opened the back door and stood by the trunk area of the gray sedan.

Tassia read some of the signs a couple of the women held in front of their bodies, hoping to capture Hyde's attention. "Can't hide my love for you, Hyde!" "Marry me, Hyde!" "I want to have your baby!" How desperate.

The driver huffed as he got out of his side and marched to the back of his vehicle. He pulled up the trunk and retrieved Tassia's two large suitcases. Tassia's plan before this project fell into her lap consisted of her vegging out on an island for an extended period of time. Luckily, she hadn't unpacked.

The driver set her second bag in the parking lot in front of the exclusive hotel. If Hyde didn't show, she would feel like an idiot. She for sure didn't want to call this same driver back if she had to turn around and go home.

"Have a good night." The driver gave her a dismissive wave while keeping his full attention on his phone and heading to the driver's seat.

He hopped inside and drove off as soon as he slammed the door closed. A few of the women standing outside cut furtive glances at Tassia, particularly when she didn't go inside the hotel, per Hyde's instructions. Some of them giggled in little groups, probably at her expense as Tassia leaned herself and her bags against a pillar in front of the circular driveway at the front door.

"I hear he's going to some club or something tonight." One woman showed her phone to another fan. "He posted something about it on his Insta."

Tassia tried not to listen in on their conversation, but she shook her head at the statement. If Hyde didn't want to go to her favorite club, no way would he be going out to some other one.

She tapped her sandaled foot to try tamping down her curiosity. Tassia pulled out her phone to confirm this fan's statement. Before she could get to Hyde's page, the women around her became excited and screamed as they looked beyond her.

Tassia turned in the direction that caught their attention. At the far corner of the hotel under a streetlight she caught sight of a tall man wearing a backward baseball hat throwing a wave to the women before he ducked into the back seat of an all-black SUV.

The vehicle rolled slowly at first to the front of the hotel. Good. Tassia imagined him stopping to get her bags and her before leaving, although she thought he would have been a little more discreet than this. These women would try to tear her apart if she jumped in the ride with him.

Once the black ride got in front of the hotel, the window in the backseat area cracked open a hair, just enough for Hyde to give a wave before the truck zoomed off into the night.

Son-of-a-bitch.

No way did Hyde leave her. Tassia knew this man hadn't played her, get her all the way out to this hotel in the middle of the night just so he could leave her.

"Come on! Let's follow him." One woman ran toward her vehicle, prompting the other ladies to run to their cars.

It took no time for the front of the hotel to clear. Good thing. Tassia didn't know whether she wanted to scream at the top of her lungs first or stomp around like a child having a temper tantrum.

No use doing anything like that. She needed to get home and rethink her life choices. Why in the world had she even trusted Hyde Love would do the right thing by her? As usual, she got sucked in by the nice-guy attitude that always tricked her. Dorian had suckered her, sweet talking her and breaking down her resistance.

Tassia pulled out her phone and started to order another Uber to pick her up. She didn't even care if the same driver picked her up and made comments about a failed job. She did have a failed job, but not the kind the driver would mean.

When a set of headlights hit Tassia from the other side away from where the driver had driven, she felt an embarrassed heat filling her cheeks while she struggled to move all her bags off to the side. At least a whole group of people wouldn't see her humiliation. This driver wouldn't know she came there to meet Hyde only to be left hanging.

Once she got her two pieces of large luggage moved closer to the curb, she hit the option to order the car. Just as she completed the order, the vehicle she saw rolling up to the hotel's front door stopped.

The oversized silver Land Rover parked in front of her, which made Tassia blink. When she heard the driver side door open, she attempted to look over the top of the vehicle to see the driver. The shadow of the driver's feet headed toward the back of the vehicle until the person turned the corner.

Seeing Hyde Love caused Tassia to stumble back while her heart pounded hard. Both took a chance on the unknown.

"You made it." Hyde smiled at her, a surprise considering what she had just seen.

"How did you do that?" Tassia peered down the road like she could see the black SUV that had driven away only moments before. "I saw you go in that other vehicle." She watched Hyde loading her luggage into the back of the pricey ride.

"Double." He smiled and gave her a wink. "I do it a lot to get some peace." At that statement, Hyde scanned Tassia from head to toe.

The look alone caused her body to flush all over. "No entourage?"

Hyde shook his head. "I told you we would be alone, um, in the car." He slammed the back before regarding her fully. "Is that going to be a problem? If so, if you want to go home now, I can take you there."

Tassia shook her head. "No problem." She followed him to the passenger's side door until she stopped cold when she saw him opening the door for her. "Did they already leave before us or will your team—"

"We can talk more on the road, but we really need to leave now." To punctuate his point, he peered over in the direction where his double had gone. "It won't take long for the fans to realize they've been had."

She had been with a man who didn't bother carrying her luggage for her. Hyde proved true gentlemen still existed. That didn't mean he didn't have something to hide.

Even if he had an agenda, Tassia wouldn't. She agreed to this trip for work. If he thought this would be some sort of vacation like he had alluded to when they had spoken, he had another thing coming.

Tassia slipped inside and strapped herself in as Hyde shut her door. Thankfully he had the air conditioner blasting considering the heavy humid weather that blanketed the outdoors, making breathing challenging.

She settled back into the cushiony black leather seat and took a deep breath, catching the distinctly sweet and clean new-car smell. It wouldn't surprise her at all if Hyde had purchased this luxury vehicle just for this impromptu trip.

When Hyde got inside, Tassia wasted no time in interrogating him. "I told my friend and my management team that we're working off-site to write this album." She pulled out her trusty phone. "I can call anyone at a moment's notice if anything goes down."

Hyde snickered before he pulled out of the parking lot. "Understood." He glanced at her. "You have a strong support team. I get it."

Her phone. "Shoot!"

"What's wrong? Did you forget something?" Hyde left the truck in park until Tassia spoke.

"When I thought you had left me, I ordered an Uber. I need to cancel it." She did so while keeping her stare on the phone.

"I'm a man of my word. I told you I would be here." He cleared his voice. "Probably a really good reason to have not picked you up from your place. I wouldn't want my fans to know where you live. Bad enough they camp out in front of my hotel. My body double is going to be working overtime while we're gone."

"You mentioned my support team. What about you?" She curved her body around to him while still clutching her phone.

"What do you mean?" Hyde rolled the big vehicle onto the interstate, bound for God knew where.

"Do you have a strong support team? Did you tell your whole team where you're going to be?" Tassia crossed her legs.

"Depends on what you consider my team is." He glanced at her. Before she could elaborate, he continued. "I've been working constantly since I was eleven." He kept his stare on the road. "When my tour ended, I told my dad I wanted some time off. His response was to propose another opportunity and to carve out a week for me." He snickered. "A week."

"You don't feel like you can say no? You're Hyde freaking Love." Tassia slipped her phone into a side pocket on her purse.

He glanced at her. "Where were you when I needed someone to be on my side?"

"Fighting my own battles." Tassia took a deep breath. When she caught his heady masculine scent again, she had to keep this conversation going. "So what team did you consult?"

Hyde sped up. "I'm taking you to one of my homes in Tennessee."

"Tennessee? Whoa."

What a strange turn of events. The beginning of the week, she never thought she would be recording with one of the most popular recording artists of the time. Now the man had her heading to his home in the south. Good thing Hyde would have a few people from his team there, maybe other musicians. That would take away the awkward feeling of being alone with him.

"I have some family there. Family I can really trust and rely on." Hyde turned the air conditioner down lower.

This discussion must have raised his temperature.

Hyde continued. "If they're really supportive there will be food and beer in the fridge."

"Are we heading to Nashville?" It wouldn't surprise Tassia that this country star would have a house there. Most did.

Hyde surprised her by shaking his head. "Bristol." He gazed over at her. "I told you. I'm heading home."

She nodded. Hyde surprised her. He seemed to be two steps ahead of her. That didn't mean she could drop her guard or forget her mission.

"And how long do you think we'll be there?" Tassia could write a song in a day. With them both working, they shouldn't be there longer than a week.

Hyde didn't answer at first. He drummed his thumb on the steering wheel. "Depends."

* * * *

Hyde always prided himself on his honesty. Being so evasive and deceptive with Tassia felt foreign to him. He never thought that he would have to sneak away like this to eke out some private time.

This whole trip had been done under the cover of darkness. After texting Clever that he would be away to do some writing for this project, Hyde had been ignoring calls from Clever all day. Once he reached a certain point, he knew phone connectivity wouldn't be an issue, at least not for him.

Hyde knew what his manager would be saying to him. Clever would want Hyde to come back and work at Charisma's studio under his watchful eye. As an adult, Hyde no longer needed to be supervised, especially not with Tassia.

He should have warned her about his body double, but he didn't know her yet. She could have shared his little secret and ruined the ruse.

"It's going to be a long ride." Hyde kept his stare on the road. He knew this route to his home, homing in toward it like a moth to a light. "You can sleep if you—"

Tassia cut him off. "I'm fine." She kept her arms crossed over her chest and her legs crossed.

Her legs remained covered under her long dress. He guessed he had the air conditioner on too low when he spotted her pulling a cardigan from her purse.

"I have drinks in the back seat." He jutted his thumb over his shoulder. "Water, sodas, and stuff."

"Prepared." Tassia snickered. "You're a regular Boy Scout."

Hyde shook his head. "I just know how challenging it'll be for us to stop." He glanced at her. "I don't want to be spotted along the way."

"Wow."

"You saw what it was like at the hotel. Some fan sees me and then the chase is on. My life isn't mine." He tapped his thumb over the steering wheel. "I can't imagine what it must be like for you in the business." He glanced at her quickly. "Must worry your boyfriend when you're out and about." The hairs on his arm raised as he awaited her answer.

"If I had a man, he wouldn't be cool with me going with you to some secret place, even if there were other people there. He either would be coming with me or we would be writing in the studio like we had planned." Tassia smoothed her hand over her dress.

"You're saying that your boyfriend or husband wouldn't trust you?" Hyde tried to hide his smile. He never saw himself as some sort of sex god.

"I'm saying it's not appropriate for an attached woman to go off with a, well, you're single, right?" Her voice dipped down a little and sounded somewhat seductive. "I think I saw that online."

"You believe everything you read on the Internet? I thought we got through that." He gritted his teeth.

"You didn't answer my question."

Persistent. Or maybe Tassia's curiosity stemmed from something else. Hyde shifted in his air conditioned seat.

"I didn't." Hyde cleared his throat. "But I suspect our relationship statuses will help us in writing."

"Because you're single?" Tassia kicked her foot back and forth.

"You don't give up, do you?" This time, Hyde laughed out loud. "Yes, I'm single."

In the darkened vehicle, he heard her sighing. He couldn't tell if the expression came from relief or pity. His gut wrenched thinking Tassia could feel sorry for him for any reason.

"What's the reason for the breakup?" The seriousness of the question missed the mark from the playful lilt in her voice.

"You didn't read about that online?" Hyde kept his stare on the road, becoming hypnotized with the white road markings in intervals along the way.

"I want to hear it from you."

Hyde glanced at Tassia to see her twirling the tail end of her braids around her index finger.

"Nothing to tell." He scratched his head under his baseball cap before replacing it. "As in I'm not talking about it." He shook his head.

"Hmm." Tassia shrugged.

He could feel her judgment in what she didn't say. "You want to talk about your last breakup?" Silence hung inside the SUV. "That's what I—"

Tassia cut him off. "I was dumped." She snickered. "You could have read about that everywhere online." She put her hand to her head. "When I offered for him to go away with me on vacation, he decided that that was too much commitment. I guess you'd have a leg up on him if we were dating. At least you don't mind going somewhere with me."

Damn. Hyde didn't mean for this conversation to get this serious. He thought with Tassia being such a spitfire that she would have been the one to dump the guy.

"The conversation is getting a little personal." Hyde sniffed. "What inspires you to write?" Maybe knowing her inspiration would help him rekindle that spark.

Tassia chuckled. "Thank you."

He felt his eyebrows knit together. "You didn't answer my question. Why are you thanking me?"

"You asked me about my writing because you do believe me." Tassia leaned her head against the overstuffed headrest behind her.

"No Internet stories. We made a pact, remember?" He smiled to reassure her.

"Yes, I remember." She smiled and it seemed to brighten the inside of the vehicle. "Lately when I write, it's all about making hits."

Hyde felt like a million centipedes crawled over his belly. "What do you mean by that?"

"I write to get people moving. Catchy hooks, lyrics about partying, and hot men." Tassia released a yawn. "Those songs pay the bills."

"Are those the types of songs you would do for this album? I don't imagine that's what Truman and Chantel want with this project." Hyde shrugged.

"Of course not. I write for the artist and the market. I would switch gears for this project though." She sighed again, but this time it came off as more wistful. "I hope once we get to where we're going that I'll be inspired by the surroundings."

"If not?" Hyde always found inspiration at his home. It would disappoint him if Tassia didn't see the beauty in the location.

"Then I'll have to write about being let down by a man again. Women can definitely relate to that." She smoothed her hand over her braided hair. "You don't listen to music when you drive?"

"I do. I thought it would be nice to get reacquainted before we brought music into the mix." Hyde missed driving and holding a real conversation with someone who didn't fawn over him or receive a paycheck from him.

"To be honest, after you denied me a job as your back-up singer, I haven't listened to your music." Tassia reached forward. "Do you have any of your stuff cued up?"

Hyde held her hand to prevent her from turning on the radio. "No. I don't like listening to myself. I'd rather listen to other artists." He turned to her and noticed that she now stared at him as he held her. Her soft skin felt smooth under his fingers. A small part of him wanted more. At that realization, he released her hand. "We can listen to your music. I heard a little bit of it on the news that one time."

"We don't have to listen to that." She shook her head. "Not my song. I just sang the hook."

He heard a longing in her voice that pulled at his heart. "How about classic rock? It's probably not your cup of—"

"Tom Petty? Grand Funk Railroad? Janis Joplin? I'm all for it. Play away." She eased the back of her seat a little.

"Whoa. Impressive. You know who those artists are?" Hyde eased the SUV onto the long stretch of highway that would get him to his home.

"I'm in the music industry. I listen to everything."

"Just not me."

Silence hung again inside the compartment.

To cut the tension, Hyde tuned the satellite radio to a classic rock streaming channel. By the third song, this time by the rock group Heart, he heard a subtle hum. He brought his attention to Tassia and found her sleeping.

Good. Hyde could only take so many uncomfortable exchanges with Tassia. He could only imagine what would happen once they got to the house. How would Tassia feel when she learned about the trip? Maybe he wouldn't have to tell her. Maybe the location could keep her distracted enough to not want to work on the album, and then the sting of him backing out won't hurt as much. From what he recognized in Tassia from interacting with her again, he suspected that she wouldn't respond positively to the truth about this trip.

Good or bad, he wouldn't care how Tassia felt. He hadn't talked to her in fifteen years. He could go the rest of his life not talking to her again.

Hours of driving and making the trip overnight stretched Hyde to his limit. Thanks to tour buses and limousine rides, Hyde couldn't remember the last time he had driven himself anywhere, not for this long of a trek. Even with the breaking dawn's bright sun blinding him, it couldn't give him that needed second wind to finish this trip. When he saw familiar street signs signaling his close proximity to his home, he sighed in relief. In mere minutes, he would be home in his own bed, but with a stranger, albeit a beautiful one, in his house. He would have to steel himself for the potential argument from Tassia when he revealed the truth.

Hyde heard a light chirping sound from his pocket. He smiled, realizing that he couldn't send or receive calls. He could get a break. When he thought about that, he glanced over at Tassia, still asleep beside him. She might have an issue with not being able to connect to the outside world from her phone. He hoped she would settle into the idea.

At the gate surrounding his estate, Hyde entered his security code and swiped a key with a microchip over it, which activated the wrought-iron gates with spikes across the top. Hyde hadn't thought he would have to go to this extreme until he came to the house one time and found a female fan camped out in his yard.

He drove through the gates but waited for them to close behind him before he continued up the mile-long driveway.

Hyde went around the circular driveway and stopped in front of his house. "Home sweet home." He smiled as he turned off the vehicle.

Hyde figured at that point, Tassia would have woken up. She hadn't when he had stopped midway during their trip to get gas. He had paid the old man working behind the counter cash and had worn his ballcap with the bill as low as he could get it over his eyes. He reached over to touch her shoulder but stopped himself. He would first see if his family did what he had asked.

He slipped out of the truck and went to the back to retrieve some of the luggage. He would take them in the house at least for his guest.

Hyde pulled the bags to the door and unlocked it. When he stepped inside, he took a deep breath. It smelled like oak and the outdoors. He couldn't help but smile as he set the bags at the base of a set of stairs. He immediately went to the kitchen and looked in the refrigerator.

Hyde had to blink when he saw a piece of paper greeting him as soon as he opened the stainless-steel door.

I told you I would stock it, pig face!

Hyde laughed as he snatched the paper and crumpled it into a ball. No time to waste. He had to get Tassia, and he needed to get some sleep. He turned around to retrieve his guest and stopped in his tracks when he saw her standing in the open doorway.

"Where is everyone?"

Chapter 9

Tassia had no plans on falling asleep during the trip. Even when she had been on tour buses, she liked staying up for as long as she could to map out her destination. She never liked being left unaware. Hyde already had her off her game between the sweet ride, the somewhat calming conversation, and the music.

At some point, the hard rock that had been playing when Hyde finally filled the vehicle with music had turned to something soothing. Thanks to her cynical side, she suspected Hyde played the music on purpose to relax her. She couldn't believe he didn't get sleepy as well and have to pull over to take a nap. Seeing this incredible house, she liked the fact that he pushed through to get them here.

"Good morning." Hyde smiled. "I was going to get your stuff in first before I woke you up."

Tassia shook her head. "I had one job." Then she snickered. When she saw Hyde's eyebrows furrow, she clarified her statement. "I was supposed to stay awake to keep you company while you drove. I didn't mean to fall asleep."

He waved his hand. "It's not a problem. Leaving in the middle of the night was my idea." He glanced at his large-face watch. "We made good time."

"You did. I just enjoyed the ride." Just saying the word *ride* had her recalling her line in the song. She glanced at Hyde to see if he had made the connection.

"I'm going to get our bags and the rest of the stuff from the truck." He strolled by her. "You make yourself at home."

When he walked by her, Tassia noticed a ruddy shade coloring his cheeks. What went through his mind that would cause that reaction? Had he thought about her and what he could do to her, to her body?

Tassia pushed the salacious thoughts from her mind and concentrated on work. Wondering what went on in a man's mind would make a good song.

She wandered through the living room with a ceiling so high, she imagined being able to do a full back flip from a high bounce on a trampoline in the middle of the room. Open, sturdy exposed rafters lined the ceiling. The rich, cocoa-colored wood matched the tone of the wood around the large, picturesque windows that surrounded the room. A plush Oriental rug supported her sandaled feet. Matching tan and burgundy furniture pieces completed the room with pillows covering almost every chair and couch. Hyde definitely had help with his decorating.

When Tassia peered off to the side of the room, she spotted a platform area with a piano and a guitar on a stand. She wondered if the instruments had been there as decoration pieces or if Hyde actually used them.

She heard a rustling at the door, and watched Hyde coming in with two more pieces of luggage and a cooler. He placed all the items by the door and closed the door behind him. A chirping sound echoed through the house.

"The front door alarm is set, but you can go out the back door and balconies, well, I guess that's if—" Hyde stopped himself and took a breath. "Welcome to my home." He held up his arms like a game-show model. "Let me show you around first." He started in the living room. "Living room of course and music room." He pointed toward the area where she had spotted the piano and guitar.

"I noticed. Do you write there?" Tassia strolled toward the space.

"Sometimes. The whole property is inspiring, so I don't restrict myself." He moved past her to the open kitchen area. "Kitchen, of course. And I checked. My family didn't let me down. Not completely." He rubbed his hand over his face like he wanted to cover a smile. "The fridge and pantry are stocked. Please help yourself to anything in here."

"Anything?" Tassia didn't mean to make the inquiry sound salacious. Seeing Hyde with stubble on his chin and looking delectable, she couldn't help it. She had expected Hyde to overlook the statement.

"Anything you need, I can provide." He cocked a smile at the corner of his mouth.

Damn. Tassia would be with this hot man for a while. She needed to pace herself. "That line would work well in a song." She strolled to the other side of a large breakfast bar away from him.

"It would, wouldn't it?" He nodded. "I like the way you think." He moved down the end of the bar to an area with a wall of windows. "Outside is a pool." Hyde pushed open a sliding door that made the outside a part of the house now. "I'll be using this a lot while we're here."

"After we finish working, of course." Tassia stepped outside with him. Hyde definitely picked a great day to bring Tassia to his home. In the early morning sun, the sky appeared so bright blue, and the lush lawn looked so deep green. The huge pool reminded Tassia of the missed trip to Fiji with India.

Hyde didn't answer her. "Over there is a hot tub." Hyde pointed to a corner area with a raised, square spa. "The wooden door on the other side of it is a sauna." He turned to her.

Tassia had to wrap her arms around herself to keep from hopping around like a giddy goofball about her luck of getting to work in this space. She could definitely see herself lounging by the pool while she wrote some hits. "Not exactly the vacation spot I was hoping for, but this is close." She shrugged. "I guess I could work here."

Hyde must have seen through her nonplussed attitude. He nodded his head. "It's like being in another world out here. You can escape your problems. I can truly pamper myself out here."

"What do you mean? Like having a personal chef or something?" Tassia pointed back to the kitchen area.

"Yes." Hyde nodded.

"What about someone to clean up?" Having extra strangers in the house might help with some of the tension she felt with being alone with Hyde until the other crew members arrived.

"Housecleaning? Sure." He nodded and strolled down a set of steps on the other side of the pool toward the back of the large yard.

"What about a pool boy and a masseuse?" She laughed.

"I know how to clean my own pool." Hyde let the other request linger in the air like he wanted Tassia to press him on that service.

She swallowed hard. "Where are we going?"

Hyde stopped at the bank of a large, calm lake behind the house. "The lake. If you get tired of the pool and want something more organic, come here." He squatted down and sat on the grass. "I love this spot." He took in a deep breath and looked off in the distance. "I recharge here. I look out at all the trees and I feel…" He stopped as though he realized how much of himself he'd started to reveal.

Tassia scanned the land around them. A dock sat off to the side, jutting out over the calm water. She imagined Hyde casting a boat from it and the sun beating on his skin. It didn't help that while she slept on the way down, she had dreamed about Hyde and his hands and his eyes.

In her dream, Hyde coasted his large hands down her naked body, over her shoulder, down her bare arm to her stomach and finally to her vagina. Even in her dream she felt her clitoris throbbing. She couldn't be sure, but she thought she might have moaned.

Even if she had, the expression didn't rouse her out of her slumber. The dream proved too good to stop. By the time she dreamed that Hyde entered her and brought her to an exquisite orgasm, she had awakened in front of Hyde's home. If she had planned on working with him, she had to push out these thoughts.

One way to snap her mind out of that thinking. "So where is every—"

Hyde jumped up to his feet. "Before we get into anything else, let me show you to your room." He walked ahead of her. "There are eight bedrooms in this house."

Tassia started to follow him when something caught her attention. "Wait. You live in the middle of nowhere, but I can see a house back there." She pointed to a small yellow house at a far corner of the property.

"Yeah. That's a guesthouse." Hyde smiled. "I own the lake and the other side of it."

Tassia laughed. "How can you own a lake?"

He opened the back door for her. "When you have it made." He pointed to the water. "All of this was land. This is one of the biggest man-made lakes in Tennessee. I have it populated with fish and other wildlife. Kind of proud of that. Plus, it offers me a bit more privacy."

The man thought about everything.

Tassia strolled through and stood off to the side to follow him.

"Like I said, there are eight bedrooms in here." Hyde walked in front of her, but stopped suddenly.

She almost ran into the back of him. Just as she started to admonish him, she watched him remove his boots and place them next to the door. She could tell he did that out of habit.

"Feel free to get comfortable." He glanced down at her feet.

"I'm in sandals. I'm pretty comfortable." She smiled.

He padded over deep mahogany hardwood floors down a hallway. "There's a master suite down here."

He stepped into the room through a set of double doors.

"Are you letting me have your room?" Tassia's heart pounded as she envisioned sharing a bed with him.

"No." Hyde pointed up. "My master suite is upstairs. I thought you might be more comfortable on a separate floor. If you would rather be upstairs, I have other bedrooms there with en suite bathrooms."

"Wow. Nice." Tassia peered around the room.

An Oriental rug with blue, gold, and tan colors covered most of the hardwood floor. Bright light streamed through the two large windows. The king-size bed looked comfortable enough to hibernate in for years.

"Are you cool with this room?" Hyde's eyes went wide, which only accentuated the dark circles underneath them.

"Yes, this is great. Thank you. Are there other bedrooms down here?"

Hyde backed out of the room. "One more bedroom near the front of the house. The rest are upstairs." He pointed up.

"Will your team be up—"

He cut her off again. "Let me get your bags." He trotted out of the room.

A creepy tickle itched up the back of her neck. She really didn't know Hyde, but she could swear that each time she started to ask him about his team, he interrupted her.

Hyde returned to the room and set her luggage by the door. "These are it, right?"

Tassia assessed her belongings. "Except for my purse. I think I left it in the living room."

"Got it." Hyde ran from the room again and came back moments later with her purse.

"Thank you." She kept her stare on Hyde's eyes as she accepted her purse. "I know you must be exhausted."

He blinked so slowly that she thought he would fall asleep in his spot.

"If you want to get some sleep, I can keep myself busy." She threw her purse onto the bed.

"Yes. I do need to get some sleep. Just a few hours." He started to back out of the room again.

"I understand. Just let me know when your team is getting here." She approached Hyde. "You said the alarm is on the front door. Does your team have the code?"

"If anyone arrives, come knock on my door and I can let them in." He offered a small smile as he walked out of the room. "Enjoy your stay. I know I will."

* * * *

Tassia couldn't put her finger on it, but she felt Hyde kept some information close to his vest. She couldn't say that her instincts with men had always been spot on. Instead of thinking about her relationship status, she decided she would work really hard on writing songs.

She opened the refrigerator door. True to Hyde's word, the space overflowed with fresh food. Tassia removed a container of yogurt and an apple. She would only take the bare minimum.

Tassia placed the container on the counter next to a balled up piece of paper. She picked the paper up and opened it. When she read the note, her eyebrows raised as she wondered who called Hyde "pig face." She gazed up like she could see through the ceiling to see Hyde.

Tassia searched through the kitchen drawers for utensils. Once she found a spoon, she snagged a bottle of water and took her bounty outside by the pool. Why did she need to remain holed up in a bedroom when she had this wonderful backdrop to use?

She went to a chaise lounge under a large blue and white striped umbrella and reclined back. Noon time hadn't officially started yet, and it already felt like a hundred degrees, even in the shade. Tassia needed the air and space.

After eating her light breakfast, she attempted to write. The first song had a catchy hook, something she had become known for in the music industry, unless people believed the gossip.

She didn't know where Hyde would be infused in the song, but then again, maybe Hyde could figure that one out when he eventually helped with the process. He could be the hook man for a change. Why not? Beyoncé had done it for other artists.

Tassia struggled on writing the second song. She attempted to keep the songs light, just what would work in a club and on the radio. Adding a second person, when she really didn't know her singing partner, proved to be harder than she imagined. Writing duets for Chantel and Truman had been easy. She observed their loving relationship. She knew them. She tried to hear Hyde's twang in the song. She couldn't. She didn't know how to fit him in her music.

The third song she started to write, about a jerk of a man, kept getting blurry as she attempted to write more. At the third hour of trying to finish this song, she eventually had to give in to the fact that her creativity train had stopped. Hard to write when she had too many things racing through her mind: the breakup, the lies, the man sleeping upstairs in this massive house.

Tassia thought about Hyde, his eyes, and his large hands, and his deep voice. He had definitely grown up to become a fine young man. Her heart began pounding hard.

"Come on, girl. You don't know this man, not after all these years." Tassia shook her head. "Don't forget. He wouldn't hire you."

Tired of writing and curiosity getting the better of her, Tassia decided to do her own self-guided tour of Hyde's home. With him sleeping, she wouldn't have any restrictions on where she could go. She had already seen the main living area, kitchen, and one music room.

Tassia walked into the house from the pool area and closed the door behind herself to keep the cool air in the dwelling. She sauntered down a hallway and stumbled upon another bedroom. This spare room did not have an attached bathroom like hers, and had been decorated modestly. Yep, Hyde had to have had a decorator help him. No way the boy who used to wear plaid shirts would know how to mix and match patterns like this.

Tassia walked back to the main area of the house and rested at the base of the stairs. She stared up to the top and directly at Hyde's closed bedroom door. What if her searching caused him to wake up and come out of his bedroom…naked? She imagined that he slept in the nude because with a body like his, why not?

Damn. She had to stop thinking of that man's body and how he slept and who he had slept with in his past, if anyone. In Tassia's mind, Hyde remained as innocent as he had been as a kid, shy and reserved. He probably saved himself for marriage, which would make him even more likeable. His female fans would hate her if they found out that she turned her back on this project if she didn't feel right about it.

To record with someone she used to work with who later wouldn't even offer her a job still stung a little. Tassia had to keep repeating Nora and Graham's words in her head each time she felt like running. "This is business. This is business." Her team had the attorneys put in an easy-out clause to their contract. She could leave if she wanted. Then would she always be the woman who ran away like C. Love had said to her in the meeting room?

Bastard.

After taking a deep breath, Tassia ascended the stairs. She avoided going toward Hyde's room and instead went the opposite way, where she went to one of the other five bedrooms that contained its own bathroom. Seeing it made her wonder why Hyde hadn't set her up in this room instead of the room downstairs. Did he not trust her or himself?

In the first bedroom, she stepped inside and opened the closet doors and found nothing. She did the same with the dresser drawers and came up empty. Her curious nature took her to the other four open bedrooms.

Her exploration of those rooms came up empty. Where did Hyde keep his treasured keepsakes? Did he have any? Did he keep them all in his bedroom?

Tassia stood outside his bedroom door. Cool air whispered from the crack under the door and over her feet. After taking tentative steps forward, she pressed her ear against the cool wood of the door and listened. She didn't even hear him snore.

Damn it. This guy was damn-near perfect.

Then she heard him grumbling or growling. Tassia couldn't tell, and she wouldn't keep standing there to figure it out for much longer. She backed away from the door and continued with her search, which included three standalone bathrooms, all complete with whirlpool tubs and separated glass-enclosed shower stalls. All of it looked lush and beautiful, something ripped out of an interior design magazine. Too bad Tassia couldn't find the heart anywhere in the home.

No pictures of his family or friends existed on any walls or shelves. She returned to the music room, hoping to see an award or some sort of acknowledgement. He had sold lots of albums. Surely, his platinum awards would be there. Nothing.

Tassia felt like Hyde used this place to escape his stardom, but not his talent. He had instruments, so he did exercise his musical chops. What else? Why didn't he show pride in his accomplishments?

Maybe Tassia assumed too much. She hadn't really been with Hyde all that much to know why he did the things he did now. Maybe he hadn't taken her to his primary residence. Perhaps that home existed in Nashville, where she assumed all country stars lived and died.

After Tassia's museum-like tour of Hyde's clean but understated home, she returned to the pool area after snagging another bottle of water and another apple. She had banged out three songs in a matter of a few hours. She wanted to write more if only to prove to Hyde that the stories told about her had all been lies. Then again, she should have done this activity in front of him. What if he didn't believe that she had written the songs and maybe had someone else do them and she copied them?

Damn. Now she thought like her haters. Tassia had to push those thoughts out of her head. She had to assume that Hyde would trust her, would believe her above all else. Again, a tall order for someone she hadn't talked to in over fifteen years.

Tassia resumed her spot on the chaise lounge and looked out across the pool and yard in front of her. Unlike at her condo in Virginia Beach, she didn't hear any ocean sounds or smell the sea-salt air. Silence filled the still air with the exception of a few birds whistling and chirping. She removed her sandals and reclined back while taking a bite of her tart green apple.

She could write about a simple life that could be had in a place like this, with maybe a man like Hyde. Who would listen to that? No. Kids wanted to dance and move and not think or care. Tassia could write songs like that all day.

She took a deep breath and rubbed her eyes. Despite the angel on her shoulder telling her to get her head out of the clouds, Tassia couldn't stop thinking about Hyde. She understood why female fans went crazy for him. Unfortunately, even a long car ride with him didn't get her close to him.

The day slowly crept into the late afternoon. She closed her eyes for a moment. Tassia didn't want to relax, especially since this whole trip should have been about work, not resting by a luxurious pool.

Considering she had slept most of the way there, Tassia should have been wide awake. The impromptu tour of his house and the food she had eaten couldn't have made her that sleepy.

Listening to the birds tweeting and flying from one treetop to another, and the quiet hum of the pool filter lulled her back to slumber. It didn't help that the noon-day sun baked her into a comfortable place while she stayed cool under a large poolside umbrella.

Tassia set her phone on a glass-and-steel side table next to her lounge chair before she fell back asleep again. Since Hyde slept, she would take advantage of the quiet time for now. She knew as soon as the rest of the team showed up, they would be working hard and having long, sleepless nights.

It felt like as soon as she closed her eyes, Tassia came out of her sleep with the sounds of splashing. When did she get transported to Sea World?

Tassia blinked and gazed up. Besides being welcomed by the night sky and being bathed by the lights lining the pool, she sat up and looked in the pool only to see what she had been dreaming about when she had fallen asleep.

Hyde swam from one side of the Olympic-sized pool to the other side. The lights reflected off the water and his slick skin. The muscles in his wide back tapered down to his waist. When he turned over and swam backward, exposing his chest, Tassia felt a bit of drool oozing from her mouth.

"Stop it." She wiped her bottom lip and sat up taller.

Hyde got to the end of the pool and put his hands on the side like he needed to rest. He turned his head and spotted her, evident from his wide eyes. He ran his hand over his hair and swam over to the side of the pool closest to her.

Once to her side, he rested his hands on the side of the pool and stared at her. "I guess you were more exhausted than me."

"Guess so." She rubbed her eyes and sat at the edge of the lounge chair. "I hope I didn't miss the team coming here. It's so peaceful out here, I probably wouldn't have heard anyone at the door."

Hyde looked to the side of the pool before he brought his stare to her. "I'm sure you didn't."

She picked up her phone and glanced at the time. "It's evening time. Shouldn't they be here by now?"

"They should…if they were actually coming." Hyde shook his head. "It'll be just us here."

Chapter 10

Hyde could see the color leave Tassia's face as he finally made his admission. He knew he would have to tell her the truth eventually, at least part of the truth. He didn't have to tell her that he wouldn't be doing this project once he had gotten completely relaxed. He had hoped he would have had more time to enjoy the solitude of his home before revealing the fact that he wanted to treat this outing like a small vacation.

"What the hell do you mean?" Tassia jumped to her feet and looked like she refrained from putting her fists to her hips while she held her phone. That didn't stop her from balling her free hand and keeping her arms stiff by her sides. "You told me that you had a team of people joining us here."

Hyde shook his head while he stayed submerged in the cool pool water. "No. I told you that no one in my team would be in the vehicle with us. When you asked if they will be following, I said yes. I'm sure my manager will try to follow what I do on social media." Even though he thought he had been clever with his deception, he didn't crack a smile. He wouldn't make light of this situation.

"Oh my God. You've kidnapped me." Tassia stumbled back toward the house.

Hyde braced his hands on the concrete side and hoisted himself out of the pool. Even though he spotted Tassia scanning his body, he had to ignore his racing heart to bring her back down to earth. "Don't say it that way. I just thought—"

"I know what you thought." She pointed at him. "You wanted to get me out here to—to—ugh!"

Shit. Did Tassia think he wanted to take advantage of her?

Hyde followed her into the house, not caring if he tracked water on the floor. He didn't have time to dry himself off or even cover himself with a towel. "Honestly, I came out here to get a break. Nothing more. You had shared you wanted the same thing. I—"

"I'm calling an Uber and getting out of here. You're crazy if you think I'm going to work with you after this." She held her phone in front of her face and started to engage the application, but her face stilled. She peered over the phone.

Hyde acknowledged what she recognized. "The beauty of this place is that it's far enough from civilization to be off the grid. No cell reception."

"Wow. You are crazy." She shook her head. "Fine. I'll walk." She marched to the bedroom he had set her up in, and within moments, she returned to the living room trailing her luggage behind her.

Hyde held his hand up to stop her. "Please. I really didn't want to freak you out."

Without stopping her trek, Tassia asked, "Did you really want to work or is all this a joke to you?"

"I am inspired when I come out here. But I also needed to relax."

"And it's all about you, right?" She threw her purse strap over her shoulder. "You got me out here under the pretense that we would be working with a team of people to get this album done. Instead, you want to goof off." Tassia stomped up to him. "I'm not sure what type of woman you think I am, but I'm not going to stay here for whatever game you're playing."

Tassia stood in front of him, snorting as hard as a charging bull. He had no doubt of her anger. A droplet of water dripped on her smooth cheek. She growled as she wiped it away.

She pushed past him. Brushing against his hard body actually gave him conflicting feelings inside. His brain and moral compass directed him to convince her to stay for the album's sake. His body wanted to pull this woman back to the bed or even the pool he had just left to touch her more.

"I don't know what's wrong with me." She stormed to the front door. "I would never do this with anyone else. Hell, I didn't even record in the same room with Aaron. And here, I'm—" She turned to Hyde, glared at him again, and grunted.

"Don't leave." Hyde had more concern about her setting off the alarm than her leaving.

"I will walk back home if I need to. But I'm not staying here." Tassia opened the front door, setting off the warning before the alarm engaged.

"Damn it." Hyde rushed to the keypad next to the door and entered the code to disengage the alarm. Then he followed Tassia as she pulled her luggage behind her. "Stop running."

"You are a liar. Now I understand why you aren't in a relationship." Tassia started down the long driveway. In her thong sandals, she wouldn't go far.

Hyde ran his hand over his wet hair. "Look. I admit I made a mistake."

"Yeah, you did." Tassia didn't stop or even turn to acknowledge him. "You could have asked me if I wanted to come out here with you."

Hyde chuckled, and that finally got Tassia to stop.

"Something funny?" Tassia finally halted her marching to acknowledge him.

"I'm tired of asking for permission to live my life." This time he put his fists to his hips.

She released her luggage handles to get back in his face. "You shouldn't have to ask for permission to live *your* life. It's when you involve other people that it becomes a problem. You should have been honest with *me*." She turned around.

"Don't move."

"Don't tell me what to do." She grabbed her luggage handles again.

"No. Really. Don't. Move." Hyde hoped the way he spoke this time, slowly and with authority, that she would take him seriously.

"Why? Are you going to try to justify your behavior? You can't. You were wrong."

When Tassia refused to stop, Hyde had to take matters in his own hands. He ran up behind her and wrapped his arm around her waist.

"What the hell do you think you're doing?" Tassia shimmied her body.

Big mistake. Not that Hyde grabbed her for any other reason but to protect her, but her wiggling delectable body felt good against his body.

"Don't move." He got down by her ear.

"Why? Is your lawn boobytrapped, too?"

"Not mechanically." With his free hand, he pointed to a bushy line of shrubs several feet away from them. "Something is in there." When Tassia didn't say anything, he helped fill in the blanks. "Could be a bear."

Tassia gasped.

* * * *

Tassia went from anger to fear in a millisecond. If Hyde told the truth, they could be in the crossfire of a dangerous animal out here in the woods and with no way to call for help.

Damn Hyde and his need for privacy.

Tassia kept her stare on the bushes until she saw what Hyde must have noticed. A section shook significantly enough in the still night that it caused Tassia to release a small scream.

"No, no, no. Don't do that." Hyde tightened his hold around her waist and covered her mouth with his large hand.

The tips of his calloused fingers brushed against her cheek by her lips. The rough touch sent a shiver down her spine. Damn it. Did her knees just buckle?

Oh, yes. She had remembered that Hyde had his nearly naked body pressed up against her. It didn't help that his wet body felt heavenly against hers. Now her heart accelerated for other reasons.

"Stand still."

Hyde's warm breath feathered by her ear as he deftly moved around her body to stand in front of her. He didn't instruct her to do so, but Tassia hooked her arms under his and held onto his broad shoulders.

As she stood behind him, she couldn't help but press her face against his back. His wet body smelled like light chlorine from the pool, but his musky essence permeated through the chemical aroma. Damn, he smelled good.

He grabbed one suitcase while she still held the other. "Back up with me." He stepped slowly backward.

Tassia matched his steps until she noticed the bushes shaking even more. "Can we go faster?" She tried pulling him even more.

"Sure. Ow!" Hyde brought his foot up in a jerky motion. "Stepped on a rock."

She had forgotten that Hyde had chased her with only a pair of swim trunks covering his sexy body. "Okay, we can take it easy."

The back of Tassia's foot knocked against the brick front step, and she stepped up while pulling him up with her. Hyde stepped backward through the front door while dragging her luggage with him.

Hyde put his body in between her and harm's way. When they both made it inside his home, her fears started to relax. She inhaled but wouldn't release her breath until they became secure behind the door.

"We should be okay." Hyde pushed her bag off to the side and stood at the door.

Even with them both being in the house, Tassia didn't want to let Hyde go. Not just yet. His protective nature had her rethinking why she had been angry at him.

Tassia's eyes widened as soon as she saw something dark crawling out from the bushes. She exhaled. "Oh my God. A bear!" She cowered behind Hyde until she watched the animal wandering around the front yard. Then she really took notice of its size. Or maybe in comparison with Hyde's huge vehicle it looked small. When it sat down in the middle of the yard and rolled on its back playfully, Tassia had to smile. "Aww, it's a cub."

Hyde held his heavy wooden front door. "It is the season." He peered behind himself. Then he brought his attention back to the front yard. "You're right. It's a cub, which is worse."

"Worse?" She released him to approach the glass door. How could this cute thing be anything but harmless and adorable?

Hyde wrapped his long, strong arm around her waist to pull her back against himself. That feeling alone had Tassia sighing. Time away from the pool did him no favors as far as drying his body. Water droplets fell on her cheek and bare shoulders. This time she didn't wipe the offending spill away.

"If the cub is here, that means mama is not too far behind." He closed the door, which engaged the alarm again. To make sure they remained secure, Hyde locked the door. "Sorry I got you wet."

"What?" Tassia didn't move from her spot. Her intimate core quivered while he continued holding her.

How did he know what his touch did to her? Could he smell her essence the way she smelled his musky scent? She took another deep breath to capture his aroma. Despite being hotter than a skillet at his lies, she could at least enjoy his being.

"Running from the pool and holding you. I didn't mean to make you all—"

"Oh." Tassia pulled out of Hyde's grasp. "That's fine. I need to take a shower anyway." She looked at the closed door. "I guess locking the door makes sense since you know that no one is coming." Tassia took a couple of big steps away from Hyde. "Just because you helped me just now, don't think I've forgotten what you've done. I'm angry with you."

"I'm sure you are." Hyde moved past her without looking at her.

"That's it? No apology?"

Hyde stopped at the bottom stair and kept still before he spoke. "I'll shower and take you back home to Virginia tonight."

Tassia shook her head so hard her neck hurt. "We just saw a bear, and you said the mama isn't too far behind. There's no way I'm stepping out that door right now."

He sighed. "Fine, I'll take you back in the morning. Not my preferred time to travel without an entourage, but you want to go."

Heat filled Tassia's face. "No. I wanted to work. I guess that's different from your agenda." She peered toward the back of the house through the large glass sliding panel doors that opened up to the pool and backyard. "You own this entire property, right?"

Hyde nodded.

"I can stay in that guesthouse." She pointed as though he wouldn't know about the small home on his site.

Hyde shook his head. "You can't."

Tassia snorted. "You've got to be kidding me. Why is that?"

He dropped his gaze. "Take my word for it. You can't."

Tassia crossed her arms over her chest. "I'm not taking your word for anything. You've already proven to be a slick liar."

Out of exasperation, Hyde raised his hands in the air. "Fine. I'm a liar. You've figured me out. I'm not the Boy Scout people say I am."

Tassia stared at him for a moment when she noticed his armor cracking. "That's a shame. The nice boy I knew fifteen years ago would have been great to work with now."

"And there's the problem. We can't be those kids again. We've grown up. We're not on a show." Hyde blinked and took a couple of steps up the staircase. "I'll shower and change. If I can get the truck into the garage without any problems, I can get you home tonight."

"What? But—"

He didn't wait for her to give him some sort of acknowledgment. He took the steps by twos and ducked into the room at the top of the staircase.

Tassia looked back at her luggage by the door. She retrieved her bags and went back to the bedroom Hyde had shown her when they first got to the house. She closed the door behind herself and locked it.

Everything about this situation felt wrong. Despite the lush and beautiful surroundings, she wouldn't be able to get comfortable, not with a man who couldn't be honest with her, a man who only thought of himself.

Tassia opened one suitcase and pulled out a T-shirt and a pair of shorts. In case they did hit the road that night, she wanted a good outfit that would travel well. She ducked into the bathroom and looked at herself in the large circular mirror over the sink. The reaction this time had her floored.

She stared at herself for a while and wondered in this moment how did she identify herself. She had gotten in a vehicle with a man she barely knew for a job. Did that make her trusting or adventurous? Her headstrong self demanded that she run. Did that make her a quitter? The stories about her not writing her own songs angered her. How could she get people to believe?

Tassia stripped and ducked into the large stall with a rain showerhead that completely doused her and relaxed her. The steam even smelled fragrant like she had gone to some rainforest and got caught in a storm. Too bad she had to experience this moment here.

At the end of her shower, she got out and quickly dried herself. She put her box braids up into a bun to keep them out of her way. Then she got dressed, finishing off her look with a pair of black-and-white Converse low-top sneakers. Before leaving the bedroom, she packed her belongings back in her suitcase, readying herself to leave either that night or in the morning. With two naps under her belt, she could do the driving if necessary.

One thing Tassia knew for sure. She wouldn't be settling in this home. If she still felt this out of sorts when he came down from his shower, she would be leaving. If she returned home, what would she be going home to? An empty beach-front condo without her friend or a job or even a purpose. Her management team would probably quit if after signing the contract she walked away from the project. Her dad, though, would be ready to tell her to come home to Maryland and give up her foolish dreams. Then there would be the rumors that she knew Hyde's camp would start that she gave up on the project because she couldn't write any songs.

Tassia did have to thank Hyde for one thing. This trip gave her lots of ideas for songs. She pulled out her phone. On instinct, she started to check her email and social media accounts. The connection error message reminded her about the dead space.

Damn Hyde.

Now she had no excuse to not write. As usual, she typed over her phone screen lyrics to a song that immediately popped in her head. She wanted to play it on the piano, but she didn't want to get attached to anything in Hyde's house.

Hell, why should she concern herself about that? He didn't care about her feelings, uprooting her to bring her to his house in the middle of nowhere.

As soon as she thought that, she heard rushing water upstairs stop. Sounded like Hyde had just finished his shower. Great. Now Tassia imagined Hyde's naked body even more. She had to get her mind off her sad personal life and keep thinking about business. He had lied to her. Then again, he attempted to work and give her a good time.

No. Hyde thought only of himself, not her. She had been with plenty of men who had been that way. She had to rethink if she wanted to do a project where she would be tied to this man through recording, performing, promoting, and maybe even touring. Hell, what did she get herself into?

Tassia finished the third song she had gotten stuck on earlier, got through a fourth song by the time she sat at the piano bench, and started on a fifth song when she reclined back against the keys, causing a clamorous noise to echo through the house.

Tassia glared up the *Gone with the Wind* type of stairs and sniffed. She wanted something to eat, and wouldn't be waiting for Hyde. She marched to the kitchen and set her phone on the largest kitchen island she had ever seen. It had a light gray concrete waterfall top and sides. Nothing but the best for the most popular entertainer in the world right now. She rolled her eyes.

She peeked into his large refrigerator and spied fresh, raw chicken breasts along with some vegetables and even some tortillas. If she could find the spices, she could make herself some fajitas.

Tassia pulled the items out and placed them on the counter next to the fridge. When she turned to retrieve one of the hanging pans over the island, she screamed and backed against the counter.

A young woman with reddish brown hair and wide brown eyes stared back at her.

Chapter 11

Tassia imagined she had to be one of Hyde's rabid fans. Her off-putting wide smile didn't help her cause.

"What are you doing here?" The stranger cocked her head.

"I was going to ask you the same thing." Tassia kept her voice steady while trying to take inventory of her surroundings.

Why didn't she bother to look for knives first? Maybe because she didn't think she would be face-to-face with a potentially eager fan.

The young woman with a petite build approached Tassia with her hand out like they had stepped into a business meeting. Tassia reared up on her toes and started opening drawers around her to look for anything that would be able to help her in this situation.

"I'm Pepper. Some people call me Pep."

When Tassia stared at the woman like she had spoken another language, she continued.

"I'm assuming Pig Face didn't tell you I was here."

At the mention of the nickname, Tassia glanced at the wrinkled piece of paper on the counter. Then she heard stomping footfalls coming down the stairs.

"Are you Hyde's wife?" Tassia's heart beat a little slower...not that she cared.

If this woman had been romantically linked to Hyde, she wouldn't be surprised that the man hadn't admitted that to her either.

Pepper wrinkled her nose and shook her head like she smelled something foul. "Oh, God, no. Eww."

At that moment, Hyde ran into the kitchen. Still in bare feet, he at least had on loose-fitting shorts and a Garth Brooks T-shirt. The man stayed rooted in country music.

"What the hell is going on?" He looked at Pepper and rolled his eyes. "Christ, Pep, did you sneak in the back door again?"

She held up a set of keys and jingled them in the air. "When you have keys to the place, it's hardly sneaking." Pepper crossed her arms over her chest.

"I'm assuming you've introduced yourself?" Hyde pointed to Tassia, who still had no idea what situation she had stepped into.

"Working on it." Pepper turned back around.

Before she could say anything, Hyde did the honors. "Tassia, this is my cousin, Pepper Wallace."

Tassia exhaled, but her face wouldn't produce the smile she wanted to have. She slowly lifted her hand to Pepper, who accepted it and immediately pulled Tassia in for a hug.

"Good to meet you. Good to meet anyone that can stand to be around Pig Face—"

"Hyde, okay?"

"For longer than five minutes." Pepper turned to him and smirked before she let Tassia go. "What's your story?"

Tassia had to collect herself before she spoke. "Your cousin and I are supposed to be writing songs for an album."

Pepper nodded. "I knew you couldn't have been one of his crazy fans." She snorted as she walked over to the island. "If you were, you would have attacked me by now, and that wouldn't have gone over well for you." She nodded her head to the right. "By the way, for future reference, he keeps the knives by the stove on the wall."

Tassia glanced at the shiny blades affixed in their spots by magnets apparently. "You scared me. I thought Hyde and I were the only ones in this house."

"You are." Pepper leaned on top of the counter. "When he needs me, I stay in the guest house."

Now it made sense why Hyde said she couldn't stay in the guest house.

"What are you doing in here?" Hyde went over to the stainless-steel refrigerator and pulled out a bottle of beer.

If Tassia had plans of going home tonight, she would have to do all the driving. No way would she let this man drive after drinking alcohol.

He turned to her. "Want one?"

Maybe with another person there on the property, Hyde could be tolerable. She nodded and put her hand out to him. After popping off the top for her with a bottle opener he pulled from a drawer, he handed her the frosty brown bottle.

"Thanks." Tassia nodded and took a sip.

Man, did she need this beer. It had a nice hoppy flavor with a subtle citrusy finish. It helped that he had it ice cold.

"Are you cooking or what? I'm starving." Pepper rubbed her stomach.

"Pep, you don't ask that of a guest." Hyde knocked his elbow against his cousin.

Even though he towered over her, she didn't budge.

"She's not a guest. If she's working with you and she's here—alone—she's practically family." Pepper laughed and looked at Tassia. "I'm teasing. I don't mind cooking." She scanned the items Tassia had placed on the counter. "Looks like it's fiesta night." She jutted her thumb over her shoulder. "Go get the chips and salsa from the pantry."

Hyde blinked. "Did you forget that this is my house?"

Pepper tucked her wavy hair behind her ears. "Yeah, yeah. Save that 'I'm Hyde Love' stuff for your fans." She pointed down. "Here, you're Pig Face." She snorted again. "Always will be." Like a whirlwind, she retrieved a large cast-iron skillet from a lower cabinet and placed it on one of the eight gas burners on the stove. Then she got out a bottle of olive oil from a cabinet by Tassia's head. "You like your food spicy?"

Tassia smiled. "Of course."

Pepper smiled wider. "I like her already." She turned to Hyde. "Way better than that airhead you were dating before, Shelby Lynne." She mimicked putting her finger down her throat and made a gagging sound.

"Oh, no. We're not dating. We're just working together." Tassia glanced at Hyde. "Supposed to be. We've worked together before, though, years ago."

Pepper stared at her before her eyes widened. "You were a Ratty Girl. I remember. I loved the scenes you were in more than—"

"Watch it." Hyde plucked his cousin on the back of her head.

"Hey!" She rubbed it before playfully punching his chest. Pepper poured some oil into the skillet. "When you called me and asked that I get the house ready, you said it was because you were taking some time off."

Hyde cleared his throat. "I was. I am. Sort of." He went to a side room that must have been the pantry area.

"Yes, I signed a contract with Charisma to do a duets album with him." Tassia took three large gulps of beer, nearly finishing off the bottle. "He said he brought me here so that we could write."

When Hyde returned, Pepper did what Tassia had been thinking about doing when she learned the truth. Pepper balled her small hand into a fist and punched the mega star on his arm.

"Hey!" Hyde placed a bag of tortilla chips on the counter along with a jar of salsa. "I let you get away with that once, but there won't be a third time or you're going in the pool."

"You kidnapped her." Pepper pointed to Tassia.

Now Tassia started to like this woman. "Yes. I said the exact same thing."

Pepper brought her attention to Tassia. "Did he even tell you I was here?"

Tassia shook her head.

That response got Pepper to grunt her disapproval.

"Not one word or I'm giving you the noogie of death." He wagged his finger at her.

"You lied." Pepper shook her head. "I'm telling—"

Hyde interrupted her. "Don't you dare say it."

"Grammy Love. She will take a switch to you."

Tassia couldn't help but snicker at the antics between these two. They acted as though time had stopped at their adolescent years.

Hyde growled.

"Get a bowl and dump the chips in it." She turned to Tassia. "Don't just stand there. I showed you where the knives are. Get me one. You take one. We have stuff to cut up."

"Like Hyde said, I'm a guest here." Tassia cocked her head.

"You were also about to cook for yourself before I came in here. And let's not forget that this guy here lied." Pepper nodded her head back toward Hyde.

"I wish you two would stop saying that." He poured the triangle-shaped chips into a bowl before he opened a jar of salsa.

"And I wish you would stop being so sneaky. You weren't that way when we were kids." Pepper accepted a knife from Tassia. "Thank you. You were the one who would tell a room full of folks when you went to the bathroom."

Hyde looked at Tassia first. "I was three when I did that. My older cousin wasn't supposed to share all of my business to a stranger."

Pepper's eyebrows raised. "You can't call a woman you brought to your house a stranger, especially if you two plan on working together." She scraped some cut up pieces of chicken into a screaming-hot pan. "You're a songwriter besides being a fabulous singer and dancer?"

Tassia glanced at Hyde first before she answered. "Yes, and I wouldn't call what I did fabulous."

"You were way better than this guy here." She nodded toward Hyde. "You sing for Charisma? I know that label." Pepper paused. "That's where—"

"Truman Woodley, yes. He records there." Hyde nodded.

"No. I was going to say Chantel Evans, well, Woodley now."

Tassia had to blink now. This woman not only knew an R&B singer, but she knew her original name. She didn't say Shauna Stellar. She didn't even call her Chantel Woodley first. Yep, Pepper and she could be friends.

"Yes, they both own the label, and I work for them. I guess you could call it that." Tassia finished off her beer, then looked around for a receptacle to dispose of it.

Hyde took the bottle that she held, brushing his fingers against her hand before he took it from her.

"Um, thanks." She went back to the counter to continue cutting up the vegetables. "Anyway, I do songwriting for them and some studio work."

"She's being modest."

Tassia stopped cutting before she peered at Hyde.

Hyde continued. "She's on that big hit song that's out now with that rapper."

If Hyde attempted to sound hip and with it, he had failed miserably.

Pepper's eyes widened as she stared at Tassia. "Holy shit."

"Language." Hyde nudged her with his elbow.

She waved him away. "Screw you, Pig Face." She kept looking at Tassia. "You sang that song."

The stone in Tassia's stomach dropped. She had hoped being this far removed from civilization that she wouldn't have to talk about that damn song. Even in the sticks, she would be known as the "hook girl."

Tassia sighed. "Yes, I'm on—"

"'Love Me Tonight.'" Pepper put her hand to her chest. "It's my favorite song."

Tassia stopped moving. She had a single that she had done for a movie soundtrack when she had first gotten to Charisma. The soundtrack overall sold well, but she knew that no one would know her from her one and only song on it that didn't make the charts.

"You know that song?" Tassia smiled.

"Know it? I bang guys on the regular to it."

"Hey! Now *I'm* going to tell Grammy Love about you." Hyde pulled out another beer and started to hand it to Tassia.

She shook her head. She wanted to be sober for this conversation.

"I can't believe *the* Tassia is here in Pig Face's house." Pepper ran over to Hyde's entertainment set.

"Will you please stop calling me that? It's getting on my nerves, and we are no longer ten years old." Hyde pulled out a bottle of water instead, unscrewed the top, and handed it to Tassia.

"Nice to see you can be a gentleman." Tassia accepted the drink. This time she let her fingers drag over his strong hand.

"I can be a lot of things." Hyde's voice dipped down low while he kept his stare on her.

The look alone had her knees quivering.

He broke his stare long enough to look at the pan on the stove. "Looks like right now I need to be a chef." He pulled a spatula from a drawer and started pushing the chicken around in the pan.

The smell of the cooked meat mixed with chili and cumin spices filled the air and reminded Tassia of her favorite Mexican restaurant. To put some space between herself and Hyde, she padded over to the bowl of chips and dipped one into the salsa.

Spicy didn't even begin to describe the flavor, but she liked it. She enjoyed the heat that hit the back of her throat and went all the way down to her belly. Before she could try another chip, she heard a familiar sound filling the house.

"By far the best song on the soundtrack." Pepper skipped back into the kitchen and sat at a barstool while Tassia's song played through the house.

Pepper swayed back and forth while keeping her eyes closed. "Magical."

Tassia smiled. To get some recognition for her work made her feel validated.

"You have a beautiful voice." Hyde had said the statement in almost a whisper, but Tassia caught it.

"Did you write this?" Pepper jutted her thumb in the air.

Tassia nodded. "I think I wrote it in a day." She returned to her station next to Hyde to finish cutting up the vegetables.

"Dude, you are lucky to have her." Pepper snagged Hyde's open beer and finished off her cousin's drink.

"I don't know if the project will go through." He glanced at Tassia. "I messed up. I'll be taking her home in the morning."

Pepper growled louder than a bear. "You did mess up. Did you apologize?"

He didn't look at her. "I think so. But—"

"Do it again." Pepper pounded her fist on the counter.

"Stop telling me what to do. We're not kids anymore."

"Exactly. You're a grown man and she's a grown woman. You two are working together. You need to tell her your plans so that you two can be on the same page." Pepper pointed at the two of them. "I know you're

talented. I can show you videos of him at county fairs when he was little."
She snickered. "And I know you can sing your face off. This could be an
amazing collaboration."

Except for the sizzling meat, the kitchen became quiet as soon as
the song stopped.

Tassia peered up at Hyde. "Is she your other manager?" She chuckled.
"She's doing a hell of a job convincing me to stay."

"Is it working?" Hyde gazed at her.

She paused before responding. "Does it work for you?"

Hyde licked his lips before answering. In her mind, Tassia imagined
him doing that to prepare to kiss her. She balled her toes under her foot as
she waited for the next crucial step. Which one would bend first?

"Jesus, will you just kiss her already, or tell her that you're an idiot?"
Pepper scooped up some more salsa and popped the filled chip in her mouth.

Hyde smiled. "Should I drop down to one knee for this?"

"What?" Tassia laughed at his odd question.

Before she knew it, Hyde went down to one knee in front of her and
held one of her hands. In that moment, Tassia imagined this happening to
her in real life, she and Hyde together. She shook her head. That fantasy
made no sense. Although she had started to get to know him, it didn't erase
the fact that he had used their situation to his advantage.

She pursed her lips as he crouched down in front of her.

Hyde stared at her with his heavenly green eyes. "Tassia Hogan, in
my years in the industry, I have learned some incredibly bad habits like
keeping my plans private, even to the people who will be working with
me. I should have told you the real reason why I wanted to come to this
house instead of tricking you. For that, I am sincerely sorry."

"Tell her you will never lie to her again." Pepper pointed to Hyde, then
Tassia. "Do it."

"Be quiet, please." Hyde waved off his cousin. "Tassia, will you please
stay on this project, write some songs, and do the duets album with me?"

This project could be great for her career. Here Tassia had the biggest-
selling artist out now on his knee asking her to do this duets album with him.

"Yes." What else could she say to a tempting offer like that?

"Now seal this deal with a kiss and let's get going." Pepper jumped
from the stool and marched to the refrigerator.

"Um, a handshake will do." Tassia shook Hyde's hand as he stood again.

"Why are you so obsessed with us kissing?" Hyde scooped the cooked
chicken onto a platter.

Pepper groaned. "I haven't had any in a while. I'm living vicariously through you, cuz."

When Tassia got to cutting up the onions, the tears flowed quickly. Damn it. She loved the vegetable, loved the taste, but she couldn't take the tears.

She had to blink several times to focus when she felt something against the back of her hand. She noticed a white, dampened paper towel. She looked up to see Hyde holding it.

"Wipe your eyes. I can take over onion duty." The smile he offered nearly weakened her. This version of Hyde could have convinced her to do more than just come to his house.

"Thanks, but I'll be fine." She accepted the towel if only to wipe her eyes quickly. The cool feeling did soothe the ache, but she wouldn't let him know that.

"If we're going to be working together, you'll need to accept help." He moved back to the pan and dumped the cut-up bell peppers into it.

Tassia finished cutting up the onions to hand them off to him. "You'll have to do the same, you know. Compromise, remember?"

Hyde kept his stare on her while the air around them stilled.

"Want to hear some embarrassing stories about Hyde?" Pepper cackled and clapped her hands.

* * * *

Hyde spent most of the night corralling his cousin to keep her from revealing too much. He did have to thank Pepper for her intrusion. Because of it, Tassia agreed to stay longer. Who knew Pepper would have known Tassia's music? Even more impressive, she didn't mention the song that had bothered Tassia so much.

"My cousin Hyde is so conceited," Pepper began, "when he was a kid, he thought the game hide-and-seek was named after him."

Tassia burst into laughter and leaned back in her chair. "Stop it. I can't take it." She put her hand to her stomach.

"I was four. Give me a break." Hyde stood and collected the plates from the dinner table.

"I can do that." Tassia stood. "Compromise, remember?"

Hyde took the dirty dishes from her hands. "Still my home. You sit." He glanced at Pepper. "Did you have anything sweet in here?"

"You mean besides me?" Pepper chuckled. "There's some ice cream in the freezer and cookies in the pantry. Oh, and that thing you asked me to get and put in the freezer. But I thought you were dieting? I thought all of you Hollywood types stayed on diets."

"Not me." Hyde scraped the remaining food from each plate before loading them in the dishwasher. "I stay in shape so that I can move around easier on stage."

"Same here. I just finished a tour." Tassia raised her arms in the air to stretch.

"Really? If I knew you were out there singing live, I would have gone." Pepper crossed her legs in the chair she occupied.

"It wasn't my tour. I, um, sang a duet on a song with a bigger artist."

Hyde watched Tassia rub the back of her neck. He knew she didn't want to go into this topic. "Hey, let me get that—"

"You don't mean that 'Ride Me' song or whatever it's called? Ugh." Pepper screwed up her lips and shook her head. "You were the best thing on that song. I can't stand Aaron."

Hyde watched Tassia screw up her lips. "You paid her to say that, didn't you?"

"You really don't know Pepper, do you?" Hyde chuckled. "She's as pretty wide open as you can get."

"Speaking of wide open, I'm going back to the other house. If I hadn't had some beer, I would go back to my place and work off this dinner." Pepper flitted her eyebrows suggestively. "By the way, are you going to be doing that thing you do in a couple of days because of your—"

"Hey." Hyde swiped his hand back and forth over his throat to cut her off. "Some things about me should be kept secret, okay?"

"You mean like your mad crush on—"

"Hey, time for you to go." Hyde stood behind Pepper and held her shoulders.

"Wait." Pepper turned and grabbed Hyde's arm as she split her attention between him and Tassia. "You haven't told her?"

Hyde felt his insides warming up to a molten level. "Pep."

His cousin rolled her eyes. "Hyde."

He had to blink when she finally used his real name and not the moniker she'd been calling him for over twenty years.

"You need to be open. You don't want to get an ulcer, do you?" She turned to Tassia. "He used to have a major crush on you."

Tassia stared at Hyde. "Really?"

"Long time ago." He waved his hand in the air to try to pass off this bit of news as dismissive. When he did dare to peer up, he caught Tassia staring at him.

"When you all got breaks in taping, he would come back home and talk about this cute, wonderful girl on set with these amazing green eyes." Pepper stood in front of Tassia and nodded. "They are spectacular."

Tassia snickered. "That could have been anyone." She shook her head. "Maybe Christina."

Pepper groaned. "Not that airhead, who still needs to be thanking you for her career." She pointed at Tassia. "No. It was you. He didn't know this, but I looked through his dresser drawer."

Hyde felt his eyes go wide. "I think we all need to go to our rooms and—"

Pepper continued. "He had a picture of you at the bottom of his dresser, right underneath his tighty whities."

Hyde exhaled hard enough for everyone in the room to hear it. "Feel better about doing that?"

"Hey, don't get mad at me because I like to keep my plate clean." She brushed her hands together. "You tell people how you feel at all times, that way if you were to drop dead right now, you can never say to yourself, 'I wished I had said whatever.'"

"If I'm dead, I'm not going to say anything." Hyde laughed at her.

"And thanks to me, Tassia now knows how you truly feel about her."

"Felt." Each time Hyde had looked at Tassia now, he saw hate and discontent covering her beautiful face...except now.

Tassia's expression softened. She regarded Hyde differently. Maybe she saw him less as that kid from back in the day and more as a man. Now he would have to figure out if those little-kid feelings still existed today.

"Whatever." Pepper cocked her head.

"To get on another topic, we saw a bear in the front yard." Hyde shook his head. "Stay in the main house."

This time Pepper shook her head. "You have that huge fence around the backyard, so nothing that can't fly is getting back there. Besides, we've been making so much noise in here that I doubt anything is still out there." She went to the back door. "And you two need to get to work." She winked and exited as quickly as she had popped into the home.

The silence that hung in between them this time felt uncomfortable. To continue avoiding talking about the huge rhino in the room that Pepper had introduced, Hyde busied himself by cleaning the kitchen. He never expected Tassia to assist him, but she stood, shoulder to shoulder, with him, wiping down counters and rinsing off dishes.

Hyde finished loading the dishwasher by the time Tassia padded up to him. "Thanks for dinner."

Hyde hoped his sigh of relief that she didn't mention what Pepper had revealed didn't come off as too obvious. "Not a problem." He put in the cleanser, closed the door, and started the device. "You want some dessert?"

When he saw Tassia snake her slender, pink tongue over her lips, he had to suppress a groan.

"No. I'm stuffed from dinner." She cleaned off the counter as though she needed to help. "Did you want to—"

"What?" Hyde tried to hide the eagerness in his voice, but he knew it came through from the way he had interrupted her.

"Work on some songs?" She reached behind herself and pulled out her cell phone. "I started on a few that I wanted to run by you if you're up to working."

Hyde looked at Tassia differently. In his plan, he never took into account that Tassia would take this project seriously. She had done some work. He had been selfish in all of this. Tassia had been right. He had every right to make demands for himself. He couldn't impose his will and desires on anyone else, especially those who had no idea about his plans.

Hell, at what point had he become his father? Hyde never used people, and now he figured out why. He felt horrible. No way could he admit this out loud, let alone confess his selfish sin to her. To make up his poor behavior to Tassia, he had to take her and this project seriously.

He nodded. "Yeah. Sure. We can work on songs." He walked ahead of her. "Let's go to the music room."

"Perfect. I can play on the piano." She followed him to the room he had designated for inspiration.

He hadn't taken her to his in-home studio yet. That would be next.

"I hope what my cousin said didn't make you feel uncomfortable." Pepper's revelation certainly put a twist in Hyde's belly.

"I was more surprised than anything else." She continued following him. "You were so quiet back then, I didn't think you liked anyone, let alone had a crush on me. Did you really keep a picture of me in your dresser drawer?"

Hyde stopped and faced her. He started to refute the story, but when he stared into her eyes, he couldn't. His mind and body refused to betray this woman's trust once again, although he still kept secrets from her. "I did. I was bowled over by your talent. I thought you were the best singer among us. I knew you were destined for great things."

This time she snickered. "Instead, you're the big star and I'm the back-up singer."

He stormed up to her. "You're not a back-up singer. You're a talented, beautiful woman with big things ahead of you." Now he started to sound like her at their business meeting not too long ago.

"You think I'm beautiful?"

Damn, he had said too much. He backed from her. "You have an appeal that some may find attractive." Great. Now he sounded like a businessman, like his father.

"What about you?"

Hyde should have seen that coming. "I think any music videos we do will get a lot of hits because of you."

Tactful. Good enough answer to get him by.

"So, Hyde."

"Yeah?" He looked back at her before he stepped into the room.

"No, I mean your name. Where did that come from? You don't hear that name a lot lately. And the fact that your last name is Love just tells the world you are closed off to relationships." She laughed.

Hyde tried to join her in her light ribbing, but part of her statement held merit. He had been burned too many times to be a good man for anyone. Not now.

"Family name. My father said a great-grandfather or someone like that was named Hyde. I did my genealogy a few years ago." He shook his head. "Couldn't find a relative with that name. Not a legal name. Not like me. By the time I had discovered it, I was already famous as Hyde Love."

"You could always change it. You could go by your middle name. What's that?" Tassia sat down at the piano bench. When he remained quiet, she regarded him again. "What? Is it worse than Hyde?"

"You think the name Hyde is bad?" He sat next to her on the bench. At the close proximity, he saw her bottom lip quiver a moment before she answered.

"Um, no. I actually think Hyde is a cool name. It's the Hyde Love of it all that makes it bad."

"No middle name." He held his hands up in surrender. "Not lying. My parents thought Hyde Love was enough. What about you?"

"Wait. I have another question about your name. Pig Face."

He didn't want to, but Hyde knew he rolled his eyes. "You remember how I was back then. Until puberty, I was a little butterball. I think I was supposed to represent the husky boys."

Tassia covered her mouth to suppress a large laugh. "You have certainly taken control of your situation. I can attest to that since I have seen your body."

"Ugh, that picture of me online." Hyde placed his hand on the smooth black and white keys of the piano.

"No. I don't mean that. I mean when you were in the pool." She kept her gaze away from him.

In that moment, Hyde wanted to look in her eyes. "Watching my diet and exercising are how I got my body in shape. Unfortunately, my cousin can't let that old me go."

"Does that bother you?"

Hyde leaned back as he regarded Tassia. "You know, no one has ever asked me that. I can laugh at it now. That's all that matters."

"Maybe that should be one of the songs." She placed her phone on the music stand.

After the blowout they had had earlier after his swim, Hyde never thought he and Tassia would be calm, civil, and with this much sizzle between them.

As much as he had wanted, Hyde had tried not paying attention to the sexy woman lounging by his pool after his nap. Even through her long dress, he caught the shape of her slender legs. Her hands with delicate fingers had been placed on her stomach. She looked like a queen.

For that reason, during his second shower, despite their disagreement, Hyde couldn't help but handle himself. He had ducked his head under the streaming cool water that did nothing to shrink his manhood or desire, and he stroked his hardening penis while thinking about Tassia, the girl who had piqued his interest as a pre-teen, and the stranger he didn't hire years ago but still had an amazing voice and a body he would want to touch.

He remembered how hard his heart pounded in his chest the more he thought about her. Hyde had growled and his body had shaken as soon as he came.

"Tassia." Probably the one and only time he would be uttering her name in this way.

If he liked betting, Hyde suspected that she would fulfill her contractual obligation but wouldn't be recording with him, not in person. He wanted that personal interaction, particularly after experiencing the spark from touching her hand while preparing dinner.

When he had gone down the hallway toward the bedroom he thought she would be in, it surprised him to see the door open. He had crept down the hallway to not freak her out when she saw him. When he didn't see her, Hyde had wondered if she truly did start walking back home. He had spotted her luggage still by the door, so he knew that couldn't be true. He had also noticed the note his cousin had left for him in his refrigerator left open on the counter. Tassia must have gotten a great laugh out of what his cousin had written.

"I like Pepper." Tassia smiled as she swiped her fingertip over her phone's screen.

"Pepper has never met a stranger. In all the time I've known her, she's never really changed." Hyde sat up taller. "I can tell she likes you. She normally doesn't fight me for just anyone." He let his fingers sink into a couple of keys to emit a sound. "I really am sorry I brought you here without telling you the full truth."

Tassia remained quiet while keeping her stare on her phone.

"Had I asked you, would you have—"

She interrupted him. "It doesn't matter now. I'm here." She cleared her throat. "I'll stay until we've finished writing."

Hyde didn't expect his heart to pound as hard as it did when she admitted that she would stay. "You don't want to go home in the morning?"

Tassia snickered. "Maybe it's the beer talking, but I don't mind being here now."

"Beer? Okay. After some sleep and a sober head, if you change your mind in the morning, let me know. The last thing I want you to feel is trapped." He had had enough of feeling like that in his last relationship until he knew he and Shelby Lynne had to part ways.

"You'll be the first to know." Tassia nodded.

"I don't know about you, but I'm a melody guy first." Hyde tripped his fingers over the keys and played the opening of one of his songs.

"Before we get to that, I need to ask you something." Tassia crossed her legs.

Hyde had to keep his full concentration on her eyes in order to not drop his attention to her caramel-colored thighs. "Sure. Shoot."

"When I auditioned for you years ago, why didn't you hire me? Wrong sound?" She shrugged. "Wrong look?"

Hyde immediately shook his head. "None of those. Wrong time. There were several reasons behind it. First, I was finally an adult, and I was trying so hard to separate from my Ratty Rat days. I didn't want people to keep relating to me as that fat, little kid. Miley Cyrus went the extreme route to have people see her as a woman and not Hannah Montana."

"I was going to ask if that naked picture of you was—"

"Not staged. Not leaked. Not supposed to get out at all." He shook his head. "It was all embarrassing."

"What are the other reasons? You mentioned there were several." Tassia swung her legs back and forth.

"Your audition was during a time when I allowed my management team to make the bulk of my decisions for me. I was in the room, but I was busy writing songs." To ease her questioning mind, he reached out and held her hand. "Trust me. Had I been paying attention—" He regarded her for a moment before shaking his head. "No, I still wouldn't have hired you."

Tassia's eyes widened. "Really? That's good to hear from your mouth." She snatched her hand from under his.

"It's obvious you are no one's back-up singer. You belong at the front of the stage. If I had hired you, it would have delayed your progress." To occupy his hand, he returned it to the keys. "You're a star." He thought he caught her cheeks changing to a crimson color.

"This coming from the biggest star on the planet."

"I'm a music lover. That's it. And I know what I like."

She swept her hand down her leg. "Okay. Thanks for the honesty. I guess we can get to work now." She picked up her phone and showed it to Hyde. "I wrote a few songs. I was very inspired."

"By the surroundings or the situation?" An uncomfortable tickle crept up the back of his neck.

"Both." She scooted closer to him on the bench. "This first one I called 'Kidnapped by the Cowboy.'"

He blinked. Before he could correct her assessment of labeling him as a cowboy, if she indeed meant him, she started playing a tune that sounded decent. Her voice, though, had his insides transformed into jelly...until he listened to her words.

Using the terms *selfish*, *ego-driven*, and *careless* felt like daggers stabbing at his gut until she got to the chorus.

"I got kidnapped by the cowboy. His will gave me no choice. Like I was his little toy. And his games gave me no joy." Tassia kept her stare on the piano keys until the end of the song. Then she looked at him. "I have more."

She swiped her finger over the screen and without his approval or permission, she sang the next song she called "Hot for Nothing" about a nice-looking man with nothing to offer.

That one had Hyde seething. She focused the songs on him, and she painted him as a villain. After thinking they had gotten through their misunderstanding, she brought them back to the past. Did she really think he would want to sing about this repeatedly and record this?

"This third song I've called 'Worthless' to, well, you'll see." She pounded her fingers over the piano keys while she sang about feeling good for nothing.

That song had him seeing red. It took every bit of his strength to not tell her how wrong she had been about him. The song titles and content had been the least of his worries about the songs.

"I was working on a fourth song, but I'm not ready to present that one."

Hyde had to stifle a laugh when he thought about the whole situation. Tassia felt ready to present these other songs to him?

She smiled when she asked, "What do you think?"

Hyde had heard every word she had said, and it brought him back to the moment he had just talked about with Tassia. He finally had made a selfless decision and here she wanted to blast him for it.

"I hate them." He felt the flames licking the sides of his face as he spoke to her and watched her smile melting.

"They're supposed to be funny. I was angry when you told me the real reason you brought me here." She turned her full body to him so that she straddled the piano bench to get closer to him.

At a different time, hell, only minutes ago, he would have wanted to kiss her pouty lips. Then he remembered the words she said through them.

After unclenching his jaw, he finally spoke. "This is a duets album. What part is meant for me?"

She chuckled. "Maybe you can do the doo-wop sound. Or better yet, you can just repeat the phrase 'I'm sorry' while I sing. How's that?"

Hyde stood. "Mistake. I knew this would be a mistake." He headed toward the door.

"Does that mean you're giving up on this project? Are you taking me home in the morning?"

He stopped. "Oh, no. I'm going to write my own songs. I'm going to have a good time with mine just like you did with yours. You have a great night."

Chapter 12

For all his bravado, Hyde didn't realize how hard it would be to write songs. Strange. He remembered being a kid and banging out a song every hour it seemed like. Then again, he had been inspired. Working alongside Tassia so many years ago provided him some great inspiration for several songs. To prove her wrong, he had almost wanted to break out those old songs to show her he could bring something to this arrangement.

Despite Tassia's songs not having any duet parts for him, Hyde had been impressed by the fact that in a day, she had written three songs. He suspected that her songs would classify as "club bangers," as she had once described them. He couldn't say Tassia didn't prove herself. She did. He had fallen on the job.

Hyde walked by Tassia's closed bedroom door to head to the backyard. Maybe if he sat by the pool like she had he could write. The last couple of days had him curious as to what occupied her time. Maybe she plotted on how to kill him. He would deserve it if he hadn't apologized. How long could she not talk to him?

Instead of thinking about that, Hyde needed to do what he had come here for. Or at least what he told Tassia he had come here for—he needed to get to work.

Hyde sat on the edge of the pool with his feet and lower legs in the water while he held a pad and pen in his hands. He pressed the pen on the paper and—nothing.

"Damn." Hyde shook his head. "Come on, man. You've done this before. You aren't that far removed from the process."

Hyde closed his eyes and did what he told Tassia he'd done when he had written songs in the past. He thought about the melody. In his head, the melody matched Tassia. It sounded full bodied and smooth with a hard-hitting beat. What he heard in his head seduced him...just like Tassia had.

He glanced back at the house halfway hoping she would be looking at him. What the hell was wrong with him? Why couldn't he open up more? Tassia didn't deserve his suspicion. She didn't need to get him at less than his best. For that reason, whenever he made food, he would leave a plate out for Tassia. Before coming out to the pool, he had made a salad and a bacon-lettuce-and-tomato sandwich.

Hyde refused to leave his spot until he wrote a completed song. Sitting on the concrete around the pool caused his butt to tingle as it went to sleep, and the backs of his legs started to sting. Even the cool water he had his lower legs submerged in didn't soothe him.

"Get it together. Think." Instead of squeezing his eyes shut and not looking at the blank page staring back at him, he confronted his nemesis head on.

This time he put the pen to paper and started writing, slowly at first. He struggled with the words until he thought about Tassia, what he put her through, and his crush. With her coming back into his life, he started to realize that maybe old feelings hadn't gone away.

After an arduous four hours of sitting by the pool, Hyde finally had lyrics to a song. He didn't know how good it would be, but he knew how honest he had made it.

He stood, dried off his legs and feet, and walked back into his house for a bottle of water. He had to smile when he noticed the offering he had left for Tassia had been accepted. Forgiveness had to come.

* * * *

Tassia knew she shouldn't have sung those songs to Hyde a couple of days ago. Since then, he had kept his distance, barely speaking to her. It surprised her that he didn't get her loaded in his truck first thing in the morning the next day and drive her back home as fast as he could.

Instead he had prepared a full breakfast with fried potatoes, scrambled eggs, bacon, and biscuits, and left the meal out for her. He had done the same for lunch and dinner. He had prepared dishes but didn't eat with her.

As her way of thanking him for at least looking out for her, she did the dishes.

Hyde couldn't stay angry with her. He made a mistake and she wrote about it. Taylor Swift had built her empire on her pain. Why couldn't Tassia do the same?

Hyde did have a point. The songs she had written had no part for him. She still had it in her head that she wrote every song for herself.

She had written duets before for Chantel and Truman. She had it in her to write a duet. She didn't know if her feelings about Hyde tempered her creativity. She had to break this cycle of holding on to past hurt. They hadn't slept together. In the last couple of days, they had barely even talked.

Tassia had remained in the bedroom Hyde had allowed her to stay in while there. She glanced by the door at her packed bags. At any moment, she knew Hyde would be scooping her up and shuttling her back home.

At that thought, a knock sounded on the closed, locked door. Tassia clutched her phone as she climbed out of bed and padded to the door. She had on a short sundress this day. Because she had taken a nap earlier, if he wanted to hit the road right now before dinner, she would be ready. Starving, but ready.

Tassia opened the door and found Hyde on the other side. His normal five o'clock shadow had been shaved off completely, showing off his chiseled jawline. Anger no longer filled his eyes. His expression held some remorse. For that reason, Tassia released the breath she held.

"I've made dinner." He nodded toward the kitchen.

Tassia smelled the aroma of seared beef and roasted vegetables. The scent reminded her of summertime and home in Maryland with her father. When she heard her stomach start to growl, she put her free hand on her belly to cover the sound.

"I'll be out there soon." She started to back into the bedroom.

"Will you come out here and join me? There's something I want you to hear." He didn't wait for her to answer.

Hyde walked away from the bedroom. Tassia contemplated not leaving the bedroom. She no longer wanted to look at these four walls. Instead she slipped on some flip-flops and left her phone on the bed.

By the time she had gotten to the kitchen, she gasped at the sight. Through the large sliding glass doors to the sunroom, she saw a scene with a dressed table and low lighting. Not candlelight. That would be too intimate. What did Hyde have in mind?

Tassia walked to the table. "What is this?"

Hyde pulled a chair out for her. "Have a seat."

She waited a beat before she went to the chair and allowed him to move it easily under her. "Thank you."

"I grilled some steak and chicken." He pointed to a platter filled with meat with perfect grill marks crisscrossed on them. "I also made some roasted zucchini, onions, and potatoes, and there's a salad there."

"I love food cooked out on a grill." She took in a deep breath. "It always reminds me of summer."

"I know." He nodded.

"You do? How would you know that about me?"

"You told me on our final day of shooting. I remembered." He smiled.

Tassia recalled that she had shared that little bit about herself to him before Burt pulled her up and dragged her out of the studio. She couldn't believe he remembered.

Tassia looked over at the food before bringing her attention to him. "You made all of this yourself without help?"

He let a slight smile peek through. "Yes. Pepper went back to her place yesterday. She wanted to say good-bye to you, but you were holed up in your room."

"Will she be back?" Tassia pressed her hands against the top of the large wooden table.

"Probably when we finally leave. She's about the only one I trust in this house to open it up for me and make sure it's okay when I go." Hyde, now wearing a T-shirt and denim shorts, walked over to a darkened corner of the room.

Her heart started pounding hard until she saw him pick up a guitar and carry it back to her. When she saw him sitting down next to the table and facing her, her heart drummed for a different reason.

"I've been busy these last couple of days." He positioned the guitar on his leg. "I was also inspired since being here." He peered at her. "And after listening to your songs."

Tassia lost her appetite but kept her stare on him. She wanted to prepare for his lyrical beatdown like she had given him.

"This one I called 'Not Good Enough.'" Hyde strummed on the guitar and kept his gaze on her.

When he sang, the lyrics talked about being a better man for the right woman. The words coupled with the sincerity and gravel in his voice did something to her. Tassia felt a throbbing between her legs that she hadn't felt sincerely for a long time. She didn't want to be that woman who fell for a man from a song, but Hyde had written a great song.

He stopped playing for a moment. "This is your part of the song." He sang her intended part that expressed how Tassia truly felt.

The section talked about wanting a man to step up to her high standards because of her worth. What she liked about the song had to be the way he told a story.

At the end of the song, Hyde placed his hand on the guitar strings before he released a long sigh. "It's been a really, really long time since I had to write my own songs. I don't know about you, but I can't say this was an easy process." He connected his stare to hers. "If I had to say one thing good about this whole experience so far, it pushed me out of my comfort zone and got me to get out of my own way. It took me two days to write this. What do you think?"

* * * *

Hyde sat rooted in his spot as he waited for Tassia to answer. Suddenly Tassia pushed back her chair, sprang to her feet, and ran over to him. He expected her to maybe get in his face and yell at him. With time alone to think, he finally came to terms with his actions. He had been selfish. He needed to show Tassia he could be a good singing partner and an even better man.

Tassia stood in front of him for a beat before she lowered her head and kissed him hard enough that it stunned him. Hyde closed his eyes and wanted so much to remove the guitar from between their two bodies. He knew if he had done that, he would have pulled her onto his lap and held her close to him.

Tassia's soft lips molded against his perfectly. She tasted like fresh berries and she smelled like wildflowers. Before he could stop himself, Hyde cupped his hand against her and brushed his thumb over her cheek, causing her to moan and dive her fingers through his short hair.

When she touched him, Hyde had to remove the barrier. He set his guitar on the floor next to him, which prompted her to straddle his lap. This intimate connection forced him to wrap his arms around her waist.

In his mind, he imagined a relationship with Tassia that went beyond this duets album. The fact that she kissed him after the song showed that she understood him. He had intended to apologize, and she got that from the lyrics. The kiss just proved that she also caught his underlying feelings for her.

Tassia moved her hips forward as she broke from the kiss. "You included me in the song."

Hyde tried catching his breath as he nodded. "It is a duet."

She kissed his cheek toward his ear. "You're a good man. A really good man."

If Tassia stayed on his lap any longer, she wouldn't think of him as a good man.

He tapped her back. "Thank you. It's just one song." He attempted to stand but Tassia didn't move off him.

"A really good song. You're incredible." The longer Tassia stared at him the more she must have sobered to her position and situation. "It'll be great for the album." She stood and braced her hands on his shoulders for a moment before she turned and sauntered back to her seat at the table. "Did you write more?" She picked up the platter full of grilled meats and selected a chicken breast. "Do you want steak?" She stared at him while still holding onto the platter.

Days ago, Hyde didn't think this woman would have spit on him if his body had been set on fire. Now she wanted to serve him.

"Yeah. That would be cool." To show he could be just as accommodating, he picked up the tray of roasted vegetables and served some to her before he put some on his plate.

Hyde sat down next to her at the table. "Glad you liked the song. Believe it or not, your songs inspired me. I didn't realize how my actions affected you until I heard you describe me as a jerk."

"Not a jerk really." Tassia cut up her food. "Maybe a conceited egomaniac."

Hyde nearly choked on his sweetened iced tea after Tassia's statement. "Oh, really? Okay, I get it." He cut into his steak. "The bad part about all of this is that I was never like this before. I used to be so open and trusting. Then I had people who claimed to be my friends sell me out and lie to my face. I had people sneaking into my personal space." He hesitated before continuing. "I've had women want to be with me to further their careers. I lost trust quick. I truly wanted a break. I relax when I'm here. I'm at peace when I'm home. I should have asked you if you wanted this trip. For that, I'm sorry."

Tassia smiled before she put a morsel of the chicken in her mouth. "Apology accepted." She chewed on the meat and moaned again.

It sounded exactly like when she moaned while she kissed him. The sound raised the hairs over his body and pumped blood into the area below his waist.

"You're a gifted songwriter." He chewed on some of the roasted vegetables. The smoky taste appealed to his taste buds, introducing a slight bitter flavor along with the vegetables' natural sweetness.

"Thanks." She shook her head slightly. "After listening to your song, I know I need to step my game up."

Good. He didn't have to say it and incur another potential argument. After that kiss, he wanted to be on this woman's good side. He also knew that he couldn't hide his feelings. He had to be honest with her.

"You can definitely write a hit, but it feels like the songs are on the surface." He waited for the blowback. To hedge his bets, he continued. "It's nice to have songs you can dance to, but what about the soul?"

Tassia opened her mouth like she wanted to argue, but then she picked up a couple of vegetables on her fork. "It's easier to write about something fun than to expose your vulnerabilities."

"You didn't seem to have a problem with that in 'Kidnapped by the Cowboy' or the other songs. You just incorporated a catchier hook." Hyde picked up his bowl of salad and started in on it now that he had tasted his main meal.

"I'll make a deal with you." Tassia crossed her legs. "You teach me to write a soulful song and let me teach you to relax a little." She raised her eyebrows.

"Why do people think I'm uptight?" He wagged his finger at her. "Remember I managed to get you to my house."

"But we won't talk about that." She smirked. "Your hit songs have been about what?"

"I don't know. Hanging with friends, finding the right person who will make you happy, being good to your family and friends." Hyde stopped and rolled his eyes. "Jesus, I am a Boy Scout."

Tassia laughed. "You know, that's not a bad thing. Not every woman wants a bad boy."

"Is that why you kissed me?" He had to know what she thought. Hyde knew how he felt.

"I kissed you because you seduced me." She cocked a smile at the corner of her mouth.

"I did?"

She nodded. "That song and this meal. I didn't know any other way to respond. You wooed me."

Hyde flicked the food on his plate as he let her words roll around in his head. His stomach fluttered in a way he hadn't felt since he had asked out Debra Miller, the daughter of one of his tutors when he became a high school senior.

"I didn't think I was your type." He leaned back in his seat. "I thought Aaron was your speed."

Tassia rolled her eyes. "Nothing ever happened between me and Aaron."

"After all of this is said and done, what will you say about me?" Hyde placed his empty salad bowl on the table.

"That you're passionate about your work, you're good to your family." She picked up her glass of tea. "And you are a phenomenal kisser."

"Wow. Thanks." He cut into his steak. "Just imagine if I had had some planning."

She smiled and it brightened up the space. "A lot could be said for spontaneity."

He nodded. "True." He shrugged. "You could also argue that there's something about your partner planning out a way to make your toes curl that is also very, very enticing."

"You mean like this dinner?"

His smile widened. "What? We both had to eat."

"And that song."

"We have this album, which reminds me. The songs you wrote…"

Tassia rolled her eyes. "Look. I was angry. I wanted to get my feelings out there."

"I know." Hyde held his hand up. "With the way they are, I don't think they belong on the album."

She stared at him. "What? Why is that?"

"This album needs to reflect both of us. Like I mentioned before, there's no part in it for me." He finished off his dinner before he dropped another suggestion. "And we should concentrate on writing and recording. I haven't shown you everything in the house."

"You mean like the upstairs?"

Hyde understood what Tassia meant. Did she want to see his bedroom? He wanted to show her that and more, particularly after that mind-blowing kiss.

"I mean the recording studio I have in my home." He watched her eyes widen.

"Besides the music room, you have an actual recording studio?" She finished off her dinner.

He nodded. "It's in the basement. I'll take you down to show you. Once we fully concentrate on business, we won't have time for anything else."

Tassia stood. "Sounds like a plan." She picked up her empty plate and grabbed his. "I'm ready to get down." She sauntered to the back door of the house and turned at the doorway. "Get down to work, of course." Her sly smile let him know that he would have a challenge before him.

Hyde took Tassia down to the basement area that practically spanned the entire home.

"Wow. This is like another living space but with a full studio in it." She scanned the room and stood at the control board. Tassia peered back at him. "We could write and record here. I mean what if we go back to Virginia with a demo album?"

Hyde leaned on the boards next to her. "We could do that."

Tassia patted his hand. "Let's do it."

He didn't move. His mind raced to illicit thoughts of them kissing like they did before dinner and going beyond. Since he had been the one to set the rules of sticking to business, he needed to get his head out of the gutter.

"Let's do what?" Hyde shrugged.

"Let's record the song you just did. I want to hear how we sound together. That will be the true test."

No. The true test would be if Hyde could record with her and keep his mind on business.

"Let me get my guitar and lyrics." Hyde went back upstairs for those items, the whole time thinking about keeping his mind on business.

After he retrieved the items, he returned to the studio and found Tassia on the couch on her stomach with her back to him. Her dress rode up so that the hem fell right below her ass. This project would be difficult.

"Here are the lyrics." Hyde crouched down next to Tassia. "This is your part."

Tassia reviewed it and nodded. "Can I change this part here?" She pointed to a line. "I don't want to keep saying you aren't good enough. The song should end with hope, don't you think?" She looked up at him, bringing her face dangerously close to his.

He remained close to her until he stood. "Let's try it both ways to see what works. Agreed?"

Tassia got up on her knees on the couch before she stood. "Cool. Let me do some warm-ups first."

"That's fine. Then we can rehearse." Hyde tuned his guitar while Tassia strolled into the studio area and positioned herself behind the piano.

She started playing a melody on the piano that almost sounded like what he played on the guitar, but it sounded better. Tassia did her vocal scales and even that sounded magical.

"Oh, I got you something else." He reached beside the couch between it and the wall and revealed a large jar of small, green square items individually wrapped. "Sour apple Now and Later."

Tassia hadn't had that candy in years. Like she hadn't eaten in a decade, she grabbed the jar from Hyde's hand and dove inside it for one of the candies. As fast as she could, she unwrapped it, making sure to peel the white wrapper from areas on the hardened taffy candy where it stuck. As soon as she got everything off, she popped it in her mouth.

The sweetness of the candy struck her first before she had to suck her cheeks in when the sour portion snuck in to her taste buds. "So good. Better than what I remembered as a kid." She put her hand to his knee. "I can't believe you remembered all of my favorites."

He smiled. "I know this isn't your home, and I know barbecuing and candy won't make up for my bad behavior. I hope this shows you that I do listen, I do care, and I am sincerely sorry."

Now Tassia saw Hyde as the nice person she had remembered working with as a kid. To see this side of him come back out reassured her. She could do this project. Considering he had shot down her three songs, she would have a lot of work to do.

"Are you ready?" Hyde sat at a stool. "Let's practice first before we record."

"You want me to join you on the piano?" She remained seated.

"Yes. I liked what you played earlier. You start and I'll join in."

She nodded and started the song on the piano. Hyde started singing his part. Because he wrote the song, he knew when Tassia's part began. Expecting to signal her, he turned toward her.

She started on her own, infusing her full self into her verse. When she got to the end of the song and sang it the original way, Hyde immediately understood what she meant about the change.

"You were right." He nodded. "Let's do this again and you sing the line you want to change."

"Did you feel that?" Tassia placed her hands on top of the piano. "We harmonize so well."

Hyde had felt it. The goosebumps on his arms hadn't gone down even at the end of the song. When they sang the song again with the line changed, his heart thrummed. Part of the reason had to do with her incredible voice. The other reason had everything to do with the fact that the song, meant to be an apology, now had her accepting his apology and forgiving him.

By the time they recorded the song and replayed it for themselves, Hyde saw Tassia in a new way.

"I think we have a hit." Tassia nodded.

"Maybe." He shrugged and tried keeping his attention anywhere but on her.

Tassia managed to seduce him with her voice and her willingness to try things his way. If he looked in her eyes, he would be done.

They continued working until almost midnight. Hyde glanced at his watch. "You don't think listeners will like this?" She moved closer to him.

Hyde didn't want to retreat from her, so he remained still. "I think it's just a demo. We've just laid this down once. It could use some work, some finessing. We shouldn't get too excited." He had to repeat that last part in his head because he couldn't deny that he wanted this woman.

"What do you think about doing this without any instruments?" She wrapped her fingers around the neck of his guitar.

When Hyde refused to give up the one barrier hiding his excitement, Tassia slid her hand down slowly until her hand connected to his. Her fingers against the various strings caused them to wail as she moved over them.

Tassia smiled and he felt powerless again. "It's okay. Let me have it."

Without a fight, Hyde allowed her to take the instrument from him. He watched her carefully place it next to the piano. Then she pulled the piano bench from its spot to a place next to him.

Tassia gazed up at him.

Damn. She had him. When she licked her lips, he could no longer see straight let alone sing.

"You want to count us off?" She nodded.

"Sure." Hyde tapped his bare foot on the carpeted floor. "Two, three, four."

He started off the song. Without the guitar or piano to back him, he heard his every word. He had to be extra careful to stay in tune. He set the octave for her part. Too low and she might not be able to dip her voice down that far. Too high and he could be setting himself up for failure.

He caught the desperation in his voice, his fear, his regret. When she sang her part, all while staring into his eyes, he melted. This time when she changed the line in the song, he felt like she had forgiven him.

At the end of the song, the room remained quiet. He heard himself breathing so hard he thought she would worry about his condition.

Tassia placed her hand on his thigh. "For all my kicking and screaming, I'm actually glad you brought me out here." She drummed her fingertips lightly over his leg. "Maybe I need to learn to be more open, try new things." She moved her body closer to him. "What do you think?"

Think? Hyde could barely talk. The touch on his leg shot an electric jolt through his body. He'd started staring into her eyes at the opening of the song, and didn't think he had blinked at all during that time. His eyeballs burned and itched, but he would be damned if he broke this connection with Tassia.

He swallowed. "I think we have a great start." He chuckled. "After the rocky one, of course."

She laughed.

"We had a good night. If we keep this up, we could be done in a couple of weeks, maybe sooner." Hyde ached to touch her hand. He wanted to feel her.

"Anything else we should do tonight?" Tassia posed the salacious question without making a move. She had even stopped drumming her delicate fingertips.

Every part of his body screamed to offer this woman a place in his bed right now. Then he heard his father in his ear telling him not to mix business with pleasure. The relationship with Shelby Lynne had been arranged as a strategic business move meant to propel both careers. What Hyde felt for Tassia now came from an honest place. He had built his career on being the good guy, polite and gentlemanly. What he thought about this woman would shock his fans.

In this moment, he didn't care about them. He only thought about what he could do to make the two of them happy.

Hyde put his hand to the side of her face. When Tassia kept her stare on his he knew he had the green light to keep going.

He brushed his thumb over her smooth cheek before he gently pulled her close to him and planted a soft kiss on her pouty lips. This time he felt transformed, like only he and this woman existed in the world.

Tassia curved her hand down to his inner thigh, dangerously close to his throbbing manhood. One side of Hyde's head wanted her to continue that hand up his legs. The other side, the business side, screamed for him to stop, to think about his career. He had fallen for a singer before and had gotten burned. He had assumed the relationship with Shelby Lynne had been real until he discovered the truth. What a great little actress she turned out to be. Nothing about Tassia felt fake or forced.

Tassia moaned during the kiss and it made Hyde want her even more. His lips vibrated against hers and he wanted nothing more than to keep exploring. Hyde slipped his tongue into her mouth. The tip of his tongue touched hers in a playful yet seductive tease. What else could she do with that lethal organ? How could he use his tongue on her body? Oh, the places he wanted to go.

Hyde sobered to the moment and pulled back from her. Tassia's lips looked seductive in a now swollen and pink state.

"It's been a long day." Hyde stood, which forced Tassia to remove her hand from his leg. "Maybe we should call it a night."

"Really? You don't want to—"

"There's something I need to do."

"I'm sure there is." She stood and stretched her arms over her head. "I really, really liked the kiss. Didn't you?"

Hyde didn't want to answer that question, but after getting her there under false pretenses, he wouldn't be holding back from her anymore. "Yes."

"Don't you think we should—"

"I don't want to blur the lines." He didn't. He had to think about this logically even though his body begged for him to take her there on the studio floor. He briefly glanced at the couch in the room and had to turn away. From the way she smiled at him, he knew he had been busted.

"Blurry lines might make for really good music." When she must have noticed Hyde's unwillingness to budge, she shrugged. "For as long as I live, I will never understand men." She shook her head. "I'm going to go back to my room to write." Tassia headed to the door.

"Great idea. I'll do the same, and we can start all over again in the morning." Not that Hyde wanted this night to end.

Hyde wanted to kick himself in the head for cutting off what could have been a wonderful night with her. He had enjoyed being creative with Tassia. He also started to respect her songwriting skills. He had something he needed to do and he didn't need Tassia to see it.

"Thanks for writing the song and for recording it." Before she left, she sauntered to him. Instead of kissing him again, she hugged him. In his ear she whispered, "And thanks for the kiss."

Holding her firm body flooded his brain with more salacious thoughts. He had to cool himself off, and he had the perfect way to do it.

Tassia released him and went upstairs. Hyde secured the studio before he went upstairs, but he didn't continue up to his bedroom on the next level. He went out the back door and down to the dock. He glanced behind him to make sure Tassia wouldn't be able to see him. With the slope of the land and him being so far out on the dock, he knew she wouldn't be able to spot what he had planned.

Hyde glanced at his watch again. He only had a minute. In the blink of an eye, he stripped out of his clothes until he had nothing on, and then without thinking about it, he jumped into the lake.

The cool water did a lot to lower his libido. He dipped down under the water and swam out as far as he could before he remained floating in the middle of the lake.

He hated himself for acting like a goofy, lovestruck teenager around Tassia. Working since before puberty restricted his dating life. He had missed out on prom and other school dances while he worked on albums and tours and had tutors on the road.

He started to swim back to the dock and had to stop when he noticed he now had an audience. Tassia sat on the edge with her feet in the water.

Oh, shit.

Chapter 13

Tassia couldn't settle herself after such an incredible recording session and that kiss. Those kisses. The first one showed her appreciation in a sexy way, but that second one had her floored.

She wanted to keep working, but after seeing him damn near run away from her after rocking her soul and after he peered at his watch for the fifth time in a span of ten minutes, she figured he wanted to do something else.

Maybe he did want to keep their relationship professional. Or maybe she really couldn't keep a man's interest. Then why did he kiss her? He initiated it this time. She didn't mind. She liked touching his muscular thigh while he caressed her face. Hyde could be tender, which made her wonder what he would be like as a lover.

"Stop, Tassia. The man is trying to be professional." She shook her head as she let her feet dangle in the refreshing water.

Tassia knew she needed to cool herself down somehow after that duet and kiss. A shower wouldn't have helped her. When she tried writing, Hyde filled her thoughts. She wished she had saved that picture of his naked behind on her phone. Without cell service, she couldn't call it up so that she could at least stare at it.

She heard a slight splashing in the water and assumed that the fish Hyde had paid to be in the pond decided to jump out and do a little moonlight dance. Or maybe frogs inhabited the water. From all the croaking and crickets chirping, it wouldn't have surprised her. Then she saw something larger than a normal pond fish and way bigger than a frog.

Something large headed toward the dock. Maybe a turtle swam in the water. Tassia wouldn't give the creature a chance to make a feast of her toes. She pulled them out of the water and remained in a crouching position until she recognized the water monster.

"Hyde?" Tassia kept her feet out of water until the hump she saw got by the dock.

Hyde lifted his head above the water. "What are you doing out here?"

"I was just about to ask you the same thing." She resumed her original position with her feet back in the water. "I thought you said you had something to do."

"I did."

In the darkness, Tassia found it hard to see his full expression. He hung his head down a beat before he peered up at her.

"Do you remember when Pepper started to ask me about something I was going to do while I was here?"

Tassia kind of remembered that conversation but had dismissed it as more ribbing from Hyde's cousin. "Yeah. Why?"

"Every year, I take a dip in the water on this day."

"Why? What's special about this day?"

Hyde hugged his body against the wooden steps that went down in the water from the dock. "Ever since I was a kid, I have jumped in some body of water on my, um, birthday."

Tassia blinked. "Today is your birthday?"

He nodded. "Technically now it is."

"No wonder you were looking at your watch. Why didn't you tell me?" She kicked her foot up to splash his face.

"I was going to tell you in the morning. It's another reason I wanted to come out here. I wanted something for me. Sounds selfish, especially since I involved you."

"It is. But I can kind of get it." Tassia waved her legs back and forth in the water. "So why swimming on your birthday?"

Hyde shrugged. "I don't know. My grandmother started it. She doesn't live too far from here. She would take me to a lake by her house on my birthday and let me swim with my friends. When I started recording, I had to make time to do the same thing, hence the picture of my naked behind."

Tassia started to laugh but stopped and looked behind herself. She had seen the strewn clothing over the dock. It hit her that Hyde had to be in his manmade pond in the nude.

She stood. Tassia should have been nice and piled Hyde's clothes closer to the stairs and given him his privacy. Instead she decided to give herself a present. She would see if he truly wanted her.

Tassia removed her dress. She gazed down at Hyde to see if he would object or ask what she had planned on doing. As fast as she could, she put her hands behind her back to undo her bra. In a swift motion, she curved her shoulders forward and let her bra straps slip down her arms, then she removed her panties.

Before anything could be said or before she could run away, Tassia jumped into the cool water with Hyde. She broke through the surface and found herself a few feet from him. In the moonlight and the couple of dock lights, he looked more sexy than sinister.

Like he didn't want her to make the next move, he swam toward her in a time that would probably have rivaled Michael Phelps'. As soon as he got in front of her, he wrapped his arm around her waist and stared at her.

"Beautiful." He crushed his lips against hers again with so much passion and intent it took her breath away.

To keep herself steady, Tassia wrapped her arms around his broad shoulders. He slid his hands down her back. In her mind, Tassia wanted him to grip her ass, show her that he wanted her.

Like he had read her thoughts, Hyde eased his hands down to her backside and palmed it in his large hands. Tassia wrapped her legs around his waist while he kept his legs moving to keep them afloat.

Hyde broke from the kiss, but this time he used one arm to swim them back to the steps at the dock. He didn't let her go while he got them to safety. He positioned her so that she rested against the steps. He gripped a step behind her head and continued kissing her, taking over her mouth and senses.

Why the hell had Shelby Lynne let this man go? Hyde curled Tassia's toes just from a kiss.

He coasted his hand down her body to her breast. When he cupped it, she had to break from the kiss long enough to lean her head back and savor the moment. With her head back, Hyde took the time to lick up her neck to her chin before he sucked the sensitive flesh near her collarbone.

"Oh, yes. Don't stop." Tassia gripped his shoulders.

Hyde pressed his body closer to hers, putting his chest against hers. Tassia could die at this moment and would have been so happy.

As she settled into this incredible moment, a feeling broke her from getting too comfortable. Tassia shrieked and peered down in the water as though she could see anything.

"What's wrong?" Hyde's deep voice sounded even deeper as he held her.

"Something's in the water with us. I felt it." She wiped her face. Why the hell had she jumped in this pond? She hadn't done something like this since before she realized brain-eating amoebas existed in them. "Something big swam between us."

Hyde smiled before he chuckled. "You mean this?" He moved his body closer to hers.

Tassia identified the elephant in the pond with them. "Let's go to my room." She turned and started to head up the steps.

"I thought we were doing really good out here."

Tassia stood on the dock and gathered her clothes. "We were, but I want more, and I have condoms in my room, unless you have some out here or in your pocket." She nodded back to his discarded clothes.

Hyde took a couple of steps up but didn't appear over it yet. "I like a woman who's prepared." He winked. "All right, Girl Scout. Start the shower."

Tassia didn't need any other prompting than that. She ran toward the house, only looking back once to see if Hyde followed her just as quickly. She spotted him under a light gathering his clothes and trotting behind her, but still managing to look like he carried some swag. How the hell could this man do that completely naked?

She stepped through the back door and nearly slipped on the floor as she rushed to the bedroom. She didn't need to fall and break something before finally getting this man into bed, or even the shower.

When she reached the room, she threw her clothes in a corner, then dove into her still-packed suitcase to find the condoms India had packed when Tassia's plan had been to go to Fiji for a vacation. By the time Hyde stood in the doorway staring at her, she located the string of packaged prophylactics in gold packaging.

In an exaggerated manner, Tassia pulled out the string and held it in front of her body before tossing them on the bed. Hyde, still holding a pile of clothes in front of his body, finally dropped them at the doorway.

Tassia couldn't help but lower her gaze to check out his goods. No wonder she thought something had slithered between their bodies. Hyde's dick sat up nice and tall and thick. Yes, this man definitely wanted her and showed it in the right way.

As he approached her, she backed into the bathroom. She had been given a task to start the shower. She needed to do that.

Tassia turned on the light and then turned to the large shower stall to start the water. It surprised her when the lights in the room dimmed down to a seductive level. She turned to see Hyde making an adjustment next to the light switch. She had no idea that the lights in the room had that capability.

When she stepped into the stall, he followed her. It didn't take him long to reconnect his hands to her waist and pull her forward so that his long, strong member separated their bodies. Even after swimming in the pond for a short while and before bathing, Hyde smelled so good. He emitted a woodsy aroma that reminded her of everything good and decent. She hoped he wouldn't be decent with her, not right now.

Tassia wanted to see if this so-called goody two-shoes had a naughty side. He had the right equipment to be a bad boy.

It didn't take long for Hyde to recapture her mouth in a kiss. Tassia placed one hand on his shoulder and let her other hand rest on the back of his neck. At the peak of the summer heat, she understood Hyde's need to keep his hair short. She almost wished he had some hair to be able to pull on it.

Warm water rained down over them from the large, circular showerhead. Tassia opened her eyes and pulled back from Hyde when she suddenly smelled her familiar wildflower body wash. She didn't even realize that Hyde had taken his hands off her body to get the bottle she had left on a shelf behind her.

He poured the purple liquid in the palm of his hand before he lathered it over her body, down her arms, over her breasts, down her belly, and on her legs. Hyde lowered himself down to his knees in front of her. He peered up and connected his stare to hers as slipped his fingers in between her thighs and rubbed her clitoris.

"Oh, God." Tassia gripped his tanned shoulders while spreading her legs apart as much as she could.

Hyde continued staring at her while he pleasured her, caressing her hardened nub enough that her legs buckled. Her knees weakened the more he rubbed her. When he leaned forward and kissed the section of her body below her belly button, she cried out.

"Yes!" Tassia put her hand on top of his head when she felt her hips gyrating back and forth in concert with his hand motions.

"You smell so good." Hyde kissed down lower, nearly getting his lips right on her slit.

If he touched her with his tongue, she would be a puddle and going right down the drain with the rest of the shower water. She wouldn't let that happen just yet, not until she got to touch him a lot more.

Hyde stood but continued his manipulations. When Tassia could keep her eyes open, she noticed that he made it a point to stare in her eyes. She tried hard to reciprocate. To keep herself grounded, she poured some of her body wash in her hand and wrapped her fingers around his shaft.

Hyde sucked air between his teeth and groaned. He nodded his head as soon as she moved her hand up and down, particularly when she pulsated her fist at his large mushroom tip.

He kept his hand moving back and forth between her legs, but then had to rest his free hand against the shower stall wall behind her head.

Just as she had done, his hips gyrated back and forth. She felt him throbbing in her hand, which turned her on tremendously. Who would have thought this country singer would have found her attractive? What was she thinking? Who would have thought that *she* would have found *him* attractive, the man who had sung and danced with her on a kids' show and at one time rejected her professionally? Now he wanted her. Boy, did she want him, too.

Tassia used her free hand to lather soap suds over his perfect, naked body, over his shoulders and down his chest to his rippled abdomen. He continued rubbing her clit while her body shook.

She kept a tight hold of his erect penis when her stomach tightened. Tassia chewed on her lower lip in hopes that she wouldn't cry out just yet. She couldn't hold back the orgasm threatening to hit her. To still his hand, she brought her legs together.

"Yes. Yes. Yes." She nodded but kept her eyes closed. "Hy. Hy." She reared up on her tiptoes before releasing the loudest scream she had ever emitted with any man or even through the worst pain she had ever felt.

Hyde hadn't even entered her and he had given her the best climax she had ever had. In return, she would do the same for him. She pumped her hand faster and faster.

"Need to stop." He squeezed his eyes closed but continued holding her pussy. To illustrate his request, he held her wrist to still her. "Need you." He pulled her under the shower head to rinse them both off before he turned off the water.

When Tassia reached for a towel to dry herself, Hyde held her hand, rubbed his feet over the plush white rug by the shower stall, and pulled her into the bedroom.

"We're both soaking wet." Tassia meant that in other ways considering Hyde had given her an incredible end to her day.

Hyde grabbed the string of condoms and ripped one off from the end. "You say that like it's a bad thing." He smiled before opening the package with his teeth and struggling to roll the filmy protection over himself.

Tassia made a mental note in her head. Hyde needed the condoms for the larger-sized men. Have mercy.

She backed toward the bed when he surprised her and captured her hand to pull her close to him. Hyde positioned her back against the wall and helped her raise her legs so that she had them around his firm ass. While he held her up with one hand cupped under her cheek, he used the other to guide himself inside her eager core.

"Shit." She pressed her head back against the wall and tried controlling her breathing, but couldn't. The deeper he plunged, the more connected she felt to him.

When Hyde got himself down to the hilt, even he cursed. "Tight. Wet. Perfect." He made slow thrusts at first. He controlled this moment, and Tassia loved it.

"Yes." She held onto his shoulders and planted kisses over his face while he grounded himself. "So good. Hitting it. Hard." She nodded. "So close."

She couldn't believe she could come again so soon. Hyde felt incredible. She tightened her legs around his body and wished in her head that this moment wouldn't end, that beyond this night, this trip, this album, there could be more between them. Could he get beyond his image to imagine her in his world? Then again, could she do the same for him?

Not drying off their bodies after the shower proved to be a smart move. The water droplets on Tassia's body quickly evaporated. Sweat replaced whatever water she had lost.

Hyde cupped her breast and gave her hardened nipple a squeeze. That prompted a second orgasm from her.

"Hy, please." She placed her face against the side of his neck and kissed the tender flesh. She tasted his salty skin and immediately craved more. She licked his collarbone as he drove into her harder and harder. When he curved his hips and hit the right spot in her core, she broke. "Yes! Hy, take it." She clawed his back and her toes curled until the orgasm subsided.

He carried her over to a dresser and placed her on top of it. As he stared into her eyes again, he started his long, slow, easy strokes.

"You are driving me crazy." Tassia braced her hands on the dresser's top and tried to control her staggered breathing.

"Tassia." He gritted his teeth, then shook his head. "So good. Beautiful eyes." He gave her a quick peck. "Soft skin." He gripped her hips and pulled her forward.

She felt him trembling between her thighs. "Tell me what you want."

For the first time, Hyde dropped his gaze and shook his head. "If you sing right now, I'll explode." He chuckled, but Tassia knew a kernel of truth existed in his confession.

To tease him, when she moaned, she added a sexy lilt to it, like when she used to sing as a back-up singer. Hyde brought his attention back to her.

She moaned again and added more layers, almost like in a church choir. The third time she moaned, she sounded more like Donna Summer in "Love to Love You, Baby."

"Tassia, damn it." Hyde's thrusts increased in speed. He pounded his fist on top of the dresser until his body shook and he held himself deep in her channel.

The position gave her a great ache that she would never be able to replicate with another toy or her own hand. This man had the magic touch, and she wanted more from him. She had to wonder if he had more to give.

Hyde struggled to catch his breath as he planted kisses on her lips and all over her face. "Best. Birthday. Ever." He laughed.

Tassia chuckled with him. "That was pretty amazing." She stroked her fingers down the side of his face. "Now what?"

Without pulling out of her, he smiled before answering. "We're grabbing all the condoms and going upstairs to the main bedroom." Then his smile melted. "And then maybe we need to talk."

Uh-oh. Tassia didn't like the sound of that.

Chapter 14

Hyde propped his head on his hand as he looked at the beauty next to him in his bed doing her best to creep away without being noticed. Tassia wouldn't even look back at him. She slipped one foot out of the bed to the floor as though gauging the proximity of the floor to the mattress.

Hyde thought he had heard her sighing in relief as she eased her other foot out of the bed, and then she oozed the rest of her luscious body from under the covers.

He guessed that she thought he still remained sleeping while she attempted her escape. In the early morning with sunlight cutting through the heavy curtains that he hadn't pulled together to keep the light out, he watched her swaying toward the door. Her hips rocked like a pendulum, and it reminded him of their incredible time together, how she moved and swayed and held onto him like a bull rider refusing to give up her seat. He wouldn't be letting her get away that easily.

"Why are you running?" His question stopped her cold at the door of his bedroom with nothing covering her body.

"I'm not running." Tassia wrapped her arms around her body, which seemed silly considering what all they had done to each other only hours ago.

Hyde watched her shoulders rise and fall when she took a deep breath before she turned to him. He did all he could to not peer down at her amazing body, full of curves and sleekness, like a luxury car that not everyone could handle.

He had had her though. He had gotten her to come multiple times.

Tassia had been just as powerful. Whether she knew it or not, she had gotten him to relax his stance on being with someone in the industry.

"Where are you going then?" Hyde sat up with his back against the ornate wooden headboard. "I thought we would—"

"We shouldn't have done what we did." She backed toward the door like she wanted to still leave.

"Can't un-ring that bell." He patted the bed. "Come back to—"

"I don't know what you think about me, but I'm not the type to sleep with just anyone." She rubbed her hand up and down her bare arm. She snickered. "It's Sunday."

Hyde felt his eyebrows rut together. "Is that supposed to mean something?"

She started to walk toward him again. "I always talk to my dad every day. If I were home, he and I would attend church together."

Although he didn't want to, he blinked in surprise. "Really?"

Tassia tiptoed back to the bed, but didn't sit down. Not just yet. "You sound like you don't believe me."

"I don't know. I just assumed that—"

She sat down on the bed. "Because I sing sexy songs that I wouldn't have a close relationship with my family or go to church?"

He remained quiet. He had made that assumption, just as she had assumed he had brought her to his house for one thing. Hyde tried to be transparent with a few exceptions.

He should have confessed to her the secret in the house. Hyde glanced at a small vintage wooden table in a corner of his room. He would tell Tassia about what he had hidden inside it at the right time. After what had happened between them, he still needed a bit of alone time with her before revealing a bit of technology he had concealed.

Tassia slipped under the comforter if only to hide her body. "That public persona is just that. A persona. I'm not easy or loose."

"Then how did I make it under your radar?" Hyde also wanted to know how he could stay there.

She peered down and a smile spread across her face. "The song." She glanced at him. "Us singing together." She rested her hand on her stomach. "I felt something. Didn't you?"

He smiled. "Of course. That's why I think—"

"No more sex between us." She shook her head vigorously. "We need to concentrate on work."

Hyde didn't agree with Tassia's request. "Oh, I get it. You're scared." He had gotten her before with that line. He would try it again.

"You're right." Tassia nodded. "I'm afraid that if we get too distracted, we won't finish what we started."

"Is that the most important thing to you?" Hyde crossed his legs at the ankles.

"Yes. Recording this album, clearing my name as far as my songwriting skills, those are the most important things to me right now. Anything else will be a distraction to both me and you. We can chalk this experience up as us taking advantage of our weak moment."

"No. For sure don't call me weak. It took every bit of my strength to make sure you were satisfied." Hyde never planned this, never expected that he would want Tassia as much as he did, and that she would want him just as much.

"Damn." She smirked.

"What?"

"That would make a really good song, too."

Hyde chuckled. "What can I say? You bring out the best in me."

He had gone to his pond to cool off after kissing her when they had recorded their song. Even that hadn't been planned nor expected. Hyde felt so right with her. He had to wonder, though, what scared Tassia from wanting more? Why did he even care? She gave him the green light to walk away without any issues. Too bad at this point, he didn't want to stop now.

Hyde peered behind himself at the condoms on the nightstand. Good thing she had them, not that he couldn't have satisfied her without them. Now that he had the opportunity to have sex with her, he knew he couldn't be happy treating her like chaste high school sweethearts, rubbing on each other and wishing for more. No way could he turn back now.

"If you don't jump in bed with random men, why the big stash of condoms?" Hyde nodded behind himself.

"My friend India. I was packing to go on vacation, and she thought it would be funny to supply me with more condoms than I could ever use in a lifetime. I never took them out."

"Lucky for us."

Tassia released a long exhale and turned on her side to face him. Hyde liked this position. He could stare in her face for hours and never get tired. Having her in his bedroom had him wishing he had invited her up the first day.

She fit. Truthfully, the large room, despite all the furniture his interior decorator said would work to fill the space, always felt empty to him. Now he knew he needed a partner. Whether that partner could be Tassia couldn't be answered right now. If left up to her, their one incredible night would remain as a one-off experience.

Tassia slipped down in bed, blinked slowly, and looked up at Hyde.

"Did you watch me while I slept?" Her voice came out quiet and croaky.

Hyde slid down to be face-to-face with her. "A little, just long enough to know that you're a cover hog."

Her bottom jaw unhinged.

"And you snore." He tried hard to hold back his laughter.

Tassia narrowed her eyes at him.

"And you throw your arms and legs all over me when you sleep." He swept her union of braids off her shoulder. "Probably a good thing we aren't going to do this again."

She looked somber. "I don't snore."

Hyde laughed and nodded. "You do, but it's actually very cute. It's almost like a baby bird."

"So I chirp?" She crawled closer to him and rested her chin on his chest.

"Not exactly. I can't explain it. It's just cute." He kissed her forehead. "You know what else is cute?"

Tassia kissed his chest. "What?"

Why did she have to do that? What happened to not having sex? That one connection pumped blood through his entire body. "During sex, you call me Hy instead of Hyde."

She blinked. "I did? I thought I said Hyde."

He shook his head. "It was like 'Hy! Hy! Hy!'"

She burst into laughter. "Now you're teasing me."

"I am, but you really did say it like that. It was sexiest thing I've ever heard. I've never had a real nickname." He rested his hand on her bare back and brushed his fingertips over her flesh.

"You surprised me." She circled her fingertips around his nipple. "Here I thought I would be showing you some tricks in the bedroom."

Hyde ignored his hardening nipple to get clarification on Tassia's assessment. "What do you mean?"

"I don't know why, but I always assumed that you were a virgin."

He sat up quick enough that Tassia had to roll off him. "Are you serious?"

She nodded. "I guess because you started in the industry so young, and your only serious girlfriend that we in the public knew about didn't last that long." She glanced down at his hands. "I've never seen a purity ring or anything, but—"

"I'm not a virgin." Hyde shook his head. "Not that there's anything wrong with it, but I'm not. The only reason people knew about me and Shelby Lynne is because of our management teams. They released statements about us. If it were up to me, I would rather keep my personal life private, that includes who I'm dating."

"Oh." Tassia moved back from him. "Seems like a good idea."

"Why does everyone in the media need to know about what I'm doing in private?"

"Maybe to show you're not afraid."

"Afraid? Afraid of what?"

She didn't answer. She continued with her thought. "Or ashamed." Tassia held the comforter up to her neck to cover her sexy body. "Maybe you're afraid of what your fans will think."

What he feared she would think had crept in her mind. "I don't live my life by what fans think. My career is something else."

She snickered. "One and the same. Your personal life is a part of your brand for your career."

"Are you saying you are the sexpot who doesn't write her own songs?" He watched her expression change from solemn to anger in a blink of an eye.

"Forget you." Tassia started to get out of the bed when Hyde snagged her hand and pulled her back.

"I didn't say I believed that." He pulled her back close to him.

"What do you believe?"

Hyde had to be honest and choose his words carefully to not hurt her. "I believe we have a great opportunity to make some beautiful music." He smiled. "You take that however you want to take it." He slid back down in the bed and placed his hand on her midsection. "I also think it's way too early to be defining anything we did. Let's just take this day by day and see what happens. Deal?"

Tassia remained quiet as she slipped down next to him. "I'd rather go with what I suggested earlier." She exhaled. "I don't do this." She shook her head. "Despite being a, um, sexpot." She screwed up her lips at him. "I don't sleep with men I'm not in a serious relationship with."

"I get it." Hyde's chest opened up as he started to be honest with her. "I don't do this either, even with the millions of women who come to my hotel room." He cocked his head at her. "I never planned on this happening between us. This was not my intention when I brought you out here. I was honest when I said I brought you here because *I* wanted a break." He positioned Tassia on her back and crawled on top of her. "But I'm so glad how things happened. I wouldn't want to do this project with anyone else but you."

"What are you doing?" A small smile peeked through her hard countenance. She didn't stop him. She wiggled her body underneath his.

"You do not want to do that. You're going to stir up some trouble." He watched her glancing over to the nightstand before she brought her full attention back to him.

"What kind of trouble is that?" She wrapped her legs around him and undulated her hips so that her nether lips caressed his previously dormant cock.

The more she moved, the harder it became. "Oh, the hard-pounding kind." He kissed her, then dragged his lips down her chin to her chest where he covered one nipple with his mouth.

Tassia arched her back and writhed on the California king-sized bed. Hyde palmed her other breast and massaged it as he continued sucking on her pert nipple.

She rubbed her hand across the back of his head. "You've got to grow your hair out. I need something to hold on to."

Hyde laughed and moved over to the breast he massaged. "I thought you didn't want to do this anymore."

She didn't respond at first. Her breathing increased as she slithered her pink tongue over her lips. "We're adults. We can be adult about this, right?"

He took her inquiry to mean that she wanted to go further in this arrangement than recording an album and songwriting. He felt positive about that direction.

Not able to hold out any longer, Hyde reached over to the nightstand and removed another condom from its wrapper.

"We need to get you bigger ones. Much, much bigger ones." Tassia licked her lips.

When he got it rolled on himself all the way, he repositioned himself back between her thighs. "I'm fine. I can work with these."

He hooked his arm under her leg and aimed himself at her moist opening. In one smooth motion, he eased his way into her and immediately got transported to the fantasy land he had created in his head, the one where they wrote all day, recorded all afternoon, and then had amazing sex all night.

Like she did the first time they had sex, Tassia clawed his back and arched hers. "So big. So good." She nodded. "Don't stop."

"You couldn't pay me to stop." Hyde kissed the side of her face. "You have no idea what you do to me, the power you have."

"You—you—you, too. Want. More."

Hyde didn't know if Tassia meant she wanted him to do more in bed or if she meant something entirely different. Did she want more out of the two of them?

He ground his pelvis as he stroked in her, knowing he would be brushing against her clitoris.

"Oh my God. Not a virgin. Not a virgin."

Her realization that he hadn't lied about his sexual experience almost made him laugh. Instead he kept going, wanting so much to hear her come over and over and over again. When she started moaning the last time and it sounded like she stood in a church choir section, Hyde had lost his mind. She sounded so good, just like when they sang in his studio. He meant it when he said that she had no idea what she did to him.

Hyde felt her intimate, slick thick walls collapsing around his shaft, tightening to an incredible level that nearly broke him. "Come, baby. Do it."

She nodded while keeping her eyes tightly shut.

"Look at me." He didn't want to finish this without making that crucial connection.

Tassia shook her head vigorously. "Can't."

Hyde felt the side of his mouth pull to a smile. "You can do anything."

"Not with you." She arched her back. "Feel it." She kept one hand on his shoulder and reached back with her other. "So good."

She undulated her hips, which proved to be Hyde's undoing. If he planned on lasting longer than a few seconds, he had to regain control.

Hyde pulled out of her, which made her snap her eyes open.

"What are you doing?" She struggled to speak in between gasping breaths.

Instead of explaining himself, he turned her over onto her stomach and brought her up to her hands and knees.

"Oh my God. Hy, Hy, Hy." She gripped his headboard with one hand.

He held her hip with one hand and guided himself inside her moist channel again. Hyde felt her body tighten for a moment and heard her cursing before she pushed herself back against him.

He gave her long, easy strokes. "You are amazing."

He slipped his free hand under her body and found her clitoris, distended and smooth. He rubbed it as he continued thrusting.

"God, need to touch you." She positioned one foot on the back of his calf, then pounded her fist against the wall. "Again. Coming." Her slender body trembled.

Tassia wailed and leaned her head back. In that position, Hyde eased his hand off her hip and brought it around to the front of her body to cup her breast. Then he leaned back on his haunches, carrying her with him so she sat on top of him.

That position allowed her to reach back and hold the back of his head while she busied her other hand by pressing his against her clit. She dragged the pads of her fingers over the back of his hand to encourage him to continue pleasuring her. No way could he be made to stop.

Hyde thrusted his hips upward in hopes of driving this woman crazy with lust and desire. If she knew that he had already gone off that edge, she would probably look at him differently.

He had to stop thinking about possibilities. Hyde built his life on certainties. He had talent. He had drive. He knew he enjoyed sex with Tassia. He didn't need any complications. If he couldn't figure out what he wanted in his life, he didn't need to involve someone else.

Hyde felt his insides tightening and his sac squeezing up. He wrapped his arm around her waist and held her tighter.

"Sexy as hell." He kissed her shoulder.

Not content to only press his lips against her salty flesh, he nipped at her skin, making her yelp. She gyrated in concert with his motions until they both came.

"You are so wrong for this." Tassia spoke between panting breaths. "We really have to stop."

"Your fault." He administered a couple of light pats on her mound. "You kissed my chest and played with my nipple first."

"I did?" She leaned her head back. "I don't remember that."

"Of course you don't. And you wiggled." Hyde kissed her neck and the side of her face.

"Trying to get away." She snickered.

"Still trying to do that?" To make it more difficult for her to answer, he nibbled her earlobe.

The soft, fleshy part rolled around his tongue as he continued holding her.

"Yes." She peered over her shoulder. "I'm going to take a shower and go downstairs."

She wriggled out of his grip to climb off the bed.

"Why?" Hyde watched her sauntering around naked in his bedroom toward his bathroom.

She stood in the doorway and stared at him. "Got to make breakfast for the birthday boy." She winked.

"Wow. I almost forgot that it's my birthday." He scooted to the edge of the bed. "You don't have to make me anything."

"I know. But I am. And then we need to talk."

"We talked. We decided that we're adults and can handle whatever this is between us. Enough said."

Tassia continued. "That's not the only thing we need to discuss. We need to get out of this house."

Damn.

Chapter 15

Tassia had sighed in relief when Hyde didn't join her in the shower, not that she would have minded. The man surprised her in so many ways. First with his songwriting skills, and then with his free-spirited side, and now the incredible way he satisfied her in bed. As great as the sex had been, she knew she had made a colossal mistake by crossing that line.

She should have stayed away, said no, resisted. Hyde had a draw to him that made her want to be with him. That scared her. If she planned on staying there to work, and only work, she had to establish some ground rules. Easier said than done. She tried doing that earlier and failed miserably but in an oh-so-good way.

Leaving the house topped her list. After over a week, she had gotten used to not using her phone to communicate or staying connected to the outside world. She missed talking to her dad.

Despite how overbearing he could be, Tassia looked forward to getting her father's words of inspiration on a daily basis. What he must be thinking right now because she hadn't talked to him since coming to Hyde's home. For that reason, she wanted to leave and at least find a phone and get connected to the real world.

After coming out of Hyde's luxurious shower, separate from a huge bathtub next to it, Tassia dried herself and emerged from the bathroom, half expecting to find Hyde sex-drenched and ready for another round. Instead she found him knocked out on his huge bed with a white bed sheet barely covering his genitals.

Hyde had his arms outstretched and one leg dangling from the side of the bed. If she could be so emboldened, she would have slid that thin sheet from his delectable body and taken that man on another ride. Then her own words filled her head. She had to keep this relationship about business and nothing else.

Tassia started to walk by Hyde, but stopped herself. She tiptoed back to him and started to tug on the sheet, easing it from his sculpted body like a museum curator unveiling a statue of *David*. As soon as she saw his nest of sandy-blond pubic hair and felt her heart racing, she stopped. If she continued and spotted his perfectly shaped shaft, she would do more than just admire it.

Damn. She wanted to lift a corner and take another peek at his impressive package. Tassia tiptoed out of the room. It felt weird for her to be walking around this strange house completely naked. She didn't even walk around her own condo in the nude like this.

Tassia ran to the room she had been occupying since coming to the house with the exception of last night. Wow, what a night. When she got into the room, she dove into her suitcase and removed a T-shirt. After putting it on, she stepped into a pair of pink panties. A brief thought entered her head that Hyde might like her in her casual outfit.

"Stop it. You're setting the rules for this, and you told him you wanted the sex to stop."

Then Hyde blew her mind again that morning. What a man. Her clitoris throbbed the more she thought about him. Tassia had to stop thinking of Hyde as the sex machine she now discovered him to be if she planned to continue working with him.

Tassia stepped into the kitchen, but peeked out into the backyard to see if Pepper had returned. She couldn't imagine doing the things she and Hyde had done and his cousin walking in on them.

After inventorying the contents of the refrigerator, Tassia decided to make a traditional southern breakfast, complete with fried potatoes, eggs, bacon, and biscuits. Cooking would bring her back to her comfort zone.

Adding each ingredient to the biscuit recipe carried the same calming effect as when she practiced yoga. Tassia poured the liquid mixture into the dry flour mix until she got a dough. Since she couldn't find a proper rolling pin in Hyde's kitchen, she continued improvising with a drinking glass that she also used to cut out biscuit rounds.

Flour covered her hands as she deposited the pan into a pre-heated oven. Then she worked on the rest of the breakfast, opting to cook the bacon on the stove instead of on a wire rack in the oven. Thankfully, Hyde did have cast-iron pans in his kitchen. True country boy.

With the bacon done, she sautéed the potatoes before she started on the eggs. Oh, hell. Tassia had no idea how Hyde wanted his eggs. Maybe he wanted them on top of her body. Her heart fluttered at the idea, and then she felt an arm around her waist.

Tassia should have jumped, squealed, fought to get out of the grasp. She placed her hand on top of the strong arm around her and leaned back. She couldn't believe how comfortable she already felt in Hyde's hold.

"How did you know it was me?"

Tassia heard the rumble in his deep timbre that vibrated her body and made her knees buckle. "Oh, Hyde. I thought it was Dwayne 'The Rock' Johnson. I was kind of hoping he had broken into your house to get to me."

Hyde laughed loudly before he kissed the top of her head. "You're cute." He uncoiled himself from her and headed to the refrigerator.

The move allowed her to take in a full view of Hyde. She figured he had taken a shower based on his fresh-smelling scent. He now wore a pair of loose-fitting shorts.

Hyde removed a pitcher of orange juice and set it on the counter. "I smelled the biscuits and bacon, and it drew me downstairs. You didn't have to do this."

"I have to admit that I'm doing this for selfish reasons, just like you bringing me here. I love cooking. It relaxes me." Tassia smiled as she placed the plate of cooked bacon on the breakfast bar.

"I didn't bring you here for you to cook for me." He leaned against the counter next to her.

"I know you didn't bring me here to do a lot of things, but I'm flexible."

He snickered. "That you are." Hyde winked.

She felt her cheeks getting hot. "How do you like your eggs?" Tassia rested her hand on top of the carton while she faced him.

"Any way except over easy. Can't stand a runny egg." He scrunched up his nose and shook his head.

"Scrambled it is." Tassia opened various cabinets to find a large enough bowl to scramble the eggs in when Hyde handed her a cream-colored bowl with two light-blue stripes circling the top. "Thank you." She smiled as she accepted it. "You said earlier that you wanted to talk to me. About what?"

Hyde retrieved a couple of plates and placed them on the breakfast bar near the bacon. "We need to decide on a theme for the album and maybe an album title." Then he grabbed some butter and jelly. "I suggest *Collusion*."

"Eww. No." Tassia shook her head before scraping the completed fried potatoes into a bowl. "In this political environment, I want us to stay as far away from that word as possible."

"That's the reason I wanted us to use it. Turn it into something positive." He watched her pouring the egg mixture into a hot cast-iron pan with some residual bacon grease.

"It also sounds contentious, like we were forced to do this."

"We were, weren't we?" He shrugged.

"Maybe. But I think it would turn off fans." Tassia smelled the biscuits and knew she could remove them from the oven. She turned off the oven but left the pan there while she split the hot scrambled eggs onto the two plates. "What about *Collaboration*?"

This time Hyde shook his head. "Too cold and business-like."

"More than 'collusion?'" She placed the pan back on the stove before pulling the baked biscuits from the oven. "We're overthinking this. We should call it how we feel about the project."

Hyde smiled to himself before he let a chuckle come out.

"What?" With quick fingers, she plucked each biscuit from the hot pan and into a serving basket.

"Lucky. I would call the album *Lucky*." He sat on a barstool.

Tassia couldn't stop the smile from splitting her head. "Keep talking like that, birthday boy, and we'll never finish this album." She brought the biscuits and potatoes to the bar along with utensils.

He poured juice for them before he offered her the bacon and biscuits first. She would never tire of his gentlemanly nature, a far cry from the men she'd dated in the past.

Could she really call what she did with Hyde dating? She wanted it to be true, which scared her. She didn't want to start a relationship, especially not one with someone in the industry, and particularly with a mega superstar like Hyde Love. She would never have peace. That said, did she really think she could be happy with Hyde?

As she picked up her fork to start eating, Hyde reached his hand out to her.

"What?" Tassia stared at him.

"I know we haven't done this since we've been here and had meals together, but I would like to pray before we eat." He took a deep breath, and on the exhale said, "I know you're missing your dad. I just thought—"

She grabbed his hand. "Great idea."

Without waiting, Hyde said a prayer he had remembered his grandfather saying before each of their big meals.

"Nice." Tassia squeezed Hyde's hand and didn't want to let it go. She would have to in order to eat—and after everything she and Hyde had done, she had definitely worked up an appetite.

Hyde slathered butter and jelly on his two biscuits before taking a hearty bite. "Oh, God. I didn't think anyone could make this as good as my grandmother. This is incredible."

"Thank you. After my mother died when I was eleven, I really got into cooking. I would help her in the kitchen growing up, I just never thought I would have taken over for her so soon." Tassia kept her attention on her food, pushing her yellow, fluffy eggs around on her plate. To get her mind off her family, she turned the conversation to Hyde. "What about you? You don't talk a lot about your family except your grandparents."

Hyde continued eating for a moment before he spoke. "Shortly after I was born, my mom left. At least, that's what my dad told me." He kept his head down as he spoke. "My dad and I lived with his parents for most of my life until I started my career at eleven and we were on that show. Once I stopped the show, I did get signed to record country music. My dad continued to be my manager. He thought he would use my opportunity to pick up women. It was embarrassing to walk in on my father having sex with a groupie after I did a set."

"Oh, wow. I can't imagine not having supportive parents. My dad always looked out for me, well, with one exception." She placed her hand on his bare thigh.

"What's that?" Hyde scooped some more eggs on his fork and took a healthy bite.

"In all the time I filmed the show, I had no idea that back home, my mother was dying of cancer." The image of her mother immediately popped in her head. She had to soothe herself by drinking some juice when she thought she would start crying.

"Oh my God. I'm so sorry." Hyde gripped her hand that she had on his thigh.

"Every time I had asked him about my mother, he said she was fine and missed me. I would talk to her a few times a week while we filmed in California. I never heard her sound weak or sick. She sounded strong. Once I left the show and went home, I discovered that my Aunt Jenny had been taking care of her, taking her to her appointments and stuff." She shook her head. "I should have been home."

"You think that's what your mother would have wanted?"

Tassia glanced at Hyde and smiled. "My dad said the exact same thing when I asked him why he didn't tell me sooner about Mom. He said that she had found out shortly after I had gotten the news that I would be on the show. He said she knew it was my dream to be in show business, and she didn't want to get in the way of my progress. I always felt guilty."

"You shouldn't." He brought her hand up to his mouth and kissed the back of it. "You talked to your mother, and she never told you about her illness, and she could have. As I see it, your parents were protecting their ten-year-old kid. You didn't need to know about illnesses and dying at a young age."

"But—"

"Despite us working like adults when we were kids, we were still kids. We deserved to be that way for as long as we could." He placed her hand back on his thigh before he continued eating. "Can I ask you a question, though, since we're talking about our childhood?"

"Sure." Tassia shrugged.

"You know I had a crush on you when we worked together."

She smiled. "Thanks to your cousin."

Hyde snickered. "Okay. Yes, thanks to Pepper. How did you feel about me?"

Tassia didn't hesitate with her answer. "I thought you were quiet and withdrawn when we weren't filming. But as soon as the cameras hit you, you were so charismatic and alive. You couldn't help but watch you perform. It's the reason I always tried talking to you between takes. I was so curious about you." She peered down at her food. "And, yes, I thought you were cute."

"Oh, now, don't tell me that and not mean it." He put his fork on his plate before drinking some of his juice.

"Oh, no. I mean it. When you did talk, I found out how smart and funny you were. And you had these amazing eyes." She sighed. "I could stare in them for hours."

"Same for you, too." He wiped his hands on a napkin. "That last day of filming, what happened that made your dad pull you out of the show?"

Tassia had hoped Hyde wouldn't have asked her this question. "It's no big deal." She waved her hand at him.

"No big deal? You missed seeing your dying mother for the show. Your dream was starting on that show. I would think it would be a big deal." He turned his full body to her as he awaited her answer.

"My dad found out that they wanted to cut my part down in order to boost your storyline. I wouldn't be a full 'Fun Crew' member. I would be a featured player." Saying it now still felt like a knife slicing her back.

"Bullshit."

She hadn't expected Hyde to react that way.

"You were the most talented in the group. You could sing your face off, even when it was the 'Happy Birthday' song. I remember you had some solo and while they filmed you, I just stared at you the entire time. You were magnificent." Hyde shuffled some food around on his plate before he completed his thoughts. "And I had heard that your dad wanted my part in the show cut down in order to give you a bigger role." He stared at her.

"Like you said. Bullshit." Now she could barely eat after hearing that. "So which parent do we believe?"

"At this point, does it really matter? What's past is past." He shrugged. "We're here now. I'm with the most talented woman on the planet. Can't beat that."

Tassia figured her face had transformed into every shade of red it could be after that compliment. "Thank you. You still have your dad as your manager. I don't. That makes us a bit different. Do you get along with him better now?"

"What made you think I didn't get along with him back then?"

"You seemed a little upset about him making you go on a diet. I remember when we talked about food, you had gotten a little uptight about the conversation and mentioned that your father had put you on a diet." She couldn't fathom the thought of her family not loving her unconditionally and putting restraints on her like dieting.

"Wow, you remembered that? Yeah, he could be a little tough." Hyde peered at her before nodding. "He used to say that I am a reflection of him, and if I wanted to do well in the business, then I had to look a certain way."

"Asshole." Tassia's inner thought blurted out before she could stop herself. "You're talented. That should squash everything else."

"Says the gorgeous woman who can stop traffic even without a stitch of makeup." Hyde put his hand to the side of her face and dragged his fingers down to her chin.

"Thank you, again. The problem with looking this way, though, is no one takes you seriously."

"I believe in you. I'm taking you seriously." He shook his head. "My dad is all about making appearances. He never wants me to stop. Ever."

"Not even on your birthday." Tassia's heart ached for Hyde. He truly had no one in his corner.

"Coming down here, sneaking away from him, has been my only break for as long as I remember. Now that I've gotten some notoriety behind my name, he's using my celebrity status to get into clubs and stuff. He's on the red carpet for events and premieres more than me. He's still using me."

"Oh, wow. No wonder you didn't want to work with me when you were presented with this project." She squeezed his thigh. "I'm not doing this to use you. I want this to be a partnership."

He smiled at her. "I know. You're an independent woman who can cook her ass off."

"I'll take that compliment." Tassia finished her breakfast shortly after Hyde. The man must have been starving.

Hyde held his hand out to her. "Come with me."

Tassia put her napkin on top of her plate. "Where? I should clean this up first."

He waved his hand over it. "We're vacationing." He must have noticed her mouth open to dispute his remark. "And working. I want you to hear something."

She put her hand into his large, warm hand. He wrapped his fingers around hers and led her to his music room. As she followed behind him, she admired the wide planes of his back, his strong shoulders, and his lean waist. In an instant, she wanted this man again.

When they arrived to the music room, Hyde sat down at the piano and patted the seat on the bench next to him. "Sit with me."

Tassia did. The cool wood met the back of her thighs, but his leg warmed the side of her leg. To get even more of the heat, she moved in closer to him.

"I want to play you another song." He placed his hands on the keys.

"When did you have time to write this one? The last one you wrote took you a couple of days."

Hyde's smile widened. "Trust me. This took longer to write."

He started singing about having a crush on a girl with pigtails. From this grown man, it sounded creepy. Maybe her initial dig at him at their first meeting held some merit.

He ended the song and turned to her. "What did you think?"

"Um, the melody was nice. I don't think this song would work on the album, and it would make you come off as a bit of a creep." She rubbed her hand across the back of her neck.

"What if I told you I wrote that song years ago…about fifteen."

Tassia stared at him and started doing the math. "That day we were talking and you wouldn't show me your song…"

"I was writing this song. 'Pigtails and Snickers' is what I had called it. I wrote it about you and never recorded it or showed it to anyone. Truth be told, I had never played it before today. I made the melody up on the fly."

She put her hand to her chest to control her breathing. "At eleven, you wrote a song about me?"

He nodded. "I didn't know then how to tell you how I felt. I didn't know what I was feeling inside at the time. And I, um…"

Tassia turned to Hyde and straddled the bench to get closer to him. "What?"

"All of my dad's talk about my personal appearance and what I knew about my part on the show, I never thought you would like me, not in that way." He sat up taller. "After you left, I started to take an interest in my appearance. I got serious with my diet and I exercised like a fiend. My hope was that one day, I would find a woman who would look at me the way I used to look at you back then." He brought his attention to her. "I can't believe fate brought us back together again." He leaned toward her and brushed his lips against hers.

No matter how long she lived, she would always remember how great Hyde's lips felt against hers, firm yet soft.

Hyde held her chin as he kissed her before breaking it and trailing his lips down her face to her neck. "If this is a dream or merely temporary, I'm going to enjoy every bit of you first."

He slid off the bench and lowered himself to his knees as she continued straddling the bench.

"What are you doing?" Tassia looked down at Hyde as he pulled her legs forward toward the edge of the bench.

"Taking a closer look at your panties." He hooked his fingers in the sides of her undergarments and pulled them down.

To accommodate him, Tassia raised herself from the seat to make it easier for Hyde to remove the pink garment. He eased it down her legs, tickling her flesh before he deposited the item on the floor. Then he spread her legs open.

"That's it." Hyde kissed up her inner thigh. "Getting my dessert."

Tassia's heart pounded hard until he swiped his tongue up from her vaginal opening to her distended clitoris. She arched her back and put her hand to the back of his head.

Hyde used his fingers to spread her nether lips before he licked her again. He massaged her labia before licking her again and again.

Tassia felt her legs trembling while she steadily tried closing her thighs around his head. When his mouth covered her clit and he pressed the tip of his tongue against it, she broke.

"Yes!" She curled her toes and drew her legs up. "Driving me—uh." She nodded. "So good." Her body relaxed against the bench. "Please tell me you have condoms on you."

Hyde chuckled as he sat back on his haunches. "No, I don't. Maybe we change the rules a little."

"How's that?" Tassia kept her head back and her eyes closed as she spoke to him. She could barely move her body.

"No sex until we write a song. Write a song…"

Tassia lifted her head. "Get rewarded." She smiled and winked at him. "That'll encourage me to work faster."

"That's if you still want to work with me."

She sat up straight. "What do you mean?"

"There's something else I need to tell you." Hyde's cheerful demeanor vanished. "I promised you after I brought you here that I would always be honest with you."

"Yeah?" She cocked her head. "If you tell me you have frozen Snickers, I am going to have sex with you right here and now."

Hyde laughed. "You haven't looked in the freezer?"

Tassia's mouth dropped open as she whipped her head around to the kitchen area. After the Now and Later surprise last night, she should have expected Hyde to surprise her with her other favorite treat. She would have to check it out to see if he told her to truth. To see his now sour expression, she suspected he had planned on laying something heavy on her.

He took a deep breath before he continued. "There is a phone in the house. You can call your dad."

Chapter 16

Hyde rose to his feet as he revealed his secret to Tassia. He wiped her intimate juices from his lips and selfishly thought about pleasuring her again. Hearing about her close relationship with her father reminded him of his own relationship with his grandfather. How could he withhold her connection with him for the sake of his peace or work?

Hyde couldn't help himself, though, after eating that incredible breakfast, he wanted to give her something to satisfy her. The way she looked at him now, he suspected she wanted to run again.

"What?" Tassia stood from the bench and drew her T-shirt down over her cleanly shaven vagina. "You told me that our phones couldn't dial out of here, that there was no cell phone connection." She snatched her pink panties from the floor.

He watched her anger simmering below the surface. Hyde had to douse that potential fuse before she exploded. "Cell phones don't have connections out here. I have a corded phone in my bedroom. I keep it for emergencies."

She cocked her head as she regarded him. "I was in your room. I didn't see one."

"I keep it in a cabinet near the bed." He took a couple of steps back. "If you want to come up and use it, I can—"

He couldn't finish his statement before Tassia zoomed by him and darted up the steps, taking them by twos. Hyde followed her as fast as he could. By the time he reached the bedroom, he found Tassia looking around the room. He spotted a wadded pink ball on top of the corner of his Oriental rug. She must have wanted her hands free to look in every location possible.

Tassia started at his dresser.

"It's not—" Hyde started to stop her search until she reached up to an upper cabinet door, which raised her T-shirt and exposed her rounded ass.

Come on, man. Keep it together. Don't look at her body.

Hyde walked over to a short cabinet and opened the doors in front. "It's here." He pulled the phone out and placed it on top of the short, wooden furniture. "I see Pepper left it unplugged. She's normally better than that when she opens my house for me." He plugged in the black phone, which illuminated a red light meaning he had a message or two…or more. More than likely from his grandparents.

Tassia dropped down to her knees in front of the cabinet and grabbed the receiver. Her finger hovered over the keys, and she hesitated.

Hyde glanced over his shoulder and grabbed a large, plush chair to put it next to the cabinet. "You might be more comfortable here. I'll give you your space." He started to leave when he felt her clutching his hand. He turned back to her.

"Wait." She pulled him. "Sit." She nodded toward the chair.

Hyde obliged her request. "Why would you want me to stay?"

"Because I need to say something, and I want to make sure you hear me." She took a deep breath. "This is strike two for you. I'm angry at you for not telling me about this." She hung up the receiver as she shook her head. "You still have this need to control the situation, and you don't trust me."

He shook his head. "Not true. I should have told you when I brought you here. I was afraid—"

"Of what? Afraid I would call the police or something?"

He shook his head. "Afraid that the peace I created here would have been interrupted." He released her hand. "After all these years of being concerned about myself, I've become selfish. I'm recognizing that now. You didn't deserve to have this information withheld from you. I'm sorry."

"Yes, you are sorry, and you're tired." She wiped her hand over her face. "After what we've done and what we're doing—"

"That's the reason I'm telling you about the phone now. I realize that—"

"Too little, too late. I'm tired of being treated as an accessory and being lied to." She rocked back and rose to her feet.

Her final concern worried him. Hyde should have told her that besides coming to his home as an escape, he had planned on ditching the duets project. Since that decision, he had had a change of heart. Why mention it now? At this point, not revealing the concealed phone had to be his worst offense. He had been honest about everything else.

Tassia shook her head. "But you need to now respect my wishes. I need to get out of this house."

Hyde started to open his mouth when the thing he feared happened: the phone rang.

Damn.

He glanced over at it. "Our peace is over." Hyde looked at the Caller I.D. screen and cursed under his breath.

"What?" Tassia tiptoed to the phone to peer at the screen.

"My grandparents." Hyde picked up the receiver. "Hey."

The screeching from his grandmother forced him to pull the receiver from his ear.

"You're here in town and I have to hear that from Pepper and not you?" Grammy Love's words cut through the phone and drove through his heart.

"I'm working." That hadn't been a lie.

"No excuse. You get over here today, right now." His grandmother huffed. "Have you eaten?"

Hyde glanced at Tassia and quickly recalled what he had done to her before he revealed the phone. "Yes, ma'am, I have." He wiped his hand over his mouth again and caught Tassia's fragrant aroma.

"What did you eat?"

His grandmother's question took Hyde off guard. "Trust me. It was a full meal." He glanced at Tassia and saw her cheeks turn a bright pink color.

"Fine. Get over here right now, Hyde Love."

Hyde knew if he had a middle name, his grandmother would have used it.

Hyde turned his back on Tassia. "That's not going to be easy. I—"

"If you don't come here we'll come to you." Then the call ended.

Hyde returned the receiver to the cradle and then looked at Tassia. "You're getting your wish. We're going out, just not where you expect." He walked toward the doorway. "But I would suggest you go ahead and call your father."

"Why is that?" Tassia stared up at him from her position on the floor.

"Because I'm pretty sure my grandmother is going to kill me. If she does, she may not let you leave." He laughed a little, but he knew he would have a lot of explaining to do to the people who helped raise him. "I'm going to get dressed. After you finish talking to your father, I really want you to move your stuff up here."

"Still trying to control this situation?" Tassia cocked her head. "What part of me being angry with you are you not understanding?"

"I know you're angry. I know I messed up."

"Again."

He sighed. "Yes, again. Nothing will get resolved if we're apart. We need to be on the same team."

"I've wanted that from the very beginning. I wonder about you, though." She plopped down on the chair. "You think you can control me, control this whole situation?"

Hyde removed his shorts, revealing his nude body. "Nope. Just making a suggestion."

He watched her scanning his body from his face down to his feet and back up again, stopping around his midsection. Her look alone had blood pumping in all areas of his body. He had to play this cool.

"The more we're together, the more work we could get done." Hyde opened a drawer and pulled out a pair of boxers. "We could write songs all day, then record, and then—"

Hyde had to stop talking when he watched Tassia removing her T-shirt. Then she sat in the chair he had moved over next to the telephone cabinet. Talk about not playing fair.

"You're right. I'm going to call my father and then get dressed after I take another shower. Someone got me dirty again." She crossed her long legs.

"What do you mean? I licked you clean." He winked at her.

That reminded him that he needed to take care of his own hygiene needs before he saw his grandparents. As much as he enjoyed tasting Tassia's sweet saltiness, he had to get his mind back on the task at hand. They would be visiting his grandparents.

"I'll decide after the call if I'll move to your room or just go directly to the airport."

* * * *

Tassia sat seething as she thought about Hyde's behavior. The entire time she had been in his home, he never revealed that he had a phone, a way for her to connect to the outside world. She didn't know what she hated more, a man who didn't care what she did or one who tried controlling her.

After all this time, she needed to talk to a man who had never let her down. To respect Hyde's privacy, she enacted the feature to block his number.

"Dad?" Tassia heard a click after one ring.

"Baby?" Her father sounded almost panicked. "Where are you? Are you hurt? I haven't heard from you in almost two weeks. I started to call the police."

"I'm fine." She curved her foot under her naked backside.

She couldn't believe she got so brave to sit naked in front of Hyde, and then call her father, not that the man could see her. If he did, he would admonish her brazen behavior.

"I told you I was working." Tassia didn't know that her work would involve having sex with a sexy if not infuriating man.

"I know, but even when you were on tour, you called me every day." The more Burt Hogan talked, the more relaxed his voice sounded.

With his renewed comfort, Tassia's shoulders eased down and her breathing slowed. "I'm working in a remote location, you know, kind of like what Meatloaf did when he recorded *Bat Out of Hell*." She knew bringing up one of her father's favorite albums would strike a chord with him.

"Are you someplace where you can't call?" A pause lingered. "Why are you calling from an unknown number? What's going on?"

"Dad, I'm okay. I promise. I'm in Tennessee." She swung her leg back and forth as she spoke to her father.

"Tennessee? Why aren't you recording in Virginia Beach?"

Tassia thought about Hyde and the reasons he told her why it would be better to work in his home. "This location opens us up creatively. We're getting a lot of writing done."

"We? Who are you there with?" Burt sounded like the same protective father she remembered who winced and tensed when he taught her how to drive, and who had given her prom date a hard time when he had picked her up for their special date.

"I'm with another singer." She swallowed hard before revealing Hyde's identity. "Ever hear of the country singer named Hyde Love?"

"Are you serious? Of course I know who he is. That's the guy who they were going to bump you out of the show for. But I stopped them. I took you from there before they could embarrass you." Burt sounded like he had taken a bullet for her, like they had gone to war. "After all these years, I can't believe you're working with him. Who else will be on the album? Chantel?"

"No." Tassia knew it wouldn't take long for her father to put the pieces together. "It's a duets album. Just him and me."

Silence.

"Dad?"

"Is your management team there?" Suspicion filled his voice.

"Um, no. We're here by ourselves." Tassia didn't wait for her father to jump to a lot of conclusions, which would have been true. "We're doing a lot of writing."

"That's one good thing. I can't believe people out there are calling you a fraud and a liar. I want to beat down every one of those people who doubt you."

Tassia smiled. She knew her dad would always be in her corner.

"But I don't think you should be off somewhere with some guy. I don't care who he is."

An uncomfortable tickle went up the back of her neck that matched the grinding twisting in her gut. Did her dad always see her as some sort of damsel in distress?

She heard through the phone some keys jingling.

"Where are you? I'll drive down and come get you."

Tassia imagined her father hitching up worn jeans that he kept hooked to blue and white striped suspenders.

"I would actually love that if I could tell you exactly where I am." She stood. "Until then, hold tight. If anything, I may need a ride from the airport."

"Does that mean when you come back you'll be coming to my house instead of Virginia Beach?" Burt's voice rose.

Tassia sighed. Although she wouldn't want to run to her father's home, she recognized that after her experience with Hyde, she might need some support. "Maybe. For now, though, I'm going to continue working here. I'll contact you when I get back home."

"Baby girl, I love you. I don't want to see you have an unhappy day in your life." Burt's voice hitched.

Her father always had her back. She had to appreciate that. Knowing she had such a great support system had her breathing a little easier. Leaving this project would be hard. If she made that ultimate decision, her management team would have to understand and respect that. They wouldn't, but Tassia would hope they would.

"I'll call you again later. Give my love to Pougie." She always ended the call sharing her admiration for her father's Yorkie.

Tassia showered again and dressed in a maxi dress and simple sandals. The ride in Hyde's vehicle remained quiet during the excursion until he broke the silence.

"Did you talk to your dad?" Hyde navigated through some backroads at a high rate of speed, but like an expert.

Tassia should have felt uncomfortable. With Hyde, she felt relaxed. "I did." She wanted to keep the conversation short and sweet.

"So how did it go?" He split his attention between her and the road. "Did you tell him you were kidnapped by a cowboy?" He screwed up his lips like he wanted to suppress a smile.

"No." She crossed her arms over her chest. "I let him know that I'm serious about my career and I may not be able to contact him every day."

"Oh." He drummed his thumb on the steering wheel. "I hope this separation from your family won't cause a problem with your relationship."

"It doesn't." She waited a beat. "And it does." She smoothed her hand over her thigh. "After talking to him, I realized that he's the only man who has my back and is willing to go to hell and back for me if he had to."

"You're saying being in my home has been hellish?" He screwed up his lips. "And here I thought you liked our, um, collaboration."

Even though she tried hard not to, Tassia couldn't help but laugh at Hyde. "You are so frustrating."

"But in a good way, right?" He rested his hand on her thigh.

Nothing in her wanted to brush it away. She liked the connection. Her heart fluttered.

"I really am sorry for not sharing with you about the phone." He squeezed her knee. Then he took a turn down a gravel road.

"As long as you don't do it again."

"Well…"

Tassia sighed. "Really?"

"My grandparents." As he said that, he rolled up to a sky-blue house with white trim in the middle of the woods. "They're a little different. And they're my father's parents, the other reason I didn't want to come here. I don't want him knowing where I am. I'm not ready to go back to the daily grind. I like what we have at the house."

"But that's not real. Real life means we get out and interact with other people."

When he parked next to an older-model red pickup truck by the front of the house, the front door flew open and an older woman with chocolate brown hair stood on the porch.

"And now it starts."

Chapter 17

Hyde loved his grandparents. He knew they could be taken best in small doses, not a full impact meet-and-greet. Since Pepper revealed his whereabouts, no way could he not visit, although he had tried hard to hold off this visit until the very end of his stay.

Mabel Love's mouth curved down until it looked like invisible fish hooks pulled down the corners of her mouth. In her long denim shorts, white sleeveless T-shirt, and flip-flops, the sight brought Hyde back to the days when he used to live in this house. He knew it wouldn't be long before Granddaddy Love would be right behind her.

"She doesn't look happy." Tassia hesitated before unhooking her seatbelt after Hyde turned off his SUV.

"Believe it or not, she's thrilled to see me." Hyde took off his seatbelt and opened his door. "She won't bite. Not too hard."

Hyde heard Tassia's door close as he circled the front of his vehicle. "Grammy Love. You look beautiful as always."

"Don't give me that." The tall, thin woman stomped down the stairs toward him. "You've been here almost two weeks and this is the first I hear from you and see you?"

The front door opened and Pepper stepped out. She smirked at Hyde and it reminded him of the same expression she would give when she bested them as kids. Hyde wanted to snarl at her but with Grammy Love now in his face, he made sure to keep his expressions neutral.

"I'm working." Hyde smiled.

Mabel glared at him for a moment before she pulled him into her arms and hugged him hard. "You are exactly the same as when you were a kid." She gave him a playful slap on his arm. "And who is this?"

Hyde suspected that his grandmother must have spotted Tassia. He released Mabel and turned behind himself. "Grammy, this is Tassia Hogan. She's a singer and a songwriter." He noticed the way she smiled at the way he introduced her. "We're working on an album together."

Mabel glanced at Tassia then looked at Hyde before she broke her embrace and approached Tassia. "Nice to meet you." She extended her hand to her.

Tassia didn't hesitate. She accepted Mabel's hand. "Nice to meet you. I've heard a lot about you."

"You mean that I won't bite you hard?" Mabel snorted. "Don't worry. I've heard that joke before."

"Because she created the joke." Hyde hung his arm on his grandmother's shoulders. "I should have called, but—"

"Don't start it." Mabel wagged her finger in Hyde's face.

Hyde knew what she meant with her statement. "No story. I just got off tour and needed a break."

"Your break couldn't include coming to see us? Or were you doing something else?" Mabel glanced at Tassia.

Hyde heard Pepper snickering behind him. "Working." He peered over his shoulder at her and shook his head.

"Sounds good, but that's not work."

Hyde felt his eyebrows furrow.

"You know where the lawnmower is in the shed." She popped him on his backside.

"Grammy, do you know—"

"If the next words out of your mouth are *who I am*, I will remind you quickly who *I* am." She stared at Hyde until he laughed along with her.

"Yes, ma'am." Hyde turned to Tassia. "You can go in the house."

"To relax?" Tassia headed toward the house.

Both Hyde and Pepper cackled.

"Dear, there's nothing about the Love family that's relaxing." Mabel hooked her arm around Tassia. "You're tall. I like that." She volleyed her attention between Hyde and Tassia. "You and Hyde would—"

"We're just working together." Tassia tried shrugging out of Mabel's grip.

Mabel leaned in close to Tassia but spoke louder than a whisper. "Yep, before I married my husband, he and I worked together at a lumber yard before he finally got the nerve up to ask me out. Just ask him." She nodded toward the porch where Efrem Love stood.

He adjusted his glasses on his long noble nose. He gave a cursory wave from the shady porch.

"Hey, Granddaddy." Hyde waved to him before pointing to Tassia. "This is Tassia Hogan. We're writing songs together and will be recording an album."

"Sounds nice." Efrem nodded. "Helping me with beans?"

Hyde glanced back at Tassia. "Guess we have our marching orders. I'm mowing, and you will be snapping beans with my grandfather." He winked at her.

"Don't be cute." Mabel nudged him toward the side of the house to make his way to the backyard. "And, Pepper, come on down and help me with the flowerbeds."

"Aww, man." Pepper kicked the tip of her sneaker against a porch post.

* * * *

Tassia didn't know how she had gone from being on tour with a top rapper to making a deal to do a duets album with a country star to now snapping string beans with Hyde's grandfather. Unlike Mabel, Efrem kept quiet except for the occasional hum here and there. He kept his attention on the long, slender green beans as he plucked off the ends before depositing the prepared beans into a colander.

Tired of the silence, Tassia decided to break the ice. "Hyde tells me that he lived with you and Mabel for a short while."

"Yep." He continued preparing each bean.

"And your son is also in the music business?"

Efrem stopped moving for a moment. "He's not a musician. He's nothing like Hyde."

She blinked. "You're proud of Hyde."

This time the gray-haired mature man broke a smile. "He's special. Real deal."

Tassia smiled. "Yes, he is."

Efrem nodded before he continued humming. Tassia recognized the tune and started singing. Her voice must have surprised him. He stopped snapping the beans as he regarded her. Then he started singing along with her.

Tassia immediately recognized how wonderful his voice sounded with the same deep baritone that Hyde had. He carried a tune better than some popular singers.

At the end of the song, Efrem adjusted his glasses on his nose again before he addressed her. "Great singer."

"Thank you. You're not too bad yourself." She chuckled.

"Do you have anything I would have heard?"

Tassia felt the heat creeping up her neck to her face. "Um, probably not."

No way would Hyde's grandfather listen to a song about being ridden in a sexual manner. Tassia couldn't admit that out loud.

"I listen to a lot of things." Efrem wiped his hands over his jeans before he pulled out his cell phone.

Tassia didn't worry about him finding her song since he, like Hyde, thought she probably spelled her name as T-A-S-H-A. Then he surprised her when the opening of the song played from his phone.

She jumped to her feet, knocking over her bowl of beans. "You don't have to listen to that. Please stop."

Efrem didn't speak. He continued listening until her part came up. He stared at her. The embarrassed heat that filled her cheeks became a full-body firestorm.

"Not my best work." She crouched down to retrieve the beans.

"Beautiful voice, even if the words aren't the best." He got down on the floor with her to help her gather what she dropped. "We all sell ourselves out sometimes. If you're writing songs with Hyde, you write from the heart." He placed the full bowl of beans on the table.

Tassia helped him back to his chair. "The song put my name out there. I secured the duet deal with Hyde because the song did so well."

He shook his head. "You're talented. You need the right vehicle to showcase your voice." He sniffed. "Go in this project as a partnership. Hyde has been used enough, especially by people who are supposed to protect him."

"You mean his dad." Tassia understood what Hyde's grandfather didn't say.

Efrem snickered. "We named Hyde's father Clever because every time I would take his mother to her doctor's appointments to get a status on the baby, he would move away from the doctor's hands and instruments. He came a day earlier than planned. We barely made it to the hospital before he was born." He shook his head. "Since then, he has lived up to his name. He hasn't been home in a while to visit us. And we get it. Clever and Hyde have busy lives."

Tassia heard the lawnmower start. She watched the highest-paid entertainer in the world mowing his grandparents' lawn. Each time he passed the kitchen window that faced the backyard, she became a little wetter. Her heart pumped just a bit harder.

"I don't think Hyde and his father have a great personal relationship." Tassia recognized a good man existed in Hyde despite his need to keep things close to the vest. "He thinks C. Love, uh, I mean Clever sees Hyde as a commodity more than a son."

Efrem sighed and rubbed his eyes. "I was kind of afraid of that. I wish those two would talk more. No matter how much money you make and how many fans you get, family will always have your back."

Tassia wanted to believe that of Clever, even hearing it from his father. Yet she didn't see it. From what she had seen of him in the media, and in talking to Hyde, and even her own experiences with him, Clever only thought about Clever. When she spotted Hyde going by the window again, and seeing the sweat pour off him, she wanted him to have so much more. He deserved happiness.

"Have you heard from Clever recently?" If Hyde had been right about his father, Clever should have been calling around trying to find his meal ticket.

"Once maybe over a week ago, looking for Hyde. At the time, we really didn't know where he was. Until Pepper told us." Efrem shrugged.

"If you hear from him again, will you call the house? I know Hyde is exhausted, and Clever pushes him hard to be a success. Maybe if those two can sit down and talk, they can both get on the same page." Tassia wanted that for Hyde.

"That would be nice if it happened. That kid is special." Efrem glanced out the window before regarding her again. "I told you how Hyde's grandmother and I came up with the name for Hyde's father. Clever and Hyde's mother came up with Hyde's name weeks after his birth."

"Weeks? What do you mean? Hyde told me that he was named after a distant relative."

Efrem rubbed his hand over his chin while keeping his gaze down. "His parents didn't know what to name Hyde because neither was ready to have him. His mother kept her pregnancy hidden from Clever until she got kicked out of her house for being pregnant and came to live with us. Hyde's mother wasn't doing so well." He shrugged. "People thought it was drugs. I think she had other mental issues that Mabel and I tried helping her with by taking her to doctors. But she was not our kid, even though her parents disowned her."

Tassia listened to the story and started to see Hyde in a different way, less like a privileged star and more like a human being with family issues like the rest of the world. Hyde started in the world without an identity. She wondered if he knew the true story about his name and if he had lied to her again. Then again, why would he lie about his name? What would he have to gain?

"When Hyde was born, Clever wanted to name him after himself, of course." Efrem shook his head. "I can show you Hyde's original birth certificate. They called him Baby Boy Love. Clever and Hyde's mother argued all the time. Before Hyde was born, it was about money and Clever being responsible. Back then I can say that Clever worked hard and cared. He wanted things to work out with him and his child's mother. He even agreed to her final baby name choice, Hyde. No middle name."

At least Hyde hadn't lied about not having a middle name. She didn't realize the full story behind it.

Efrem continued. "Shortly after Hyde was named, his mother split. We have never heard from her since, and Clever searched for her."

"Wow. I had no idea." Tassia's hands shook as she continued snapping the ends off the woody green beans.

"We've never told Hyde about his past." Efrem glanced at Tassia.

"I don't understand. Why tell me this?"

"I can tell you're a kind person. We told Hyde that his mother left and that's all. He doesn't need to know anything else, but you need to know if you want to understand him better, and I think you do." He stared at Tassia. "Be kind to Hyde. As his name suggests, he does have a lot to hide. But he also has a lot to offer. He was a good kid. He's an excellent entertainer because usually the ones with the most to hide shine in other ways. He could be a really good man if he learned to let go."

"He has more to learn than that. Respect would be nice." Tassia still held onto the fact that Hyde didn't want the songs she had written on the album. "He's calling the shots on a lot of things, um, related to the album, I mean."

Efrem stared at her and didn't say anything for a long time before he spoke again. "Pepper told us how you got here."

The anger Tassia had regarding her trip there had been doused. She didn't know if Hyde's fear of working with her or presenting the two of them in public had anything to do with their TV past or if he had shame about being with her.

Efrem cleared his throat. "Mabel and I did our best with Hyde when he was here. As soon as he started working and spending time with his father, he changed. That sweet, open kid became withdrawn and shy. Then he started living up to his name." He patted the back of Tassia's hand. "Be patient with him."

"We're just working together." She smiled to support her story.

"He didn't look at you like you're just working." He settled back into the wooden kitchen chair. "And quite frankly, you weren't looking at him like just a co-worker, either."

Tassia started to refute his claim. She had to tell him about Hyde's overbearing nature, and the fact that he'd brought her there under false pretenses. She would also have to admit to herself that the man could make her toes curl in a nanosecond, and had her hitting notes when she came that she didn't think would be possible. Throw on top of that Hyde's undeniable talent and he almost had it all. Almost.

"Mister..." Tassia waved her hand in the air to get him to complete the rest. She wanted to be respectful while shooting down his assumptions, albeit accurate ones.

"Call me Efrem. Everyone does." He continued snapping the ends off green beans and tossing the scraps into a separate bin.

Knowing this family, they probably had a compost bin somewhere. Tassia could have sworn she heard chickens clucking. Mabel hadn't been kidding about putting the platinum star to work.

"Okay, Efrem. The record label and our management team are counting on us to produce some hit songs for them pretty soon. Probably not a great idea for us to take this time off to not be working." Everything she had said had been true.

Efrem didn't need to know that this conversation made her more uncomfortable than telling her father to back off a little.

"Miss Hogan."

"Call me Tassia, please." No way could she have this older gentleman calling her *Miss* anything.

"Do you know how long Hyde has owned his hideaway?"

Tassia felt her eyebrows knit together at his question.

"His home by the pond."

"Oh. No. He didn't tell me. I assumed—"

"Eight years. He had it built by an out-of-town contractor team, then he had the roads rerouted so that if any of them did try to make a visit, he would be difficult to find. And in all the time he owned his house, he has never, ever invited anyone there, not even that Shelby Lynne gal, who I couldn't stand."

Tassia blinked at his statement.

"She was too self-centered and only cared about appearances. She didn't care to know about any of us." His gaze dropped to her hands. "And she for sure wouldn't snap beans with me." He tossed a bean in the nearly full colander. "That tells me that you're someone special. Hyde brought you to his house, and he introduced you to us."

"Don't look into that too deeply. I told him I wanted to leave the house after being stuck inside for almost two weeks." She had to corral this conversation back to something tame.

"Consider this. Hyde could have taken you anywhere. He brought you here. That tells me something. It should tell you something, too."

A door opened and Tassia thought that would be the end of the conversation. Efrem continued. "Be good to him and he'll be damn good to you."

Hyde strolled in looking like a good-looking sweaty boy next door. It occurred to her that since being at his house, he hadn't worn his trademark backward baseball cap. Now he had on a well-worn cobalt blue cap with the bill over his eyes. Short grass clippings stuck to his sneakers and his legs around his ankles. His white T-shirt stuck to his body.

"I work out. I shouldn't be this exhausted. I'm beat." Hyde lifted his hat by the brim and wiped his sweaty forehead. He started to head toward the refrigerator when Tassia stopped him.

"You want something to drink? I'll get it for you." She opened a couple of cabinets and could not find drinking glasses until she peered at Efrem, who cleared his throat and nodded toward another set of cabinets behind her.

Tassia grabbed the biggest one she could find, filled it with ice, and then turned to Hyde.

Before she could even ask what he wanted, he blurted, "Sweet iced tea, like a good southern boy." He winked at her.

Good thing she held onto the refrigerator door. Her knees buckled for a moment before she pulled out a pitcher of the amber liquid and poured it into the prepared glass. When she handed it to him, Hyde slid his fingers over her flesh.

"Thanks. You didn't have to do that." He took three healthy gulps that polished off the beverage.

"You want some more?" She held her hand out to him.

The air around them sizzled as she stared at him.

"I'm sure he wants a lot of things, but he needs to get back outside and finish his work first." Efrem nodded toward the door.

Hyde chuckled. "Yes, sir. See you two for lunch."

Lunch consisted of ham sandwiches with a side of fresh-cut fruit and the best-tasting tea Tassia had ever had. They sat in Hyde's grandparents' sunroom where they could still enjoy the sun without sweltering or dealing with bugs.

Instead of eating and running like Tassia thought she would want to do considering Hyde's foreboding warning about his family, she wanted to stay through dinner. Because of the friendliness of his family, including Pepper, Tassia had even considered spending the night there with them. Spending time with Hyde recently felt like a honeymoon, even through arguments and disagreements. With Hyde's grandparents and cousin, she felt like she had come home.

Tassia helped prepare dinner with Mabel, who even shared her family's recipe for the perfect fried chicken. Tassia peeled the potatoes and helped with the homemade yeast rolls. Working side by side with Mabel reminded Tassia of being in the kitchen with her mother before Tassia started on the Ratty Rat show.

By dinnertime, Hyde looked like he had a permanent smile affixed to his face. Whenever Tassia looked at him, he winked at her.

"Pep, did you not put any food in his house?" Mabel pointed to Hyde's cousin.

"I did. I stocked the fridge and freezer and even filled up his pantry." Pepper tucked one leg under her as she sat in her chair.

"Why is the boy eating like he hasn't seen food in years?" Efrem nodded toward Hyde, who stopped eating his third piece of chicken and second helping of mashed potatoes with gravy and green beans to answer their questions.

"Pepper stocked me nicely, and I eat a lot at the house."

Tassia cleared her throat before picking up her frosty glass of tea to take a sip. In her head, she thought about what Hyde had done to her shortly after breakfast and singing the song he had written about her so many years ago.

"I miss this food." He pointed to his plate.

"He did tell me that it's his favorite meal in the world." Tassia picked up her fork but stopped when she noticed the room had gotten quiet.

"And here I thought you two only had time to write songs while you're, um, together." Pepper gave him a saucy wink.

"Hyde told me this back when we were on the show together." Tassia remembered a few things about him, too.

"Interesting." Mabel raised her eyebrows as she glanced at Hyde.

"Grammy, don't." He shook his head.

"What? Can't a grandmother want to have great-grandchildren one day?" Tassia nearly spit out her drink. "Whoa. We're just—"

Mabel waved her hand in the air at her. "I know. I know. You two are just creating this album. I get it. But one can hope." She cupped Hyde's cheek. "I do like her." Mabel brought her attention to Tassia. "Even after you two finish this project, you are more than welcome to come by here and visit anytime. You're good people. I can tell you were raised right. And my husband said you can sing like an angel."

Efrem nodded.

Tassia had to be thankful that Hyde's grandfather left out the fact that Tassia sang about riding a cowboy in a different way.

"Thank you for the compliment. And I appreciate the offer." Tassia meant it.

Being in Tennessee, she had half expected not to be welcomed in Hyde's family's home, and to be treated like a second-class citizen. These people welcomed her and treated her almost better than her family.

After dinner, Tassia helped clean up and put items away while Hyde did as his grandmother instructed and packed food to take home with them.

"If you ever need a break, you call us anytime." Mabel handed Tassia a piece of paper that had her name, phone number, address, and even her email address on it. The woman wanted to make sure to stay in contact with her.

"Thank you, Mabel. You are awfully hospitable to someone you just met." Tassia tucked the paper into her purse.

"I have great instincts when it comes to people. I have a feeling I'm going to know you for a while, even if my knucklehead grandson ruins it by doing something stupid." Mabel pulled Tassia in for a hug. "Take care of yourself and Hyde."

"I will. I promise." Tassia went over to Efrem. In his ear, she whispered, "Please call if you hear from Clever."

He nodded. "I will. Family should stick together."

Efrem's words hit her deeper than simply getting Hyde and his father on the same page. At the end of this project, who would be in her corner besides her father?

On the ride home, Tassia kept quiet most of the way, mainly because of her full stomach. She also had to process the day. Hyde had done something that he had not done with any of the women he had dated seriously. He had never taken them to see his family. He did with Tassia. What did that mean?

"I can't wait to get back home." Hyde rubbed his head. "I feel like I have dirt covering every part of my body." He glanced at her. "Thanks for being so good with my family. I know they can be pushy."

"They were great. Reminded me of my own family." Tassia put her hand on her purse over the pocket that contained his grandparents' contact information. "Your grandfather shared something with me that I wanted to share with you."

Hyde smiled. "I can only imagine what he would tell you." He must have noticed her somber expression. His smile melted. "What did he say?"

"He told me about your parents and their early struggles when you were born." Tassia had admonished Hyde for not being transparent. She had to be the same way with him, and this information seemed important. "You didn't have a name the first couple of weeks of your life."

Hyde remained quiet for a moment before he snickered. "That explains a lot."

"He also said that your mother had issues." Tassia held his free hand. "She was the one who named you before she left you and your father."

Hyde remained uncomfortably quiet the entire ride home.

"Your grandfather said he told me because it would give me more insight about you while we work together." She swallowed hard.

"And why tell me this now?" His voice lowered.

"Because I can't ask you to be honest with me if I don't give you the same courtesy." She squeezed his hand. "You're not your name. You've established yourself to be your own man."

Hyde nodded. "Nice to hear you say that." He lifted her hand and kissed the back of it. "I appreciate you telling me this."

"You're welcome." Tassia cleared her throat. "This is not what I was thinking of when I said I needed to get out of the house." She watched Hyde keep his stare on the road.

Just as she started to say that she had enjoyed her day, Hyde interjected.

"As you know, I'm not perfect. I'm not trying to hold you back. If anything, I think you should be shining more." He pulled into the gravel road that went to his place. After entering a code at his gate and swiping a badge, the gate opened. Once through, he waited on the other side until the gate closed. "I'm sure when you asked to go out you wanted to do something else other than go to another person's house and stay in it all day."

Glad the irony didn't get lost on him either.

"I enjoy spending time with you. I don't want it ruined by spectators and critics looking to pick apart anything and everything we're doing." He pulled up to the house, and instead of parking out front, he drove around the back of the house, engaged a button on his visor and opened a garage door to pull inside. He turned off the vehicle as soon as he parked and closed the door behind them. "If you don't want to stay here, I understand. But I'm going to do everything I can to convince you to stay, write with me, record with me." He squeezed her hand this time. "Have a good time with me."

Tassia remained quiet. She didn't expect Hyde to open up like that, but she liked it.

"I'm going to take a shower. You feel like writing tonight?" Hyde opened his door.

Tassia nodded.

"Okay, I'll see you down in the recording studio in about thirty minutes. Is that cool?"

"That works."

Hyde opened the door leading into the house and waited for Tassia to go inside. After putting on the alarm, Hyde trudged upstairs, leaving Tassia alone on the main floor.

She thought about a lot of things that had happened that day. What she constantly got reminded of had to be Hyde and the way he interacted with his family. Throughout it all, he tried hard to protect her.

Tassia went to her bedroom and packed up all her belongings in her suitcases, and then took them and her purse upstairs to Hyde's bedroom where she heard the shower running. She left her cases next to the phone cabinet before stripping out of her clothes and shoes and padding over to the bathroom.

Hyde had his back to her as soap suds oozed down his body to the shower floor. Tassia tapped him on his shoulder before joining him.

"Feeling a little dirty myself." She chewed on her lower lip as she regarded him.

"I thought you would want to go home." The back of his head blocked the shower spray from hitting her.

"What? And miss all this?" She raised her hands in the air. "Besides, I never want it to be said that I'm a quitter. I'm not. I'm also a really, really big fan of yours now. That puts me at stalker level."

Hyde laughed.

"I even moved my stuff up here."

"It's about time." He started to reach for her and she put her hand to his chest to stop him.

"Yes, it is about time I do something else." She got on her tiptoes to give him a sweet kiss before she dragged her lips down his face, to his chin covered in scruff, and his thick neck.

When she got to his chest and licked his nipple, she felt his body loosen.

"What are you doing to me?" Hyde brushed her ponytail braids from her shoulder before she lowered herself to her knees.

"Taking advantage of you." Tassia slid her hands up his strong thighs before she cupped his sac and wrapped her fingers around his shaft. She felt him throbbing in her fist before she drew her hand up and down his long member.

"Are you giving me pity sex?" Before Tassia could answer, Hyde barreled through. "If so, I'm all for it."

"You are a best-selling artist, great singer, and a good man. You have nothing about your life that warrants pity." When Tassia swiped her tongue over his tip, Hyde took no time in turning off the water and staring down at her like he needed to give her his full attention. She covered him with her mouth and held him there for a moment before humming as she eased her way down to the middle of his now erect penis.

"Oh my God." Hyde put his hand to the back of her head. "You don't have to do this."

Yet the hand at the back of her head told a different story.

Tassia pulled her mouth back from him slowly before gazing up at him. "You want me to stop?"

As Hyde nodded his head, he said, "No."

She laughed. "You're giving me mixed signals." She swirled her tongue around the tip. "You want me to stop?"

He shook his head and said, "Yes."

She liked seeing him this out of control. Tassia moved her mouth down him again while stroking the base of him at the same time and massaging his balls. It didn't take him long to start thrusting his hips, slow and easy at first.

When Tassia moved her mouth faster, he matched his thrusts with her movements.

"So good." Hyde's thighs trembled. "Can't hold out."

Tassia didn't expect or want him to hold anything back from her. She pressed her tongue against the tip of his penis and extracted some of his salty pre-cum.

She moaned again, knowing the vibration must have felt good to him. Hyde groaned and placed one hand against the wall as he left his other hand at the back of her head.

"Tassia." He said her name between gritted teeth before coming in her mouth.

She wasted no time in swallowing his essence as she slowed down her movements.

"Jesus, I need to take you over to my grandparents' house more often if I'm going to get treatments like this." Hyde tried catching his breath in between laughing.

He helped Tassia to her feet and did not hesitate to kiss her.

"Now we need to get dressed and get down to the studio." She placed her hand on his chest when he attempted to hold her. "No sex until we write and record."

"Then let's go. I'm ready to get creative, and I don't mean with the songwriting." He winked at her.

Chapter 18

Hyde had never enjoyed the creative process of writing and recording more than now. It helped that he had a great partner. Tassia gave as good as she got, and he didn't just mean with sex, although sex with her couldn't be compared to anyone he had ever been with ever.

He didn't want her to think he only wanted her for sex, even though after each song they wrote and recorded together, they made love until his body could no longer take it. He wouldn't have the experience any other way.

"Ten songs in." Tassia smiled as she tapped her finger over her phone screen while she rested her back against the arm of the couch in the recording studio. "How are you feeling?" She had her legs stretched out and over Hyde's legs while he had his back pressed against the other side of the couch.

"Physically? Wiped." Hyde laughed. "But in a very, very good way. These last three weeks have been amazing."

Tassia rubbed her foot up Hyde's leg. She looked sexy wearing one of his old T-shirts and in her lacy panties. "I think so, too. I never felt so…"

"So what? Finish your thought." He set the pad and pen he held onto his lap.

"This is going to sound strange, but I finally feel heard, if that makes sense."

Hyde smiled hard enough that his face felt as sore as his back and thighs. "You have no idea." He grabbed her ankles and lifted them enough so that he could slip under her and go to the other side of the room to get his guitar. "But you're wrong. You haven't been heard, not by me or Charisma."

Tassia wrinkled her forehead. "What are you talking about?"

"You remember that song you wrote called 'Kidnapped by the Cowboy?'"

Tassia rolled her eyes. "Okay, I get it. It hurt your feelings and I shouldn't have written it."

He waved his hand at her. "No. *I* was wrong. *I* should have never told you that that song and the other ones you had written weren't good enough for the album. They were and they are."

She sat up. "No. You were right. I was getting my feelings out and I didn't have a part for you in it. It won't work."

"Listen. I'm going to play the melody for it, what I think the song should sound like. Will you sing it?" He had a plan and hoped she would be on board.

Tassia sighed hard. "I think you just want to hear me sing."

"I will never turn that offer down. You ready?" He counted her off before he started strumming his guitar.

She started singing the lyrics from when she played it for him initially. After she got through the chorus and just before she started the second verse, Hyde cut her off and infused his part.

"I'm a man who knows what he wants. A straight-up beauty not acting like a debutante." He watched her mouth drop open as he sang. "Can't take my time with you. The last time I waited, I turned around and I lost you. Didn't mean to take you away. But with me is where I want you to stay. I would never treat you like a toy. And you'll never regret getting kidnapped by this cowboy." He continued playing, hoping Tassia would continue her part.

When she didn't, he peered up at her and saw her slowly coming to a stand and padding toward him. She crouched down at his feet when she got to him and pressed her hands against his guitar strings.

"You put in a duet part to my song?" Her voice came out light, almost fragile.

He stroked his fingertips down the side of her face. "It is a duets album, darling."

She turned and kissed his hand before she continued. "Did you finish it?"

He nodded. "I was hoping you would keep singing your part of the song."

"I couldn't. I was too overwhelmed." She laid her head on his lap. "You did it."

"*We* did it." He stroked her hair.

Tassia lifted her head and shook it. "No. You did it. You got me to believe in something I didn't think was possible. I didn't think anyone could be generous in this business, especially someone at your level. I didn't think there were men out there who could be this open and kind. And I didn't think…"

She stopped right at the moment Hyde suspected she wanted to put her whole heart on the line. Did she feel the same way he felt? Had a simple pre-teen crush turned into so much more?

Hyde started to open his mouth to let her off the hook and admit his feelings when she stopped him by standing.

"I want to hear this whole song from beginning to end. And then I want to hear what you did with my other two songs." She strolled over to the piano.

"And then we'll record them. And then—"

"And then." She smiled.

"Yeah, one of my favorite parts of this process." Hyde stood and sauntered over to Tassia to kiss her on her forehead. Then he sat down closer to her before they started playing together.

He felt so in sync with this woman who he had only known as a child. Grown up, she still contained that fighting spirit and beauty that drew him to her.

By the time they recorded "Worthless," where in his verse he refutes everything she says about not being worthy of love and respect, Hyde carried a hard on that couldn't be missed. He looked over at their stash of condoms and saw one left.

Damn. They would have to venture out and buy more. No way did he want to stop this practice of having sex after a recording session.

"I want to hear the songs." Tassia left the piano and joined Hyde in the control-room area where he had the songs already cued up to play.

"I'm ready." He took off his T-shirt and turned around to make her see what their hard work had done to him.

She peered down briefly before she removed her shirt, revealing her panties. "More than you would ever know."

Before Hyde made another move, he pushed the playback option to play all thirteen songs they had recorded so far. In his head, each one sounded better than the last one. He leapt from his chair and framed her face in his hands. Once he kissed her, he couldn't think of anything else.

He felt Tassia pulling down his shorts. It took her no time to wrap her fingers around his shaft and give him a hard stroke up. He palmed her ass cheek in one hand and massaged her breast in the other while continuing to kiss her hard. He snaked his tongue in her mouth and Tassia started to moan.

Those sounds from her always shook him. Hyde pulled her panties down. The motion made her break from the kiss and turn to the place where they kept their condom stash.

"Damn." Tassia must have noticed what Hyde had observed earlier.

"It's okay. We can get more." He eased her down to the couch before picking up the last package and tearing it open.

"There are other ways I can pleasure you." To prove her point, she licked the underside of his erect penis up to the tip.

That action halted his motions for a second before he continued. "You are killing me."

Tassia giggled. "Sorry, but not sorry."

Hyde rolled the condom on before positioning himself between her lean thighs. In one smooth motion, he entered her, causing her to embed her fingernails into his shoulder and suck air between her gritted teeth.

"Sorry, but not sorry." He kissed the side of her face and her neck as he thrust into her hard and deep.

Tassia wrapped her legs around him and tightened her hold. Not necessary. Hyde had no plans to leave this position or leave this woman unsatisfied.

He rolled her hardened nipple between his thumb and index finger, making her moan and whimper. She arched her back, and he felt her slick inner walls constricting around his shaft.

"Already, baby?" He liked teasing her. He had never been with a woman who reacted to him as fast as she did.

Tassia nodded and kept her lips clamped shut.

"Tell me. Talk to me. Let me hear it." Hyde slithered his hand underneath her ass to cradle it as he continued pumping into her, harder, faster. He would ignore his aching back to give his all to her.

"Best. The best." She nodded. "More. Don't." She shook her head. "Stop." She framed his face in her hands and kissed him on every area that she could. "I like being here with you. Don't want to go."

He curved his hips and hit a spot inside her that she must have liked. He felt Tassia's body stiffen before she started screaming and beating on his back with her fist.

By the time the last song of theirs played, Hyde felt the buildup inside him cresting at the surface. He could no longer hold back.

"Tassia!" He braced his feet against the arm of the couch as he pushed himself hard in her and held himself there, depositing his seed into their last condom.

Hyde tried not to move while small tremors overtook his whole being. By the time he settled, he opened his eyes and gazed at the beauty under him.

Tassia smiled. Even with a sheen of sweat covering her face and body, she looked gorgeous. "You are going to ruin me when we go to record. I'll expect this every time."

"I'm sure we can find a quiet spot somewhere at Charisma." He kissed her forehead. "A dark hallway." He brought his lips down to the tip of her nose. "An abandoned office." He kissed her lips. "A closet."

At the last suggestion, Tassia laughed. "I would love to see you and me in a cramped, musty old closet."

"Is that a challenge?" He didn't pull himself out of her. Not just yet. He liked feeling connected to her.

"Of course. But then again, our whole relationship has been a challenge."

He caught something in her eyes that he didn't like. The hopefulness that she had before looked dimmed and almost extinguished. He couldn't have that.

"I have a surprise for you." He finally pulled out of her and deposited the used condom in the adjoining bathroom trashcan.

"You are full of surprises. I can't imagine what this could be." She rolled onto her side as she watched him.

He held his hand out to her. "Come on. We're going to shower and get dressed. We're leaving the house tonight."

* * * *

Tassia had no idea what Hyde had planned, especially since the first stop in their trip had them going to his grandparents' house. Not that she didn't like Mabel, Efrem, or Pepper. When Hyde said he had something special for her and that they were getting out, she thought it would have been to a nice dinner somewhere or to a show, not back to the place where he had grown up.

"What are we doing here? Game night?" Tassia tried to keep her voice light, but she suspected that she may have sounded a little bitter about a second outing revolving around his family.

Hyde shook his head. "Nope. Stay right here."

Efrem opened the front door for his wife and granddaughter, and locked it when the two ladies departed and went to separate vehicles. Then he approached Hyde's side of the car. Hyde rolled down the window to talk to his grandfather.

"You aren't going to drive, are you?" Efrem adjusted the worn-out baseball cap on his head.

Hyde cursed under his breath. "That's right." He turned to Tassia. "We can sit in the back seat and my granddaddy can drive us."

"Wait. Where are we going? What are we doing?" Tassia didn't get all the cloak-and-dagger stuff. Although none of the clandestine actions scared her, it all raised her curiosity.

"You'll see." Hyde put his SUV in park and got out. "Do you mind?"

Efrem shrugged. "Your Grammy and I assumed you wanted it done that way anyway."

Hyde got out and into the back seat and waited for Tassia.

"You might want to get back there with him." Efrem nodded behind himself.

"My God. Are we going through Klan country or something?" Her heart started racing.

Efrem laughed. "No, dear. You're famous so it might get out about you being in town."

Tassia considered the whole situation and finally figured out that Hyde had planned on taking her out to a public place. The idea of that pumped her blood even more.

She hopped out of her side of the vehicle and got into the back seat where she found a couple of coolers separating her from Hyde. Were they going to do a late-night picnic? All kinds of ideas rolled around in her head as they pulled off, following behind Pepper's deep-purple pickup truck and Mabel following behind them in their all-white SUV.

Hyde draped his arm across the back of the seat, probably with the hopes of touching Tassia. He brushed his fingertips over her shoulder.

"Where are we going?" She kept her stare on the fairly empty road in front of them.

"You'll see."

Even in the darkened cabin, she caught Hyde winking at her. Secretive until the end.

The three vehicles got on the interstate for about fifteen minutes before getting off an exit to a location that seemed like it could pass for their downtown. Stores lined the quaint street they drove through to their destination. Another ten minutes on the road, Tassia finally saw their last stop.

"A drive-in movie theater?" She didn't think places like these still existed.

"It's been a while since I've been. I thought you would enjoy it." Hyde pointed to the marquee. "There's an action movie playing with some romance in it."

"I'm more of a comedy fan." She smiled.

"Oh, really? Good to know for the second date." He brushed his thumb over her shoulder.

As the cars lined up at the drive-up box office, Hyde slipped on a hoodie and then a black baseball cap before throwing the hood over his head and sitting with his head down. When they got closer to the clerk, Tassia followed Hyde's cues and turned her back away from the window just in case the cashier recognized her.

"Three adults," Efrem said to the cashier.

Tassia caught a pause before she finally heard the cashier say, "Here's your receipt and the radio station or the app to download if you want to hear the movie through your vehicle speakers. Just make sure your vehicle isn't running. We also still have the stand speaker if you want to use it."

"Thanks." Efrem rolled up the window and pulled into a space in between Pepper and his wife's vehicles. He turned the SUV off and turned to the duo in the back seat. "You two all set?"

"Yes, sir. We'll listen to the movie on the speaker." Hyde got out of the back seat and gave his grandfather a hug before he got back into the front seat to set up the speaker.

After placing it in the window and rolling up the window as much as he could, he took off his jacket and used it as a makeshift curtain in that window. Then he carefully moved over to the passenger side and hung a towel in that window before getting back into the back seat.

"I will never make fun of your Boy Scout ways again. You have everything planned except for one thing." Tassia held up her index finger.

"What?" Hyde rested his hand on top of a cooler while he awaited her answer.

"Bathroom. What if one of us has to go?" She shrugged and laughed.

He held up a can of shortening. He removed the lid to show the empty container. "You can go in here and we'll toss it—"

"Eww! I can't believe you even thought of that."

Hyde laughed. "I'm always prepared." He put the can behind the third row seating. "I have plenty for us to eat and drink." He started pulling out items. "Bottles of water, soda, sport drinks, juices, beer, and little bottles of wine."

"Wow. You are prepared. We both can't drink alcohol." Tassia took the wine from his hand and inspected the bottle as much as she could in the darkened cab.

"Wow. You are a church girl, aren't you?" He winked at her. "We could do some drinking. My granddaddy can drive us back home since I know he and Grammy don't drink."

She put her hand on his lap. "Yes, but I wanted to do other things when we got home."

"Really? Then I'll hold off. I know how much of a screamer you are." He laughed.

"You are so not funny." She laughed with him. "What do you have in there for food?"

Hyde opened another cooler. "Let's see. Fruits. Got some cut-up watermelon, strawberries, apples, grapes. I also have some sandwiches, hot dogs, chips, pretzels, popcorn, candy."

"Babe, did you think we were never going back to the house?" She marveled at all the food he had for them both and the time it took for him to plan this whole excursion.

"I like giving you options." He reached behind them. "I also have a blanket in case you want to put it on the hood and lay out on it."

Movie trailers populated the tall, white screen in front of them.

Tassia threw the blanket across Hyde's lap, which made him furrow his eyebrows. "Or I could use it to cover you up in case someone walks in front of the truck."

"What are you doing?" His face stilled when she undid his zipper to his shorts.

Hyde took off his baseball cap and threw it on the driver's seat while Tassia undid his shorts and reached in for his limp member.

"I'm going to make sure everyone is awake for this." She curled her legs up on the seat and moved in closer to him while she stroked him, slowly at first. "I have always wanted to go to a drive-in movie theater if only to do this."

"Really?" He spoke in between harried pants. "You like fooling around in public?"

She nodded. "I like the danger of getting caught. What about you?"

He didn't verbally answer. Hyde reached over and cupped her breast over her T-shirt and bra.

"You like that? Or is this better?" With her free hand, she lifted her shirt and pulled up her bra, allowing him to touch her bare skin.

"Oh, God. So soft." Hyde nodded.

The movie started but Tassia didn't care. She didn't take her stare off Hyde as she continued stroking him. She had to know when she had him ready to explode.

His legs twitched the longer she played with him. She felt him curving his hips upward like he needed to encourage her. When she caught his stomach spasming, she knew she had to have him close to coming, especially when she caught him reaching for himself like he wanted to catch whatever he emitted.

Tassia removed the blanket and covered his bulbous tip with her mouth.

"Christ. That's it." He put his hand to the back of her head in time to deposit his full load into her mouth.

She swallowed every bit of his essence, enjoying the saltiness and the thickness as it oozed down her throat.

"We were supposed to be enjoying the movie." Hyde managed to smile in between speaking and breathing heavy.

"I'm enjoying it." Tassia sat up and got a bottle of water from the cooler to drink and cool herself down.

"Kind of hard to do with the windows all fogged up." He brought his backside up to fasten his shorts again.

She peered up at the windshield and noticed that it had a cloudy cover over it. "I blame you and all of your heavy breathing." She did all she could to suppress her laughter, but it erupted anyway.

"Cute. You wait until we get home. I'm going to wear you out." He gave her a playful swat on her bottom.

"You mean more than before? Yikes." She fanned her face. "You know. I am on the Pill, and right when I got home from the tour, I got tested, although every time my ex and I had sex, we used protection. I'm safe."

Hyde regarded her for a moment before he smiled. "I got tested right when Shelby Lynne and I broke up. I haven't been with anyone else since." He interlaced his fingers with hers. "Are we saying what I think we're not saying?"

She brought her face to the side of his to get close to his ear. "I want to really feel you tonight."

Hyde pulled her onto his lap. "You mean like this?" He eased his hand in between her legs to the seat of her panties.

Without pulling them off, he pushed the seat to the side and eased his middle finger into her moist channel.

She writhed on his lap. "Hy."

"Hi. How are you?" He stroked his finger in and out of her.

Unable to control herself, Tassia undulated her hips. "Yes. Hy. Hy."

"I said hi. Can you not hear me?" He snickered.

"Teasing me." She held his chin and gave him a quick peck on his lips.

"I like teasing you as much as I like tasting you." With that statement, he pulled his finger out of her and slid it in his mouth to enjoy her juices.

She had to suppress a growl when he removed his digit that had almost gotten her spot. When Hyde did nothing in the way of going back to his previous action, she let a whine emit. "Please."

"Please, what?" The corner of his mouth hiked up.

Unable to wait and unwilling to play his game, Tassia took matters in her own hand. She slipped her finger under her panties and massaged her moist nether lips first. To enjoy the moment, she closed her eyes and leaned her head back while still on Hyde's lap.

As soon as she slipped her middle finger inside her intimate area, she let out a small cry. The sound must have been enough for him.

In the blink of an eye, Hyde positioned Tassia on her back and pushed up her dress. Then he pulled her panties down all the way and parted her thighs. His first lick pushed her over the edge.

She had to cover her mouth to diminish her cries of ecstasy, but the more he licked and laved her, the more she wanted to shout to the moon and back. Her legs trembled the more his tricky tongue did the work her vibrator couldn't do.

Hyde massaged her clitoris and gave it a squeeze at the same time he dove his tongue inside her.

"Hy!" She arched her back.

No jokes or funny quips from him this time. He continued licking her until Tassia came hard. She had to pull her dress up to her mouth and cover it to keep her screams under wraps.

When Hyde lifted his head, she caught him wiping his mouth with the pads of his fingers and licking off the juices. That alone had her wanting to take him right there and then. Since she started this risqué playing, she couldn't fault him for finishing her off properly. Too bad she could barely move her satiated body.

"I love drive-in movie theaters." She tried catching her breath.

Hyde laughed at her. "You know I have a movie theater in my house. We could have fooled around in there if you wanted."

Tassia sat up and shook her head. "There's something about being naughty in public. Such a turn on."

Hyde picked something up from the floor of the backseat area. "Are you going to put your panties back on?"

She grabbed the garment from him and held them in her hand. "Do you want me to?"

He smiled as he shook his head.

She tossed them back on the floor. "Commando it is." Then she leaned against his hard body and let him wrap his arm around her. "I think this is the best date I've ever had."

"Really? I was going to impress you by taking you to a bowling alley." He laughed as he rubbed his hand up and down her arm.

The small crack in the driver's side window where the speaker hung allowed some air to come into the cabin of the car to clear up the windshield.

Now that playtime had ended—for now—they could really enjoy the movie…except for the constant beeping.

"What is that?" Tassia peered around her. "Is that noise in the movie?" Through a clear section in the windshield, she saw that the scene contained a full-on action sequence complete with car chases and gun play. She had expected to see the hero of the movie disarming a bomb or maybe getting a text message or something.

Oh, no.

"What is that?" Hyde sat up.

"Shit." Tassia jutted in between the two front seats and snatched her purse from the floor. She dove inside and pulled out her phone.

She had forgotten about her phone since she hadn't used it in weeks. Now close to Wi-Fi and civilization, the device automatically connected to everything at a time when all she really wanted to connect to now sat next to her.

The email icon on her phone showed more than 500 messages. She had over a hundred text messages that she missed. She didn't even want to look at her social media accounts. The peace and quiet that Hyde had wanted for them both got interrupted in a blink of an eye.

"Airplane mode. Put it in airplane mode now." Hyde pointed to her phone.

She did as instructed and even turned her phone off for good measure. "I never thought I would hate being linked to the real world."

"I hope in the short time your phone did manage to connect that no one has been trying to track you and reach you. If so, we're going to have to wrap up our time here and get back to Virginia." Hyde appeared calm, but the tenseness in his voice spoke volumes.

Tassia hoped nothing came from this. For now, she would try to enjoy their time there until the other shoe dropped.

A pounding sounded on the passenger door by Hyde. He released Tassia before he opened it. Pepper stood on the other side.

"I need food." In her black-and-white Converse sneakers, denim shorts, and her Black Sabbath T-shirt, she looked like a teenager.

"You need help and maybe Jesus." Hyde looked back at his stash. "What do you want?"

"Meat. Sandwich, hot dogs, and some chips." She peered into the back seat for all that he had.

"Here." Hyde handed her a bag full of treats and drinks.

"Thanks!" Then she wrinkled her nose. "Why does it smell like sex in there?"

"You're annoying, you know that?" He started to close the door.

Before he did, Tassia noticed a teenager walking by peering at Hyde and his cousin arguing. The young woman tapped her friend on the arm and nodded her head toward the vehicle.

"Hyde, close the door. I think you've been spotted." Tassia tugged on his shirt.

"Shit. Enjoy the food." Hyde closed the door and made sure all the doors had been locked. "It'll be okay."

Tassia didn't know if Hyde said that to convince himself or her.

"It's dark. Her friend will argue with her and tell her that she's crazy. We're still okay."

Tassia nodded. In her mind, she knew their utopia had ended.

Chapter 19

Hyde's mind had been on a lot of things lately, mainly Tassia and keeping her safe and happy. He had kept a close watch on their surroundings. He hadn't noticed anything suspicious yet. He hoped for the short time they remained there, nothing would happen.

"Are you writing?" Tassia looked up from her position on her belly next to Hyde in his bed, where they now spent most of their time.

"I look like I am, don't I?" He smirked to not raise her suspicions.

"Good." She rose up on her knees and straddled his legs.

"What are you doing?" He gazed at the beauty before him and would have let her do anything to him that she wanted.

She removed the pad and pencil from his hands and placed them on the nightstand next to the bed. Then she cradled his face without saying a word.

Hyde remained silent, too, as he gazed upon her, wondering what she would do next and what he should tell her, what had been rattling around in his mind since their drive-in movie date a couple of nights ago.

Both naked, Tassia scooted closer to Hyde's body until her slick pussy touched his penis. When she kissed him, it pumped blood all through his body.

He held her around her waist, holding her close and wanting this moment to last forever. He had enough money in the bank to keep them both happy for years. Just because he wanted a break, time to slow down, didn't mean she did.

Tassia slid her slender tongue into his mouth. She flicked the tip against his tongue and let them do their dance until she moved her hand down to his nipple. She circled it with the tip of her finger.

Hyde moaned as he held her breast in one hand while resting his other hand on her waist. He lowered his head to suckle her. He flicked his tongue over her hardened nipple and felt her body shake and tremble with each flick and tease.

He moved his mouth over to her other breast and gave it the same treatment. When he felt her hand reach down between their bodies to his now hardened cock, he stopped moving and let her drive.

Tassia brought herself up high enough to impale herself on his hard shaft. Entering her without a protective layer brought in a whole new sensation to him that he didn't think could be possible. She squeezed her legs around his body and undulated hers while holding onto his shoulders.

Hyde kept his stare on her eyes, never breaking eye contact, not even when the phone in his room rang. He squeezed Tassia's ass cheeks in both hands to give her an unspoken clue that he remained connected to her in mind, body, and soul. A call from his grandparents or Pepper wouldn't stop him.

She rode him harder and faster. Her breathing became labored as she held onto him like a bull rider on her last ride. He felt the desperation, too.

"Come on, baby." He kissed her clavicle. "Give it to me."

She continued increasing her speed to her grind. Hyde's fire had already been stoked. He wrapped one arm around her waist, braced his hand on the mattress behind him, and drove himself up to meet his and her needs.

"Hy." She rested her head on his shoulder as she met his thrusts with her undulations.

For the first time, Hyde came with her at the same time. That had never happened to him, and he loved that it happened with Tassia.

The gravity of the situation must have hit her, too. Tassia stared into his eyes for a moment before smothering him with a soul-stirring kiss.

She broke from it long enough to say, "I've been avoiding making love to you in this position since we started."

Hyde cocked his head. Did she think she would be bad at it? He had to tell her that she rocked his world, but first he had to know why she avoided it. "Why didn't you want to do it this way? Is it uncomfortable for you?"

She shook her head. "I didn't want to be the woman who sings about riding her man and actually doing it."

He shook his head. "Do you think any of that matters to me?"

"I knew it wouldn't, but it mattered to me." She remained on top of him as she spoke. "I know it put my name on the map in the music world, but it feels like it's my scarlet letter. For the rest of my life and beyond, it'll be a footnote in my career. I sang a song about how I like to have sex, and I didn't even write the song."

"Then don't worry about it. The people who care about you will know the truth." He pulled her forward without disengaging her. "For what it's worth, you could have written that song. Wow. How have we not done that position in all the time we've been here?"

"Because everything else we did felt so good, too." She rested her hands on his shoulders.

Hyde must have gotten too quiet too quickly and for far too long.

"Are you with me?" Tassia tapped Hyde on his arm.

He shook his head. "No. My mind is all over the place."

"What are you thinking about?" She wiped her hand over his head.

He had already been thinking about this conversation for a while but didn't know how to broach it. "Thinking about you."

"You are? What about me?" She rocked back and forth on him.

"You're very talented. You can sing." He tapped his finger against her phone that she had on the nightstand next to his notepad. "You can write. You of all people deserve to record an album." He took a deep breath. "And I'll fund it."

"What?" She put her hand to her chest.

"If you see yourself releasing an album with Charisma, I'll produce it so that you can record it there. Otherwise, you can come to my label and I'll support you there. Or we'll do something independent. You are too talented to not have had a solo album already."

He thought Tassia would have been jumping for joy at his news. Instead, she stared at him with question and suspicion in her eyes.

"Why are you making me this offer now? What's changed?" She played with her braids as she awaited his answer.

He nodded. "You're right. Something has changed. I promised I would never hold anything back from you. I love you."

She blinked at the same time he did. Hyde had never been that guy to open up first in a relationship, but Tassia changed him for the better.

"Don't feel obligated to say it back to me, especially after I say this. I love you too much to put you through the hell that is my life. I don't want you always looking over your shoulder and being concerned about who's looking at us."

Tassia got up on her knees and faced Hyde. "I'm only concerned about that because you are. I couldn't give a damn about the stares. I've been through that. And people are going to hate me for more random things than being with you." She held his hand. "Creatively, I feel like my best self with you. Emotionally, I'm the happiest when I'm with you. Of course, it didn't start off that way. And you make me feel safe, and not because of the security measures you have around here. It's because you do everything that you can to make sure I'm happy and satisfied."

"That's great. But understand that I've managed to do that in a bubble." He pointed out the window. "The real world is worse."

"I know that. But I've been the one who has been trying to convince you to get out there. You told me to stop running. You have to stop hiding." She held his hand against her chest. "I'm ready. Whether we had slept together or not, the slings and arrows were going to come our way because of this project. People aren't going to like a country singer with an R&B singer. I wasn't ready for that before. I am now. I—"

Hyde put his finger to her lips. "Don't say it."

She turned her head. "Don't silence me now."

It had been bad enough that he dragged her out here to his home. Hyde couldn't subject her to his rabid fans. He shouldn't have told her that he loved her. After what they had been through, from childhood to now, no way could he part from her without her knowing the full truth.

He had to keep her quiet in other ways. He kissed her, soft at first. In his mind, this would be their final kiss. He knew something would happen that would ruin this happy world he had manufactured.

His fault. He tried finding happiness and he did. Who knew it would have been with an old crush? He could no longer live selfishly.

"Stop. You can't tell me you love me and then want me to walk away from you." She shook her head. "And you can't buy me off. I don't want your record deal. I want you."

"I want you, too, but not like this. Not in this realm. It won't work." He shook his head.

"Are you afraid that your country fans will—"

"Don't go there. Don't make assumptions about people who listen to country music."

Tassia growled. "Damn it, Hyde. For once, fight for me."

"What the hell are you talking about?"

"Back when we were kids, you saw me go and didn't think about contacting me again. I auditioned for you years later, and you didn't hire me. Now we're here together. We feel something for each other, and you're willing to let me go again? What happened to that guy in the song you wrote who said he wouldn't let me go again?"

He shook his head. "I can't see you get hurt."

"Stop trying to protect me like I'm fragile. My dad did that when he didn't tell me the truth about my mother or when I left the show. I won't have that now. I need you to be strong enough to let me handle myself. Can you do that?"

Hyde started to answer when he saw something out of the corner of his eye that got his attention. At first, he thought it was a seagull because of its white appearance and breadth of size. Then he figured out quickly what he spotted hovering at his bedroom window.

"Shit!" He tossed Tassia to the side away from the window and grabbed his remote that dimmed his windows in an instant.

"What's going on?" She held the comforter under her chin.

"Drone. Goddamn drone." Hyde stepped into some shorts lying on the floor and pulled them up. "Take a shower and get dressed. We need to get out of here."

"No." Tassia crossed her arms and looked like a defiant child.

"If the paps are onto us, they won't leave us alone. We need to leave and—"

"And what? Go where? You have to protect your home."

Hyde went into his closet to the back and unlocked a safe. He pulled out the shotgun his grandfather had given him the first time he had gone hunting. When he reappeared in the room, Tassia gasped when she saw him.

"I am protecting my home. We're leaving right after I do something." He stormed over to the French doors leading to the balcony that sat off to the side of the window. The idiot running this drone wouldn't see him coming.

"Hyde, wait!"

He didn't. He opened the door, took aim at the flying intruder, and shot once at his target, hitting his mark before it came crashing down to the concrete patio below.

When he returned to the bedroom, he found Tassia breathing heavily. "I did-did-didn't know you had a gun here."

Hyde had to calm himself down when talking to her. She now got to see his true country side, the part of him willing to defend himself and the ones he loved. "I live out in the country and I hunt." He watched her hands trembling. He started to comfort her when he heard something he never thought he would have heard in his home: the doorbell.

"What the hell?" He stomped down the stairs.

"Oh, God. Hyde, don't. Just call the police. You still have the gun in your hand." Tassia followed him with the comforter wrapped around her body.

Hyde knew what he carried to the door. He suspected whoever got through his security gate and made it to his door had no idea what he could and would do.

Without bothering to look through the peephole, Hyde unlocked the door and whipped it open. He had to blink when he saw Pepper standing on the other side.

"Pep, you have a key. Why didn't you use it?" He watched her look sheepish and silent, two things that never describe Pepper.

"I called you. I tried to tell you." Her voice came out in almost a whisper.

"What are you talking about?" Then Hyde heard the door slam and saw what Pepper must have meant.

The last man Hyde wanted to see strolled around a fully loaded Audi. The golden color of it matched the man's tan as he sauntered to the door and stood next to Hyde's cousin.

After draping his arm around her shoulders, Clever Love said, "Hey, son." In his free hand that dangled by his side, he held a remote control.

* * * *

Tassia had too many thoughts going through her head right now to think clearly. Hyde had shocked her by wanting to produce her first solo album, but in the same breath said he didn't think they should date after admitting he loved her. He didn't even give her a chance to say anything before shocking her more by pulling out a gun to shoot down the offending drone that caught their afternoon delight.

Not content to remain standing behind her man—and she still considered Hyde to be her man no matter what he had worked out in his head—she rushed to his side with her comforter dress wrapped around her body. What she would have done if the person on the other side of the door had turned out to be some robbers, she didn't know. She knew she couldn't leave Hyde's side.

When she saw C. Love at the door with Pepper, a range of emotions went through her. She knew that as Hyde's father and manager, he wouldn't be there to harm him. From talking to Hyde, she also knew that his father wanted him to work non-stop. This trip wouldn't be a good one judging by the way Hyde's jaw flinched.

"Aren't you going to invite us in?" Clever said as he drew Pepper in closer to him like a lure for Hyde.

Hyde would probably say no to Clever, but not to Pepper. Instead of verbally answering, he took a step aside while holding the door open.

"Thank you." When Clever walked by Hyde, he held up the remote. "I suddenly lost the image after I heard a loud bang." He glanced down at the gun Hyde held. "Am I to assume that—"

"What are you doing here?" Hyde's fuse must have been short.

"Looking for you." Clever strolled into the living room, tossed the remote on the coffee table, and made himself at home on the couch. "After your slick trick with your body double a few weeks ago, I have had people out trying to find you." He wagged his finger at Hyde before he turned to Tassia. "And you. I knew it couldn't be coincidence that both of you disappeared at the same time. Your dad didn't know where you were." He volleyed his attention back to Hyde. "And your grandparents didn't know where you were...at first."

Hyde marched into the living room, but kept standing. "How did you find me?"

"Luckily, your Love Birds," Clever turned to Tassia, "that's what his fans are called. One of them posted that they thought they may have seen you at some local drive-in movie theater. And I thought, there's no way my son, who's worth almost a billion dollars, would be caught dead in some rinky-dink drive-in. And then I had another piece of luck. I've had detectives keep an eye out for debit and credit card activity as well as cell phone activity."

"Oh my God." Tassia didn't mean for her thoughts to materialize as audible comments. Now she understood Hyde's need for space and privacy.

"As soon as this one's phone pinged off a tower close to my parents' house, well, I hightailed it down here." He crossed his legs and stretched his arms out across the back of the couch. "When I saw my dear, old dad, he shared with me that your new lady friend really wanted you and me to talk. She seems to think we don't get along."

Hyde turned to Tassia, who now felt her face burning with embarrassed heat. Clever had none of the true parental concern that Burt had for her. She pushed her father to the side. Maybe she needed to reexamine her familial relationships.

"Is that true? Did you want him to come over here?" Hyde faced Tassia.

"Not really. I asked your grandfather to call if he heard from him. I thought maybe you could go to your grandfather's house to all talk, man to man." She approached Hyde but he moved away from her.

"I said everything I need to say to my *manager*. The last time I told him that I desperately needed to take some time off, he wanted to only carve out a week for me." Hyde snickered. "A week. He doesn't care that

I'm exhausted and worn out and just beaten to death. There's always something else."

"Yeah, and that something else was the interviews you missed. You also missed a televised performance. And did you know that Oprah's been trying to reach you?" Clever planted both feet on the floor and rested his elbows on his knees. "Your little disappearing act had fans worried about you. That's really bad for your business."

"Too bad it was wonderful for my personal life and health." Hyde glared at his father.

Clever scanned Hyde from head to toe. "I don't know. You're looking a little soft in the middle. I need to get you back into the gym."

"Stop it." Tassia could only take so much from this man. "You're talking to your son. Did you forget that along with his birthday?"

Clever jumped to his feet. "You want to tell me who I'm talking to? I'm talking to the commodity that I have groomed from a chubby kid on a TV show to the hottest artist out there in the world, not just in country or in music. The world. He has the ability to influence people to buy a brand or not." He pounded his chest. "I did that. That was me."

Hyde shook his head. "No. That was all me. I put in the work."

"Work?" C. Love snickered. "What work have you been doing here?" This time he scanned Tassia up and down. "I'm guessing by your attire, you two have been—"

"Don't you go there." Hyde held up his hand to his father to halt whatever disgusting thing he wanted to say.

"Let me take a guess here. It was her idea to come out here, right?" Clever pointed to Tassia.

"Wrong. All me." Hyde pounded on his chest this time.

"Oh. Okay. I bet you she convinced you to stay. Maybe offered you something. She's not as popular or rich as you. I'm sure she used other, um, currency to persuade you to—"

"Get the fuck out of my house." Hyde pointed to the door. "You are not going to come in here and disrespect me and my guest."

Clever got in Hyde's face. "Listen here, boy, I am still your manager. What I say goes. What I'm telling you and what I tried to tell you from the beginning is that this project is a bad deal. She is using you."

"What? No." Tassia shook her head. "I didn't even want to do this at first. I was ready to walk, remember?"

"She also came with baggage. She doesn't write her own songs." Clever shrugged.

"Bullshit. I've been with her. We've written songs together. I know she's talented."

"Did you also know that her father pulled her from that rat show when he found out that they were going to pair you up with her?"

Tassia shook her head. "That's a lie. My father told me that they were going to cut my part down to make Hyde the star."

Clever cackled. "And you believed him? Sweetie, your father told the writing team and the producers that he didn't want his kid having to carry dead weight. You want proof? Contact Christina, that's if she'll take your calls. She was there listening to the whole conversation." He looked at Hyde. "Are you sure she told you the entire truth?"

Tassia watched the kernel of doubt that Clever planted in Hyde's head staring to grow. His expression changed from anger to contemplative like he didn't know who to believe.

"Hyde, if that truly happened, I'm sorry. I would never say anything like that about you, ever." She held his free hand. "I love you."

Clever laughed out loud and clapped his hands. "And there it is. You are willing to pull out all the tricks, unless this is not the first time you said that to him. Is it?"

Shit. It wouldn't have been if Hyde had let her talk.

"Hyde, I am one step ahead of the paparazzi. Trust me. It won't take them long to find you two if I found you." Clever turned to Tassia. "If things don't go the way I want, I will post that video I have recorded of you acting out that line in your song on Hyde. Did you ride him the last three weeks?"

Hyde took the hand he used to hold his shotgun to shove his father back. "Lay off her. Your problem is with me, not her. Don't post anything."

"I won't as long as you cut this little vacation short and come back to work. You've already wasted millions of dollars. Even Shelby Lynne was asking about you. I think she was concerned about your wellbeing." Clever put his hand on Hyde's shoulder. "Bottom line. You have some important decisions to make. One is whether you go into this project with an embarrassing story to start it off or a feel-good story of you helping children in Ethiopia."

"You are not going to spin my working time away with a lie." Hyde shook his head. "And if this duets album is the last thing I do in my career, I'll still be fine."

"You might. Think about your friend here. I think she has a little more, and you'll pardon my phrasing, riding on this than you do." Clever laughed. "It's a no-brainer. Let me do what I do best, and forget about everything else."

Hyde remained quiet for an uncomfortable period of time.

"Come on, son. You've played around enough. Time to pull out of this project like you said you would."

Tassia blinked. "What?"

"Oh, Hyde didn't tell you?" His father put his hand to his chest. "Yeah, the day the contracts were signed, he told me that his plan was to back out of the deal. He does not want to keep associating with his *Ratty Rat's Fun Crew* castmates. But I'm sure he told you all this already, right?"

"Wow." Tassia felt hollow inside. "So your plan wasn't just to relax. You were going to ditch me."

Hyde faced her. "It's not exactly like that."

"Then tell me what it's like. While you do that, tell me how your definition of love includes hiding information from the person you said you love." She backed away from him.

Clever continued. "Remember what I always tell you. You have to remember who the star is here." He pointed to Tassia. "If you do this project with her, she will shine more than you just like back on the show. You don't want that, right?" He moved in closer to his son. "And you don't want to be associated with that Ratty Rat time, do you?"

Tassia watched Hyde as he processed his father's toxic words while not explaining his actions. C. Love managed to worm his way into Hyde's head and poison him again. Hyde still hid his true feelings. Tassia lost Hyde. She had no place there with him.

"I'm going to shower and change." Tassia looked at Pepper. "Did you drive here on your own?"

Pepper nodded.

"Good. Would you mind taking me to the airport? I need to get home."

Pepper looked at Hyde and Clever. "Um, sure. But you don't have to go. You can—"

"No. I need to go, and I think Hyde needs his space. He needs to figure out what's true and what's a lie." She glared at Clever before she made her way back up to Hyde's room.

Once there, she slammed his bedroom door and then slammed the door to the bathroom. She couldn't believe she would end this great experience with Clever blackmailing her and his son. She had hoped Hyde would have been on her side. From his expression, it looked as if he believed his father.

Tassia took the fastest shower she could, packed her belongings again, and came clunking down the stairs with her bags. When she saw Hyde standing up from the breakfast bar like he wanted to approach her, she darted out the door ahead of Pepper.

Tassia had hoped that a bear would appear again to maul her to death. It would have been a kinder expression than Hyde not believing her and siding with his father.

Pepper met up with Tassia by her car and helped her with her bags. "Are you sure you want to go to the airport right now? You could spend the night—"

"No." Tassia shook her head. "I need to get with people who truly love me."

"You're leaving one right—"

"I'm ready."

Pepper didn't say anything else as she helped Tassia load her suitcases in the trunk. Tassia had had enough of not being believed. Just like with Dorian, she would chalk this up as an experience. Unlike with Dorian, her heart truly broke from walking away from Hyde.

What the hell would she do now, especially since they had a project together to finish?

Chapter 20

Shortly after Tassia left his home without a word or a good-bye to him, Hyde showered and packed his belongings as well. Pepper never returned after taking Tassia to the airport.

He shouldn't have let her go. Hyde had so many things to process in a short amount of time. He piled his luggage by the door.

"Now that the distraction is gone, and you've cleared your head, we can get back down to business." Clever complemented the statement by rubbing his hands together.

His father had actually called Tassia a distraction. How could Hyde let her go? Why could he not see clearly how his manager had manipulated him until now?

"There's one thing I need to do before I leave here." Hyde took his things out to his SUV that he now had parked in front of his home.

"What's that?" Clever, wearing a white button-down shirt under a cream-colored suit, put his hands to his hips.

"Follow me." Hyde took his father on a high-speed chase through winding backroads to get to his grandparents' house.

When he got out of his vehicle, he noticed his father remained behind the wheel of his SUV. Hyde wouldn't wait or even try to coerce him to join him in the house. If nothing else, he would use the time to properly say good-bye to them. He would have to catch Pepper another time. He would need her to properly close up his house.

Hyde walked up to the door and knocked like he had always done for as far back as he knew. Unless he played in the backyard, his grandparents never allowed anyone to run back and forth in their house through the front door. They could through the back door.

Efrem answered the door and smiled. The smile melted when he spotted the other vehicle and its driver. "What is he doing here again?"

"I asked him to follow me here." Hyde walked into the house. "Since he sees me as his meal ticket, it won't take him long to come in."

Mabel walked in the living room from the closed-off kitchen area. "Baby, what are you doing here? Where's Tassia?"

The second question would be harder to answer than the first. How the hell did he make this mistake again? He had to be crazy or stupid...or both.

"I'm going back to work, Grammy." Hyde gave her a kiss on the cheek. When he heard the front door squeaking open and saw Clever coming through, Hyde felt compelled to answer the second question his grandmother had asked him. "Tassia left when I failed to react." He turned away from his grandparents to face his father. "My manager has some embarrassing video and pictures of me and Tassia, and he threatened to use them against her if I didn't do what he wanted."

"Oh, hell." Mabel threw the dish towel she held down to the floor. "I didn't raise you to—"

"To what?" Clever raised his hands in the air. "To starve? To scrape for everything I have? I was resourceful. Last time I checked, that wasn't a bad thing."

"It is when you use people." Efrem put his hand on Hyde's shoulder.

Hyde appreciated the support from his family at this time.

"We're family. Tassia is a sweet girl and mega talented. You shouldn't have threatened her like that." Efrem shook his head. "You're nothing but a bully."

"No. I'm a damn good manager." He glared at Hyde. "And father."

Mabel cackled. "Father? You and Hyde's mother parted ways, and you left Hyde here for *us* to raise. What we failed to do with you we more than made up for in Hyde."

He kissed his grandmother's cheek. "Thanks, Grammy. But I did let you down in one way. I should have never have let Tassia go thinking I didn't have her back. I love her."

He heard a gasp behind him and couldn't tell if it came from Efrem or Mabel.

"Love won't put fans in seats or food on your table." Clever crossed his arms over his chest.

"Sure. But at the end of the day, I need someone to confide in, to be in my corner, to love. If all you have in your life is the work I'm putting in for you and nothing else, I feel sorry for you." Hyde took a step closer to the man who gave him life.

Clever laughed. "You feel sorry for me? Please. I'm fine. I made you."

Hyde shook his head. "Stop saying that. You got me to the right places at the right time, but I did the work. I took the vocal lessons and dance lessons and tutoring and did all the touring and interviews and promotions. You rode my back the entire time. And I believed you. Every damn word. You made me believe that I was nothing. Everything you said back at my house brought me back to how I felt when I was a kid, where I thought I was nothing without putting others down. As soon as I saw Tassia's hurt look and watched her leave me, I knew better." He took a deep breath. "It's taken me a long time to get to this point but I think I can say it."

"What? Are you firing me? Is that what this weak-ass intervention is about?" Clever got in Hyde's face.

"I was going to tell you I love you, man." Hyde had to step out of himself as the performer and look at the man before him. "Tassia told me what Granddaddy told her about you and my mother, how you struggled. It must have been hard for a young man to raise a baby on his own. You sacrificed your time to take me to auditions and did everything you could to make sure I made it. Good or bad, you did do a lot for me. I recognize that. You got me to where I am today. I'm not unappreciative of your efforts." To show his father the sincerity of his words, he pulled him in for a hug. "I do love you."

Clever hesitated before he reciprocated the hug. "Thank you, Hyde."

Hyde pulled back from him and nodded. "And you are right. I am firing you."

Clever's eyes went wide.

"I need to go in a new direction with my career that you don't seem to be on board with. Plus, I don't like your management style. It'll work for newbies coming up in the business. At this point in my life, I don't need to hustle as hard as you want me to. You don't see Beyoncé out there doing as much as I do, and she's doing pretty well for herself."

"You ungrateful—"

Hyde held up his hand. "Oh, no. I am grateful, which is something you haven't fathomed for yourself."

"You tell him." Mabel nudged Hyde's arm to egg him on.

"For as hard as I have worked for you for all these years, I have yet to hear a thank you or any kind of gratitude from you."

"You expect me to kiss your ass or something?" Clever took several steps back.

"A thank you would go a long way." Hyde released another deep breath. "I'm letting you go as my manager, but I hope we can work on our relationship." He put his arm around his grandfather. "All of us."

Clever glared at them but said nothing. Then he must have collected his thoughts enough to spew more venom. "Everything I did, I did for you. Getting you paired up with the blonde, not hiring someone who would outshine you, the stories about her songwriting."

"Whoa, whoa, whoa. Back all that shit up." Hyde felt his blood turn to lava. "Let's start back from the beginning of what you just said."

Clever released an exasperated sigh like all of this bored him. "On that TV show, the writing team wanted to pair you up with that gal."

"Tassia?" Efrem scratched his head.

Clever nodded. "Yeah. I knew she had an incredible voice and would outshine you. What did I always tell you about getting outshined?"

Hyde recalled his last conversation he and Tassia had had back as children on the show. His father had that kind of thinking drilled in his head even back then.

"I, instead, got them to aim their focus on you and Christina. I thought her cute and bubbly personality would bring you up a bit, and it did. I also planted the seed that maybe it was time to rotate Tassia off the show, or at least lessen her part. But they weren't having it. Then her father came up and had ideas of his own, and eventually he talked himself out of keeping her there, which worked for me."

"But not me." Hyde put his hand to his chest. "I've sung with her. We would have been amazing together."

"Woulda, coulda, shoulda." Clever shrugged.

"What about the audition?" Hyde barely remembered her auditioning for him back when he concentrated on the writing.

"Oh, she showed up again like a bad penny. With some age and experience, she sounded even better. Luckily, you weren't paying attention and you left the decisions up to me. I couldn't let some back-up singer outshine you. I passed on her."

The lava in Hyde's veins threatened to erupt. "And the songwriting stories?"

"I did know before the meeting who they had planned on pairing you up with for the duets album. I had some people make calls to that Chatty Charlie show and give them a tip that Tassia had not written all of those songs. I figured that if you worked with her, which I had kind of hoped you would, that people would think you had written all the songs and not her. And if it didn't work out and you wanted to walk, you would have had a great reason to bail." Clever clapped and raised his hands in the air like he had done something magical. "See. Always thinking."

Meanwhile, Hyde stood there fuming, wondering if he punched his father right there and then if his grandparents would ever talk to him again.

"Why did you want me working with Tassia if, by your own account, you didn't want me working with her before?"

"Remember I said you were missing out on a certain demographic with your sales? I thought your association with her would have helped you snag the urban market. You would have had street cred. Fucking her has to up your status a little."

Hyde balled his hand into a fist, ready to knock his own father's teeth down his throat.

"You are not the child we raised." Mabel shook her head. "Our son wouldn't use people like that." She gripped Hyde's arm. "Don't you do what he did and think it's okay."

Hyde patted her hand. "Don't worry. I won't." Then he brought his attention to his manager. "I knew you were a bastard, but I didn't know you were this much of one. If you dare leak or release a picture of me and Tassia at my house, or get someone else to do your dirty work for you, I will sue you for every dime you have. Revenge porn is illegal, and Hulk Hogan didn't do too badly for himself when he sued that magazine that posted pictures of him in bed with someone who wasn't his wife."

"You would do that to your father?" Clever put his hand to his chest.

"No. But I would do that to a former manager." Hyde hugged his grandfather and grandmother. "I can't stay here and argue with him. I need to hit the road and try to make up some ground with the woman I let go of again." He approached Clever. "You now have some time on your hands since you're basically unemployed." He saw Clever start to say something but Hyde cut him off. "You will be compensated for your time and efforts. Trust me. It will be more than fair. And then I don't want to see you on the business side. But I would love to see you back here for their Fourth of July celebration, and during the holidays. Even an asshole deserves some family time, as long as he can redeem himself."

"You're making a mistake." Clever shook his head.

"No, you are if you don't recognize what I'm offering. You have enough money to enjoy the rest of your life without working. Stop running and relax a little." He patted his father's shoulder before leaving the house. "But stay the fuck out of my personal life. You get anywhere near Tassia or say a cross word about her, I will be on you like stink on shit, and you will not like the new Hyde."

With that done, he had another important mission to accomplish. He had to get his woman back.

* * * *

Tassia peered down at her phone when it rang again. At this point, she knew the caller. Not one to back down from a fight, she picked it up and answered it.

"Tassia." Hyde's voice, as usual for the last week, sounded strong. "I know you are listening to me. I haven't backed out of the duets project. I still—"

Tassia disconnected the call. She didn't need or want to hear Hyde's apology or excuses. He had his chance to explain himself that last day she had been at his house. Hyde had remained quiet.

Her phone rang again. This time, Tassia wouldn't remain quiet.

"Stop calling me." She shook her head like he could see her. "It's done."

"It can't be." Hyde now sounded defiant. "I'm not ready to give up. I was wrong. I believe you. I should have told you that day when—"

"Yes, you should have." She started to disconnect the call again.

"But you shouldn't have run away from me. We need to talk. Please give us a chance."

Tassia's mouth hung open, but she couldn't speak. Instead, she disconnected the call. How dare he say that she ran.

She sat on her father's couch with her feet curled up under her and his precious TV remote in her hand. She flicked through channels until she stopped on Chatty Charlie's show. Just like before, her image popped up next to the older man who now had on a silver jacket with purple sparkles covering it. He definitely had a favorite color.

Although she didn't want to, she stopped to listen what this old gossip had to say about her this time.

"Oh, this poor child." The host feigned remorse. "First she gets accused of not writing the songs she sold to lots of artists, but now the word is out that she did some riding of her own on a very well-known and popular artist."

The audience oohed and ahhed at that bit of news. Tassia felt heat building up in her belly the longer she listened to this troll.

"My sources tell me that the two were tucked away in a secret location for weeks where the dude just hit it and quit it and left her hung out to dry. But, hey, she should be used to it by now. She got dumped by a roadie. I mean. Who gets broken up with by the guy hauling cables and speakers?" He jutted his thumb over his shoulder. "This loser here."

The audience laughed at the same time that Tassia's phone rang. For the past week, she had been avoiding almost all calls, even the ones from her management team. When she saw India's name across the screen, she had to answer it.

"Don't look at Chatty Charlie's show." India barely let Tassia get her greeting out before she barreled through the conversation. "It's going to piss you off."

"Too late." Tassia leaned on the arm of the couch and continued watching the show.

"My sources haven't confirmed who this mystery man is." A blacked-out silhouette appeared next to Tassia's picture on the screen.

It didn't escape Tassia's notice that the image next to her looked like he wore a backward baseball cap. Damn.

"If you've been paying attention to pop culture recently, you know that someone else has been suspiciously missing from the scene about the same time. Folks, I'm not a mathematician, but even I know what one plus one is." He pointed at the two images on his screen. "These two are hooking up."

"What an asshole." India groaned through the phone. "I have people who can break his jaw if you want me to get that going."

When Tassia saw that the host moved on to a different celebrity, she muted the TV. "Why? If not him, it'll be someone else. And this time, his story is not entirely untrue. Hyde did hit it and quit it."

The look on his face when Clever detailed Hyde and her past histories together would forever be burned in her memory bank. He didn't believe her. He didn't trust her. How could he say he loved her if that foundation didn't exist?

"Girl, you don't think you meant more to him than just sex and a record?"

Tassia shook her head as though her friend could see her. "No. If I did, he would have defended me."

"Has he called you?"

"Yes, and singing that same 'I'm sorry' song. I'm not hearing it."

"Are you saying that the duets album isn't going to happen?"

Tassia had wondered that herself until Hyde mentioned that he wanted the album to still happen. "If you talk to Hyde, he still wants to do the album. Why would I want to still work with him when he was planning on ditching me all along?"

"Hyde has been blowing up your phone wanting to get back with you. He still wants to do the album. And he apologized for what he did. Sounds like he's done a whole lot more than Dudley did."

"Dorian." Not that Tassia wanted to remember that disaster of a relationship.

"And you two did the exact same thing." India laughed. "He believed his dad. You ran home to yours. Think about that."

Tassia didn't want to think about that aspect of her departure.

"Do you know what your next step is going to be?" India asked.

"I don't know. I don't know anything anymore."

India huffed. "You know this. I'm your friend. If you need anything, I'm here for you."

Tassia smiled, a first in days. "Thanks. Right now, I need to lick my wounds and heal. I'll get back out there soon enough."

When Burt walked into the family room, Tassia decided that now would be a good time to iron out another big issue that had been plaguing her. Now that she had some time to decompress, she had enough strength to talk to him about it.

"Hey, let me holler at you a little later. I need to have a conversation."

"With Hyde?" Excitement filled India's voice.

"No. My dad." Tassia wanted to say, "The other important man in my life," but calling Hyde *important* would mean he meant something to her.

Too bad he did.

"Talk to you later." Tassia disconnected the call. She turned to Burt. "Hey, Dad." She cut out the "Daddy" name as soon as she saw him in the airport to be picked up.

The flight home did nothing to calm her down or make her forget about Hyde. After everything she had shared with him, she would have thought he would have believed in her more. Blood is thicker than water.

"Hey, baby girl."

Tassia winced at that name, but said nothing. "Have a seat. I need to talk to you."

Burt took a seat and pushed his glasses up his nose. "If it's about your obligation to do that album, you have none. You can stay here and—"

Tassia held up her hand. "I have a team of people I pay to advise me on my career."

Burt blinked at her candor.

While she had her dad on the ropes, she continued. "What I need to know from the man who I employed over fifteen years ago is the truth about my show departure."

He cocked his head. "What do you mean? I told you the truth."

"You told me that the reason you pulled me from the show was because the producers had planned on beefing up Hyde's part and cutting me down to a featured player part. Is that the truth?" When her father slowed to answer, she added more to the question. "If I were to call Christina, would she say the same thing?"

Not that the popular pop star would even take her call. She hadn't spoken to her since leaving the show. Christina probably couldn't pick Tassia out of a lineup if she had gotten arrested, even with singing the infamous hook in Aaron's song.

"Dad, you have withheld the truth from me before under the guise of doing what's best for me. I'm tired of people thinking I can't handle the truth or that I'm not tough enough to take care of myself. I want the truth now or—"

"Or what?" He poked out his chest.

"Or I walk and will get back to you whenever I can." Tassia would stand firm on her word.

She wouldn't cut her father out of her life completely, but she wouldn't be as available. Maybe being so dependent on him made him think she couldn't rely on herself.

"Okay, fine. That day I talked to the producers and writing team, they had told me their idea of putting the performers together for future episodes. They were planning on pairing you up with Hyde."

Tassia's heart raced at finally hearing the truth from her father and knowing that she could have started the basis of a friendship and relationship with Hyde years ago. Now all that seemed like a memory.

"And why did this anger you so much that you had to pull me away from the show completely?" She crossed her arms over her chest.

"I could see the writing on the wall. You were the more talented one. Despite his raging success, I still think that. You would have carried him because—"

"He was dead weight, right?"

Burt's mouth hung open.

"Yeah, I saw Clever Love and, believe it or not, he told me a different story. I had to hear the truth from someone else's manager." She chuckled. "No, someone else's father. You lied to me, for years, you lied."

He held up his hand as though that would calm her. "You don't understand. You represented millions of African-American little girls. How would it be if—"

"Don't you dare say it." She planted her feet on the floor. "The show was about inclusion and diversity."

"With a rat." Her father smirked.

"The only rat was the person who lied to me. Here Hyde believed the story that Clever had told him about me being shallow and using him, and you lying and keeping secrets from me for my own good. Hyde tried defending you when I told him that my mother had cancer while I taped the show and you never told me."

"You were ten. You didn't need to know about your mother's condition." He shook his head vigorously.

"Hyde said the same thing. I was still a part of the family. You should have said something instead of keeping me in the dark."

"Your mother and I made that decision together. We did what we thought would be best for you. I didn't realize you were still holding on to this pain."

"I didn't realize it either until I saw Hyde believing his father over me and siding with him."

As soon as she said the words, it hit her. As India had mentioned, she and Hyde had done the exact same thing. Both had been led by their parent through lies and manipulations, yet, they both ran to their families.

Blood was thicker than water.

"Look, baby girl—"

"I'm not a baby." Tassia stood. She briefly looked down at her outfit to notice that she had on pink-and-white striped cotton sleep shorts and a My Little Pony T-shirt. She glared at her father. "I'm a grown woman who needs to be handling my business, personal and otherwise." She started to walk by her father. "I left a good man in Tennessee without sitting down and talking about our issues."

Burt sat up taller, but Tassia put her hand on his shoulder to still him.

"I love him, Dad. Fat, thin, white or otherwise. I love him. He saw my talent and appreciated me before I even learned to love myself. I don't know if we can get back to that special time we had, but I'll always have that memory. If you'll excuse me, I have to make some calls and get my life back in order. I can't keep hiding out and running to my daddy when I have problems." She thought about Hyde's words to her after they had sex the first time. "I need to stop running."

"Even to me? You can't run to me when you need help? I'll always be here for you." He stood and held Tassia's shoulders.

She patted his arm. "I know. I need to learn how to stand on my own. I won't do that if I'm steadily hiding behind you. And I won't be able to have a positive relationship if I don't stay to work things out. Guess I'll know better the next time." She kissed her father on the cheek and headed to her bedroom.

Tassia needed to stop her personal pity party and start living. Whether with Hyde or not, she had to make her way back to life. The first step would be to tackle her career. Time to get her team together.

Chapter 21

Chantel held Tassia's hand in a waiting room area before the official press conference began. The connection shocked her as it normally did. Tassia looked at her boss in amazement.

"You've had a rough couple of weeks." Chantel kept her voice low.

Tassia didn't need to rehash the gossip about her songwriting skills or the fact that she may or may not have bedded and been dumped by the hottest man in entertainment. All of it hurt, but she gained some wisdom and backbone to ignore the negativity. She wished she could have figured out a way to not miss Hyde.

"I'm fine." She patted the back of Chantel's hand. "I appreciate your support. Keeping me on Charisma and all."

"Of course. We have always believed you. As a matter of fact, our legal team is mounting a cease and desist order to Chatty Charlie to stop spreading lies about you or he'll be sued."

Tassia smiled at that bit of news. She would have been happier if she could have talked to Hyde before this press conference. Despite her last confrontation with her father at his house when she had vowed to make things right with Hyde, fear kept her from calling him. To hear him reject her would have crushed her.

"It didn't surprise me when we heard from Hyde's camp that he was still on board with the project. Since Clever Love is no longer Hyde's manager, we could never get a confirmation on whether he would be here for this announcement." Chantel looked almost remorseful as she patted Tassia's hand.

Tassia tried putting on a brave face. After ignoring the man, she couldn't blame him for ditching the project now. It also surprised her to hear that

Hyde no longer had C. Love managing his son's career. It made her wonder if that decision came about because of what had happened between them.

Truman stood next to Chantel. "You ladies ready?"

Tassia turned to Chantel. "Seems weird to do a press conference. Feels very old school."

Chantel smiled. "That's the point. I want to give it an almost presidential feel. I think this project is that important."

Tassia and Chantel nodded. Truman stepped out first while holding his wife's hand. In a show of solidarity, Chantel held Tassia's hand even as they stood at the podium in the lobby of the Oceanfront Hotel in Virginia Beach.

"Good afternoon, and thank you for coming." Truman took off his trademark cowboy hat as he spoke to the eager media that steadily snapped pictures and recorded the press conference with huge cameras.

The ballroom where the press conference took place had been stripped except for a few chairs for the press and the podium with various microphones.

"We're here to formally announce an upcoming project." Truman glanced at Tassia before he said the news. "Charisma Music is putting together a duets album that will have our artist, Tassia Hogan, who you may remember from the hit song "Ride Me" by Aaron, and country singer and superstar, Hyde Love."

At the mention of his name, the flashbulbs from the cameras intensified and loud murmurs echoed off the walls.

"Announcements have gone out on all social media networks. We're hoping to release the album in the spring of next year." Chantel leaned forward to speak into the bank of microphones.

"Will a tour follow?" one reporter in the crowd asked.

"It depends on their schedules." Truman's tactful answer would hopefully keep the ravenous group at bay.

"Where's Hyde? Why isn't he here to say anything?" another reporter asked.

This time Tassia stepped forward. "Of the two of us, he has more demands on his time. But he is still committed to this project." At least, people in her camp and at Charisma kept telling her so. "You'll see this announcement on all of his social media feeds right now, too." At least she had been told that by Chantel and Truman. Since Tassia still hadn't talked to Hyde since their final phone conversation, she had no idea where Hyde stood.

"Will your recent bad publicity about you not writing any of your songs hurt your sales?"

That question angered Tassia enough that she gritted her teeth.

"Uh, no." Chantel squeezed Tassia's hand like she wanted to calm her. "Those stories are false, and our legal team is going after every news outlet that has recently reported this as being factual. Tassia is a phenomenal songwriter, who—"

Chantel stopped speaking when music piped into the room. Tassia didn't recognize it at first. Guitars and a solo piano playing complemented each other until the singing started. Then it hit her. The demo version of "Kidnapped by the Cowboy" filled the expansive room.

Hearing Hyde's strong, soulful voice had Tassia's knees weakening and her stomach churning.

She turned to Chantel. "I didn't know Hyde shared these with you."

Chantel moved back from the microphones. "I don't know what you're talking about. He didn't send us any demos. Are you saying this is you and Hyde?"

Tassia nodded. "If he didn't give these to you, then…"

She peered behind the sea of reporters and caught a view of something she had been wanting to see for the last couple of weeks. Hyde Love stood behind the group that had had their full attention on Tassia, Chantel, and Truman. Even without his trademark backward baseball cap, he still looked the same to her, still hot, still sexy.

Then one reporter turned and caught Hyde.

"Oh my God. It's Hyde Love!" The reporters and cameras all turned to him as he made his way through the group to get to the podium.

He shook Truman's hand first. "Sorry for being late." He kissed Chantel's cheek. "Thanks for the invite." Then he stared at Tassia. "Hi."

Tassia fought to keep from smiling like a silly schoolgirl. She had to remember that he had chosen the word of his father over hers. Then again, hadn't she done the same thing?

"Hi, Hy, um, Hyde." Tassia remained on the side of Chantel away from Hyde.

Even from where she stood, she smelled his familiar musky scent. The aroma reminded her of everything right and good about being with him in Tennessee.

Hyde turned to the media. "Hi, everyone. I'm Hyde Love."

Laughter rippled through the group as though the man needed any kind of introduction. The fact that he did introduce himself made him even more appealing.

"I apologize for getting here late. I wanted you all to hear a sample of one of the songs from the upcoming duets album. It's only a stripped-down demo without a band behind us or a producer working it over. What did you think?" Hyde scanned the group.

Tassia saw a lot of head nodding.

"And Tassia wrote the song. I just did my part of it. I know some allegations had been made about her skills. Believe me. She is hardworking and talented." Hyde glanced at her for a long moment.

A female reporter stood up. "What will the album be called?"

Hyde chuckled. "Funny you should ask that." He peered over at Tassia. "We were talking about that and wondering the same thing. A title hasn't been decided yet. I had a couple of ideas." He said nothing until he locked stares with her. "My suggestion is 'Love and Strength.'"

"Why that?" A cameraman aimed his camera directly at Hyde.

"Is it true about the rumors that you and Tassia—"

"Yes." Hyde didn't wait for the woman to finish her question, and Tassia couldn't breathe.

This man, who had at one time admitted to not wanting to put his business out in front of the media, now had shared with the world that they had more than a working relationship.

"I'm tired of hiding. I've known Tassia Hogan since I was eleven on the *Ratty Rat's Fun Crew* TV show. I was too shy to talk to her then, but I'm making up for lost time now." He moved away from the microphone to get in front of her. "I've made a lot of mistakes these past couple of weeks."

Tassia, not willing to let him off the hook just yet, nodded. "You sure have. You believed your dad."

"And I shouldn't have, especially since I know all the things he did, which I'll share with you later." He reached for her hands.

Tassia pulled them away. "You assume there will be a later?" She tried keeping her voice down but couldn't. Emotions ran too high in her.

"I hoped." He pointed to her. "But you ran."

Tassia remained quiet. He had her.

"I think we both have a lot to discuss, including…" Hyde reached into his pocket and pulled out a robin's-egg blue hued ring box.

Tassia heard Chantel's gasp before she heard the media gasping. When she saw Hyde dropping down to one knee in front of her, she wanted to faint.

"Tassia Hogan, I have made plenty of mistakes in my life. One was letting you go not once, not twice, but three times." He smiled. "If this were baseball, I would be out. But it's not, and I'm hoping you will give us a chance." He held her hand. "I don't do public displays of affection."

Tassia laughed. "You're doing a great job of it now."

"With you, I want to shout from every rooftop in the world that I love you." He kissed the palm of her hand. "Not talking to you these last couple of weeks has been torture. But it allowed me to write one more song. I called it 'Redemption.' I just need you to help with your part of it. And I need you back in my life."

She ran her fingertips down the side of his face. "I might be able to squeeze you into my schedule."

He smiled even wider. "Is that a yes?"

She nodded. "I've missed you so much." She finally looked at the ring in the box.

The diamond looked as big as a bird's egg. Hyde slipped it on her finger and jumped to his feet to hug her. While everyone in the room applauded, he lifted her off her feet.

"I never want to be away from you for this long of a time again." He kissed the side of her face. "I've missed you so much." This time he kissed her lips.

The sounds in the room became muted as Tassia fell into the passionate expression. She missed and needed this man back in her life.

"I will never run from you again. I promise." She nodded.

"And I won't hide anything from you ever. I'm taking more control of my life, and that starts with who I want as my wife." Hyde eased her back down to the floor.

"I can't wait to call you my husband. But there's one thing we need to do."

Hyde's forehead wrinkled. "What's that?"

Tassia pulled him down so that she could whisper in his ear. "When I write my part of your 'Redemption' song, we need to—"

"Oh, yes. I think that'll be contractual." He winked at her.

Tassia laughed. "I love you so much."

"I love you, too." He nodded to the back of the room. "I have my guitar. You care to do some singing?"

"With you? Of course."

Epilogue

Two years later

"And the award for Album of the Year goes to…" The lead singer of a popular rock band struggled to open the red envelope before he read the winner's name. "Looks like a pattern tonight. Hyde Love and Tassia Hogan's 'Strong Enough' duets album."

Pepper, wearing a sparkly short dress, along with Graham and Norma raced up to the stage again to accept the award on Hyde and Tassia's behalf.

"Turn that off, especially since they didn't use my legal married name now." Tassia waved her hand as she sat up in her hospital bed. "Come say hi to your son."

Hyde turned off the hospital TV and sauntered over to his wife, who held the second most precious thing in his life. He brushed his index finger over their baby's arm, causing the sleeping darling to splay his little fingers.

"He's going to play piano. Look at those fingers." Tassia kissed him on his forehead, covered in a small white beanie. She peered up at Hyde. "We did this."

He wiped his eye with the back of his hand. "All of my professional life, I thought all I needed was to win an award." Hyde shook his head. "What I really wanted was a family to call my own." He pressed his lips against Tassia. "I love you, baby."

"I love you, too."

The hospital room door opened. With the curtain around the bed drawn, the identity of the guests didn't become apparent until Mabel, Efrem, and Burt's heads popped around the pale blue fabric.

"The nurses said we could come in." Mabel went to Tassia first and kissed her cheek. "My first great-grandson." She openly cried as she looked down at the bundle in Tassia's arms. "May I?"

Tassia smiled. "Of course."

Mabel picked up the baby from her arms and went over to a rocker in the corner. Efrem and Burt followed her. "Did you two decide on a name? Who am I holding?"

Hyde looked at Tassia, who only smiled at him.

"We would like to introduce you to Noah Four Love."

At the same time, Mabel, Efrem, and Burt said, "Four?"

The sound caused little Noah to start crying a little, which Mabel remedied with a little rocking and cooing.

"I messed up three times with Tassia. Fourth time for me was the charm." Hyde held Tassia's hand.

With his family there together, he now felt complete.

Love & Harmony Series

Don't miss any of the books in the Love & Harmony Series

Crazy in Love
Love Like Crazy

Meet the Author

Crystal B. Bright graduated with a B.A. from Old Dominion University with a major in Creative Writing and a minor in Communications with an emphasis on Public Relations. She earned her M.A. from Seton Hill University in Writing Popular Fiction. For more information about Crystal and her writing, please visit her website at www.CrystalBrightWriter.com. You can also find her at https://www.facebook.com/crystal.bright.397, or follow her on Twitter @CrystalBBright.